PARTING GIFTS
by Lorraine Heath

Also by Lorraine Heath

SWEET LULLABY

PARTING GIFTS

LORRAINE HEATH

DIAMOND BOOKS, NEW YORK

This book is a Diamond original edition, and has never been previously published.

PARTING GIFTS

A Diamond Book / published by arrangement with the author

PRINTING HISTORY
Diamond edition / December 1994

ISBN: 0-7865-0061-1

Diamond Books are published by The Berkley Publishing Group, 200 Madison Avenue, New York, New York 10016.
DIAMOND and the "D" design are trademarks belonging to Charter Communications, Inc.

PRINTED IN THE UNITED STATES OF AMERICA

10 9 8 7 6 5 4 3 2 1

To my sister, Theresa, who
read every word I ever wrote
and asked for more.

Acknowledgments

I wish to express my sincerest appreciation to Ann Goertemiller at the University of Texas Southwestern Medical School Library for her assistance in researching medical information available in 1881. Any misinterpretation of the information is mine.

I want to thank the librarians and staff of the Plano Public Library system for always finding the facts and information that elude me.

And to the members of my critique group: Carmel, Barbara, Barb, and Ellen. Thank you for taking the time to read each chapter as I finished it and for giving me your honest opinion. You taught me the value of humor and the strength of tears. This book is as much yours as it is mine.

PARTING GIFTS

❧ 1 ❧

Maddie Sherwood listened as the boisterous laughter rolled out into the night. She knew the kind of house behind which she stood, the type of women who lived within its walls, how they earned their keep. Their cheeks were rosy, their bosoms full, and they had the energy to laugh.

When was the last time she'd laughed?

She felt her stomach lurch as the aroma of carrots, potatoes, and beef wallowing in a thick broth wafted out into the alley. Her mouth watered, and tears welled unbidden in her eyes. She clutched the worn calico of her dress as though that alone could stop the aching hunger growing in her hollow abdomen.

A chill wind whipped through the deserted alley. She turned her back toward it, her tangled hair a frail barrier against the harsh elements surrounding her. Only two days before, a lingering spring had begun to ease its way into summer, and warm breezes had caressed the land. She had accepted Mother Nature's promise of warmer weather and traded her coat for a hot potato. The week before, she'd exchanged her shoes for stale bread and moldy cheese.

Now she had nothing left to trade but her dreams.

The back door squeaked open, spilling pale lamplight into the alley, the light's feathery fingers reaching out to touch her. A robust woman braced her arm against the threshold, her stance thrusting out one hip so she had a place to plant her other hand. "Don't like people loitering out behind my place," she said, huskily.

The woman's raspy voice revealed her identity. Maddie's brother, Andrew, had often spoken of Bev, the madam who owned this establishment in Fort Worth's notorious Hell's Half Acre. She entertained outlaws and judges alike and had a reputation for running an honest parlor house. Nothing came out of a man's pockets that he didn't take out himself.

Maddie wished she could walk away, but it was more than the weakness in her legs that kept her rooted to the spot. It was the tarnished truth. "I've no place else to go."

Bev stepped out of the doorway, her scarlet taffeta gown whispering across the ground as she sauntered toward the waif leaning against the dilapidated fence. She put a finger beneath the young woman's chin and tilted her face up toward the moon. "You sure are a scrawny little thing. Hungry, too, I'll bet."

She gave a slight nod.

"Nothing in this life comes free, honey. I got some hot food, a warm bath, and a soft bed I could give you, but you'd have to give me something back."

"I can clean your house—"

Bev's throaty laughter echoed down the alleyway. "Honey, I don't make money off a clean house. If you're willing to share that soft bed with a few gentlemen each night, then I'd be willing to let you sleep in it."

Maddie closed her eyes. She felt the shadow of warmth radiating around her as Bev positioned her body so it served as a buffer against the wind.

"Honey, you won't die from what I'm offering you. For the most part, it ain't all that unpleasant. Ah, hell, now and then you get a man that's a little too rough, a man who never heard of soap, but for the most part, the men are just lonely. For a few minutes you make them forget just how damn lonely they are."

Maddie opened her eyes, an unpleasant tremor of anxiety

coursing the length of her body. "I've never . . . never been with a man."

Dropping her arm around the girl's shoulders, Bev drew her against her ample bosom. "Well, that's even better, honey. The first time should be special. I'll see to it that it is. Now, let's get a little food in that belly and wash you up a bit."

She balked as Bev began to lead her toward the open door.

"Come on, honey," Bev urged, her voice laced with knowledge. "If there was any other option open to you, you woulda been doing it by now."

Wiping away the silent tears dampening her cheeks, Maddie followed Bev inside, down a narrow hallway to a room that was cloaked in shadows as though secrets lurked in the corners.

Maddie only ate enough stew to stop her stomach from growling, accepting the promise of a proper meal once she'd finished servicing her first customer. With the knot in her stomach tightening, she didn't think she could have eaten more had it been offered.

The bathwater was lukewarm, and she wasn't altogether certain she was the first to use it. She scrubbed up quickly and just as quickly dried off. She combed the tangles from her hair. She slipped into a red silk gown, positioning the thin straps on her bare shoulders so the bodice covered her small breasts.

Reaching deep within herself, she dredged up what little dignity remained. She walked into the middle of the gilded parlor and clambered onto a table. Pushing away the unsettling thoughts of all that would transpire before this night ended, she fixed her gaze on a thin crack marring a distant wall.

Licking her lips, she again tasted the whiskey Bev had made her drink. The acrid odor of thick cigar smoke assaulted her nostrils as men crowded around her. Although they were forbidden to touch her until they'd paid for the right, she felt as though chilled fingers skittered along her flesh.

The bidding, which included shouts, laughter, and lewd

comments, began. She kept her eyes focused on the crack in the wall, wishing she could fly across the room and crawl into it.

"Come on, honey, give 'em a taste of what they'll be getting," Bev urged, tapping her painted nails impatiently on the table.

Maddie knew she'd make more tonight as a virgin than she would any other night of her life. Bev had given her explicit instructions on how to draw the highest bid, but following those instructions was a harder task than she'd imagined. She reminded herself how hungry she'd been, how cold, how alone. Slowly, she moved her trembling fingers up to one of the straps. As the hoots increased, she slipped the strap off her shoulder and brought the bodice of the gown down to reveal one breast, her eyes never leaving the crack on the wall.

"One thousand dollars."

As a hush descended over the room, Maddie closed her eyes, not certain she wanted to look at the man who'd bid such an exorbitant amount.

"Oh, hell, you could have waited until we'd seen more," a man bellowed, disgust and disappointment apparent in his voice.

A chair scraped across the floor as a pleasant masculine voice resounded throughout the room. "You want to see more, then pay for the privilege."

Maddie opened her eyes and watched a tall, brown haired man walked across the room. The crowd parted, allowing him access to his prize. He focused his attention on Bev, his smile slight.

"Do you anticipate any further bids?"

Bev smiled. "I reckon not, honey. Imagine you'd top 'em anyway, wouldn't you?"

He nodded slightly and extended his hand up to Maddie. She slipped her hand into his, relishing the strength and warmth he provided as he helped her step down to a chair and then to the floor. Discreetly, he slipped the strap of her gown onto her shoulder and adjusted her bodice before easing his coat around her shoulders.

"I'll show you to the room," Bev said as she heaved herself out of the chair.

"For a thousand dollars, madam, I expect to have her for the entire night." He quirked a brow. "In my hotel room."

Bev laughed. "You show me that thousand dollars, and we'll see what we can work out." With a flourish, she turned and marched toward the back of the room.

The man placed his arm around Maddie, drawing her possessively against his side, escorting her through the throng of men as though he owned her.

As the beans soaked in butter melted in her mouth, Maddie wondered if anything had ever been as delicious.

"When was the last time you had something to eat?"

With regret, she swallowed, unable to savor the taste as long as she'd wanted. "I had something to eat earlier in the evening." Avoiding the man's eyes, she pierced a piece of chipped beef and brought it to her lips, inhaling the spicy aroma, just before she slipped it into her mouth. His actions weren't at all what she'd expected.

Once they were in his hotel room, he'd had a hot, steaming bath prepared, removed his coat from her shoulders, and draped a blanket from the bed around her. He'd had food brought up and given her the choice of bathing or eating first. She'd chosen to eat, although from time to time she glanced over at the welcoming sight of the water misting within the wooden tub.

"Maddie. Do you mind if I call you Maddie?"

She moved her head slowly from side to side and toyed with the potatoes. As they'd ridden in the buggy to the hotel, he'd asked her name. It was the only thing he'd asked of her since he'd escorted her out of the parlor house. He'd told her his name was Charles Lawson.

"Maddie, look at me."

She lifted her gaze to his. His eyes were a deep dark brown, reminding her of the fudge her mother had made at Christmas. And they were kind, filled with compassion and understanding.

"Maddie, did you want to work in the parlor house? Was it truly your desire to become one of Bev's girls?"

Tears flooded her eyes. Reaching across the table, he caught them with his thumb as they escaped onto her cheek. He gave her a soft smile. "How did you manage before tonight? Who took care of you?"

Sniffing, she ran a finger beneath her nose. "My father. My brother."

"What happened to them?"

"They were killed during a stagecoach holdup."

"When did this happen?"

"Two weeks ago."

He sat back and studied her. She shifted in the chair, wondering what he was thinking, hoping he'd ask no more questions of her.

"Surely, your father's estate left something to you."

She shook her head. "We never had much. My father's trade caused him to move around a lot." She forced a quivering smile. "He promised we'd settle here. Said he'd buy a house . . . a small house with a white fence going all the way around it." She lifted a shoulder slightly. "But it didn't work out."

"So you have no place to go, no one to help you?"

Her eyes darted around the beautifully furnished room. She'd never in her life seen anything so grand. "I don't have any skills, either." She brought her gaze to rest on his brown eyes. "I guess that won't be true after tonight, though."

She watched a deep scarlet flush his cheeks. She'd never before seen a man blush, didn't know men did blush. Certainly, her father, her brother, and their traveling companions never blushed.

Scraping the chair across the hardwood floor, Charles stood and walked to the window. Pulling the curtain aside, he looked down on the quiet nighttime activity. A few carriages rolled along the street. People strolled along the boardwalk, stopping occasionally to look in a store window. He had a long list of things he needed to do while he was in Fort Worth. The young woman eating in his hotel room was not one of the items on his list.

He'd gone into Bev's looking for a little companionship, someone to take his mind off his troubles for a few hours. He'd been sitting in the corner, nursing a solitary whiskey, trying to decide which woman would earn his coins. Then this young woman had climbed onto the table, and Bev had announced in her deep, throaty voice that the girl's virginity would go to the highest bidder. Suddenly, his troubles became insignificant.

She'd seemed so small in the room crowded with men. Her golden hair cascading about her shoulders hadn't concealed the fact that the garish gown she wore had been made for a more buxom woman. It was evident hard times had befallen her. Yet she possessed a beauty, a dignity that hunger couldn't disguise. An innocence that youth claimed with tenacity; an innocence that would be torn asunder as easily as her maidenhead; an innocence that once stolen could never be returned.

The men in that room had been bidding for the privilege to plunder that innocence, to be the last man to gaze into trusting eyes, the first man to gaze into eyes consumed by the knowledge that nothing in this young woman's life would ever be beautiful again.

He wondered if any man standing in that room knew that what he was bidding on so fervently was priceless to this young woman.

So many things in life were priceless: a woman's first experience with love, a mother's touch, laughter. Recently, Charles had found little in his life to bring him laughter. He glanced over his shoulder at the woman sitting at the table.

He had been but nineteen when he'd taken Alice as his wife. He'd visited a brothel or two in his youth. The women's eyes had always seemed dead, lifeless. He'd dreaded taking the sparkle from Alice's eyes. He'd given her as much gentleness and love as he could, hoping to ease things for her. Afterward, her eyes had reflected a love for him deeper than before.

He smiled at the fond memory. He'd been her first, her

only. The wonder of it had always shone in her eyes.

He thought of the children that their love had produced. They knew little of a mother's love, the difference a woman's presence could make.

Turning abruptly, he walked across the room and dropped into the chair. "I'd like to make you a proposition."

"You don't have to proposition me. You've already paid a thousand—"

"I paid a thousand dollars to get you out of that hellhole. And that's all."

She used her fingers to comb the silken tresses back from her face. "I thought you wanted . . . I mean the bidding . . . you bought the right. . . ."

He smiled sadly. "I'm impotent."

Maddie knew it was rude, but she couldn't stop her eyes from forming wide circles nor her mouth from dropping open. She snapped her mouth shut, then whispered, "Impotent? That means you can't—"

"No, I can't. I got trapped in a stall with an angry stallion a little over a year ago." He released a self-debasing laugh. "It's a wonder I can still piss."

She lowered her eyes as the heat rushed to her face.

"I'm sorry. That wasn't a very gentlemanly thing to say, was it?"

She shook her head before lifting her gaze to his. His eyes held more sadness within their depths than any man's she'd ever seen, more than her own eyes held, she was certain. She tilted her head. "Then why were you there?"

Once again, she watched the crimson coloring creep up beneath his tanned cheeks. He smiled lightly. "A man still likes to look, occasionally to touch."

"I would think that would make your condition that much harder to live with."

"Much in life is hard to live with, Maddie. All we can do is make the best of the situation, take the hand we're dealt, and try and bluff our way through. Isn't that what you were doing tonight?"

And what she'd probably be doing tomorrow night and the night after that. A shudder of revulsion raced through her body. She'd still be a virgin tomorrow. She'd stand again upon that wobbly table, smelling the smoke, studying the crack in the wall. Only tomorrow, Charles Lawson wouldn't be there to take her away.

He enfolded one of her hands in both of his. His were warm, hers cold. His steady, hers trembling. His large, hers small.

"Two years ago, my wife died during childbirth. I loved her, Maddie." He smiled in remembrance of a happier time. "I still do, and I miss her something fierce. I don't expect to ever love again, but I have three children. I want them to grow up knowing a mother's touch."

He closed his hands more securely about hers. She felt the slight tremor in his hands as he cleared his throat.

"I'd like for you to marry me."

Maddie felt her heart lurch within her breast, her breath leave her body. She didn't know this man, but then would she have known any of the men who would have helped her step down from that table? "Marry you?"

"I know I'm asking a lot of you because there's much I can't give you: my heart, children of your own. But I can give you respectability, food on the table, a roof over your head." A miniscule light sparkled within his eyes. "I own a small stagecoach inn just north of Austin. It provides me with a modest income, but it needs a woman's touch as much as my children do. You'd work from dawn till dusk—"

"But why marry me? You could hire me to care for your children."

"It's important to me that my children come to think of you as their mother. And as I mentioned earlier, I still enjoy an occasional touch. I would want you to sleep in my bed, to hold you at night. That, as innocent as it would be, would still be inappropriate if we weren't married."

"You must know other women—"

"Those women . . . most women . . . want a man who can do more than hold them at night. I'd be asking them to give up the same things I'm asking you to give up, but I'd give them nothing of equal value in return for their sacrifice. At

least for you, I'm offering a life better than the one you'll
have if you go back to Bev's."

"But you don't even know me, the kind of person I
am."

"Don't I?" he asked, gently. "What was so damn interesting about that crack on the wall? I think you'd spend
your life looking for cracks and trying to hold your tears
at bay."

Momentarily taken aback by his keen insight into her
feelings, she withdrew her hand from his and clenched it
within her lap. He shoved himself away from the table.
"Sleep on it. You can let me know in the morning."

"I don't need to sleep on it, Mr. Lawson." She met his
gaze squarely. Within his eyes, she recognized the desperation that had brought him to this moment of asking a woman
willing to sell herself to numerous men to be content with
only one man. To be content with one man who could never
truly be a husband to her. "I shall be honored, sir, to become
your wife and a mother to your children."

She watched as relief washed over his features. She
thought she detected a slight glistening in his eyes before
he turned away and studied the fire in the hearth. When at
last he spoke, his voice was hoarse.

"Good. My children so enjoy gifts. It is my hope, Maddie,
that you shall be the finest one I ever give them."

❧ 2 ❧

As the stagecoach rumbled over the rough road, Maddie watched the passing scenery with disinterest. She'd been a fool to marry a man she didn't know, to marry a man based on feelings she thought she detected in his eyes. She clenched her jaws, her fists, and her heart. She knew at last why he needed a mother for his children. He, himself, was a drunken sot.

The night when he made his proposal, he slept on the settee in the hotel room while she slept comfortably in the soft bed. The following day, he took her shopping.

Then they went to a small Methodist church where an austere, unquestioning minister performed the ceremony. They exchanged their vows quickly, with little emotion. Afterward, they browsed the cow town for little trinkets to give the children upon their arrival home.

That evening, after dinner in the hotel dining room, Maddie excused herself while Charles stayed behind to finish his whiskey. She went upstairs to prepare herself, not in the manner a woman usually prepared for her wedding night, but in a way she hoped would leave some special memory of her first night sharing a bed with a man.

She slipped on a nightgown with tiny flowers embroidered on the bodice. As she began to loosen her hair, Charles stumbled in, weaving across the room until he fell into the bed and passed out.

That night, Maddie slept on the settee. The following morning, he awoke as though nothing had happened.

She'd seen other men nursing their hangovers, but Charles appeared to have none of their symptoms after a night of heavy drinking.

"You neglected to inform me you imbibe," she said tersely.

His cheeks flamed red, and he looked around the room as though only just realizing where he was. It took him several moments before he gathered the courage to meet her gaze. "I'm sorry. I don't know what got into me."

Whatever had gotten into him on their wedding night, apparently got into him last night as well. Shortly after they arrived in Waco, she went for a leisurely stroll through a town she'd heard much about but never before visited. She returned to the room and discovered Charles sprawled across the bed, dead to the world.

She refused to speak to him this morning, had been tempted, so tempted to return to Fort Worth or to just stay in Waco. But she supposed the same drunk every night was better than a different drunk every hour.

Leaning forward, Charles dug his elbows into his knees and took her hands in his. "Maddie, I need to put things right between us before we arrive."

Ignoring him, she suddenly found interest in the rolling, tree-covered hills.

"I owe you an apology for last night."

Grateful they were the only two people traveling within the confines of the coach, she snapped her head around and pierced him with her gaze. "Do you want to get a jump on things and apologize for tonight?"

Blanching at the hurt and disappointment clearly visible in her eyes, he ran his thumbs lightly over the tops of her knuckles. "I deserve that, I know. I fight these spells, I truly do. They don't usually come this quickly together." He squeezed her hands. "I'll fight them harder."

So much of her past was painful, filled with moments best forgotten, but she wanted, needed him to understand her aversion to his distasteful habit. "My father's . . . friends . . . would get so ugly when they'd had too much whiskey to drink."

He brought her fingers to his lips. "Did I get ugly?"

"No, you didn't even smell sour as they often did. If you hadn't walked so crooked and passed out, or been sprawled across the bed as you were, I might not have known you'd had too much to drink."

"I'll take more care in the future not to walk so crooked and not to pass out. And I promise not to sprawl across the bed."

His eyes held such sincerity she wondered if she'd ever stay angry at this man for long. But more, she knew she owed him a debt of gratitude. He'd saved her from a fate worse than dealing with a drunken husband.

"Were you thinking of your wife?"

"No." He released her hands and gazed out the window. "Actually, I was thinking of you, hoping I hadn't done you a disservice. So much of life is unfair, Maddie. I hope you won't come to regret the choice you made."

Teetering with the motion of the roiling coach, he moved awkwardly across the narrow space separating the seats, sat beside her, and pointed out the window. "There's home."

As the stagecoach slowed, Maddie glimpsed a two-story structure surrounded by majestic oak trees with banners of moss swaying in the slight breeze.

"It's so large," she said.

"It does seem huge when the floors need to be scrubbed or the windows washed, but when we have guests, it seems very small."

"It'll always seem big to me."

She felt the excitement and apprehension churn her stomach as the stagecoach rolled to a halt, rocking slightly before settling into stillness. She patted her hair, making sure it was still neatly secured in a dignified bun beneath her hat. She smoothed out the skirt of her serge traveling dress and took a deep breath.

"You look wonderful," Charles said, touching the crease in her brow.

"I should have confessed . . . I haven't been around children much."

"You'll do fine."

She nodded, gathering from his smile the courage she would need to meet the children who would now call her mother.

A resounding click echoed around her as the door to the coach opened. She lifted herself off the seat, bending at the waist as she prepared to leave the coach.

She saw the large hands first, coming to assist her, clamping down on her waist, steadying her. Instinctively, she placed her hands on the chambray cloth covering the broad shoulders. Then she lifted her gaze.

And there she remained, suspended in time, falling into the obsidian depths of the blackest eyes she'd ever seen.

The man lifted her out of the coach, an errant breeze blowing his black hair across his brow. Slowly, so slowly, he set her feet on the ground, no more than a whisper's breath separating their bodies. She was now looking up into his rugged face. Where the sun had beat down on it before, the shadows now played, disguising his features, softening the sharp edges.

Charles stepped out of the stagecoach. "Jesse."

The man's gaze remained fixed on Maddie's, and she wondered to whom Charles was speaking.

"I'd like you to meet Maddie . . . my wife."

Jerking his hands off her waist as though she'd suddenly caught fire, the man stepped back. "Your wife?"

Charles slipped his arm around Maddie and drew her against his side. "Yes, we were married in Fort Worth."

The man's thick black brows furrowed deeply, and she wasn't certain if it was the term wife or married that was foreign to him.

"The doctor must have had some good news for you then," he said.

She was surprised to see her husband pale at the man's words.

"No, nothing's changed, but I don't want to discuss it here," he snapped impatiently. "Where are the children?"

"In the barn."

"The barn?" Charles latched onto Maddie's hand and

began pulling her through the yard. "I don't like them playing in the barn."

Maddie stumbled over a rock, regained her balance, and somehow managed to keep pace with Charles's frantic steps. Considering what had happened to him, she fully understood his panic at the thought of his children playing around animals. He fairly flew into the barn. She rammed into him when he stopped abruptly.

"Last stall."

She jumped as the deep voice echoed throughout the huge cavernous structure. She threw a pointed look over her shoulder which she hoped would serve as a warning to him not to make it a habit to sneak up behind her. Then she was jerked forward as Charles once again pulled her along. Dutifully, she followed.

The sight of the last stall brought with it the strong scent of hay, the fading scent of livestock and manure. A boy, with hair the same shade as Charles's, was hunkered before a pile of hay. He picked up one coin after another and set each aside, his lips moving as though he was counting. In the hay behind him, the bottom of a pair of coveralls was visible. The coveralls tumbled out of the hay, and a small girl righted herself, flicking her golden hair out of her brown eyes.

"Cain't find it," she announced and scooted over toward the boy.

"Look again. It's gotta be there. Uncle Jesse said there was ten, and we only found nine."

Maddie glanced at the taller man standing beside her. Until this moment, until the boy had referred to him as his uncle, she hadn't seen the resemblance between the two men. Hard lines and creases were etched within Jesse's face, features sculpted to a certain degree by nature's elements. His mouth was as full and broad as Charles's, but where Charles's lips tipped up as though he was always ready to smile, Jesse's remained a perfect line as though waiting for the situation to tell him how to mold them. The contours of their noses were identical, straight and bold. Their eyes were shaped the same, but carried different colors, Charles's dark brown, Jesse's deep black. Creases brought on by smiles outlined Charles's eyes. She thought Jesse's creases were more likely to have been brought on by squinting against the sun or wind.

A squeal resounded, and Maddie turned her attention back to the pile of hay. A tiny girl, previously hidden, scrambled out from beneath the hay. With a tattered rag doll draped over her arm, she squatted beside the boy.

"Did you find it?" he asked.

She shook her head vigorously, sending her riotous curls, as golden as her sister's, into further disarray.

"What are you looking for?" Charles asked.

The children's heads popped up and smiles filled their faces. Charles moved into the stall and knelt, relishing the feel of tiny arms going around his neck, wet kisses planted upon his cheek, exclamations of joy filling his ears.

The boy was the first to step back. "Uncle Jesse said there was ten five-cent pieces in this pile of hay. Said we had to stay here till we found 'em all, but we can only find nine." He shot an accusing glance at his uncle. "I'm thinking he lied."

Jesse stepped into the stall. "I'm thinking you didn't look hard enough. What's that over there?"

When the boy went to investigate the indicated corner, Jesse slipped a hand out of his pocket and dropped a coin beside the smallest child's feet. The little girl grabbed it up and clutched it in her chubby hand.

"I find!"

The boy spun around, his eyes narrowed in suspicion. "Texas Rangers ain't supposed to cheat."

"I didn't cheat. I said there were ten coins, and now you have ten coins."

"They ain't supposed to trick people, neither."

The boy stalked over and began gathering the coins.

"I didn't mean to trick you."

The boy glared at his uncle. "Then why'd you hold one back?"

Jesse looked at Charles. Charles lifted a brow, his expression stating clearly, "My boy's not stupid. You got yourself into this mess, you get yourself out."

Jesse hunkered down beside the boy. "I'm sorry, Aaron. I had chores I had to tend to. I asked you to watch your sisters so I could get ready for the stagecoach coming in. You didn't want to, so I gave you a game to play that couldn't be finished until I decided it was time for it to be finished."

"It wasn't fair," Aaron grumbled.

"Neither is not helping out when there's work to be done," Charles said.

Standing up, Aaron studied his scuffed boots. "I don't like watching my sisters."

"Sometimes we all have to do things we don't want to do." Charles tipped up his son's head with a finger beneath his chin, meeting his gaze squarely. "Next time Uncle Jesse asks you to help him, I'd appreciate it if you'd do so willingly."

When silence was the boy's response, Charles lifted the boy's chin higher.

"Yes, sir," Aaron mumbled.

"And I'll talk to Uncle Jesse about not cheating anymore."

Nodding slightly, Aaron looked toward his uncle, knowing he'd lost a little and gained a little. Jesse also nodded, acknowledging a partial defeat before standing and moving out of the stall, relinquishing the children back into his brother's care.

Charles clapped his hands together. "Now, then. I've brought you all a very special gift this time."

Reaching back, he held his hand out to Maddie. She placed her hand in his, surprised to find his trembling. He pulled her forward. She knelt in the straw and looked at the dirty faces.

"I've brought you a mother," Charles said quietly as he squeezed her hand.

She smiled, not certain what sort of welcome she'd expected, but three children staring at her with mouths agape wasn't it. Charles placed his hand on the blond head of the smallest child. "This is Taylor."

Taylor stuck a grimy finger in her mouth. He gently res-
cued the finger and pulled the child onto his knee. "Taylor's
never known a mother. Can you say Ma?"

Shaking her head, she buried her dirt-smudged face against
Charles's chest.

"Can you tell her how old you are?"

She peered at Maddie with one eye open, the other still
pressed against her father's chest. Within her lap, she began
to work her fingers, bending some fingers with the help of
her other hand. When she'd accomplished her goal, she held
up her hand, two fingers extended.

Maddie smiled. "Two years old. Isn't that wonderful?"

Nodding, she moved her face away from Charles's chest.

"Wouldn't you like to give your new mother a hug?"
Charles asked.

Taylor slid off his knee, walked to Maddie, and slipped
her chubby arms around Maddie's neck. Maddie placed her
arms around the child, squeezing her. She'd never before
been hugged by a child, had not realized that a child's hug
could claim her heart. She wanted to say something kind
and loving to the child, but her throat was clogged with new
emotions. Taylor released her hold, dropped onto Maddie's
lap, and claimed her place.

Charles pulled the other girl onto his lap. "This is Hannah.
She'll be five in a few weeks."

"How wonderful," Maddie managed to say.

"Will you bake me a cake?" Hannah asked.

Maddie nodded. "I'd like to do that very much."

Hannah smiled and wrapped her arms around Maddie. "I
love you."

Maddie once again felt her throat constrict, her heart
expand. She looked at Charles, and he was smiling.

"I'll love you, too," Maddie promised, knowing it
wouldn't take much for her to love all these children.

"I'm eight years old, and I don't need a mother," a small
male voice announced defiantly.

The harsh clearing of Jesse's throat caused the boy to
look up guiltily. The brusque sound startled Maddie. She

lost her balance and toppled to her bottom. The boy laughed until another curt clearing of Jesse's throat caused him to stop.

"That's Uncle Jesse's warning sound," Hannah whispered near Maddie's ear, her small hands cupping the words. "When he does that, you'd best straighten up or else."

"Or else what?" Maddie asked, her voice low although she knew everyone in the barn was privy to the words being spoken.

Hannah lifted a small shoulder. "Don't know. We always straighten up."

Maddie smiled. "It is a scary sound, isn't it?" She glanced up, her smile fading. Jesse was watching her intently, too intently.

"I won't call her 'Ma,' " Aaron said.

"You don't have to," Charles said. "She and I have discussed it. If you prefer, you may call her Miss Maddie, but regardless, I expect you to give her a chance and treat her fairly."

"I ain't gonna hug her."

"Maybe you could just shake her hand so she'd know she was welcome," Charles suggested.

Aaron studied his father. Then his glance shot up. "Did Uncle Jesse shake her hand?"

"No, he didn't." Charles twisted his body slightly and smiled at his brother. "But he came fairly close to hugging her."

Maddie felt the heat rush to her face. Jesse averted his gaze and studied the pile of hay, a deep crimson covering his face and creeping down into the opening of his shirt. She wondered if blushing was a family trait.

"Well, then, I reckon I could shake her hand," Aaron said grudgingly.

He stuck out his hand. Maddie placed her hand in his. His fingers closed quickly around hers. Then he released his hold and shoved his hand behind the bib of his coveralls as though hiding it would save it from disgrace.

Charles stood. Reaching down, he brought Maddie to her

feet. She slapped the dust off her skirt and picked the hay away, anything to avoid looking at the man standing beside her husband.

"Jesse, the small trunk on top of the stagecoach is Maddie's. Will you carry it to my room, then see to changing out the horses? The whip said they want to leave within the hour."

"I'll get right on it."

Charles touched each child's head. "There's other gifts in Maddie's trunk. Why don't we go see what they are?"

The children squealed in delight and scampered off. Maddie watched as Jesse ambled out after them. He stood a little taller than Charles and was broader across the chest and shoulders, as though he'd spent his life working outdoors.

While in Fort Worth, she'd seen the town's mascot, a black panther, pacing in front of the courthouse where he'd been chained. This man's movements very much reminded her of the panther's. Sleek, powerful, predatory. She found it disconcerting that this man wasn't chained.

Charles placed his hand on her waist. "Would you like to see your new home? It doesn't have a white fence around it, but I think you'll be pleased."

With his arm around her, they walked toward the inn that served as a resting spot for travelers and a home to the family who lived within.

The house was constructed of solid cedar logs. Cypress shingles graced the roof. Contentment surged within Maddie as she stepped onto the wide veranda that circled the house. Above her, another veranda, accessible through doors from the inside and stairs outside, circled the entire second floor.

Smiling, Charles pushed open the door. Maddie slipped past him into the foyer. Stairs ascended to their left, double doors sealed the room to their right. Charles opened the double doors. "This is where our overnight guests generally spend their evening."

In awe, she stepped into the room. It was designed for the comfort and relaxation of weary travelers. A sofa rested before the fireplace. To one side, a half-dozen chairs circled a mahogany center table. Against one wall, a grandfather clock clicked a steady tattoo as its pendulum swung lazily from side to side. A spittoon sat in one corner, a cabinet housing liquor in the other.

"On the other side of the house is a smaller room the family uses in the evenings. It's not as fancy, but I think it's more cozy. I'll show it to you later."

He escorted her back into the foyer and stepped through a wide opening into a large dining room. "This is where we serve our guests their dinner."

She heard the rapid pounding of small feet. Then the children rounded the corner.

"Uncle Jesse won't let us open the trunk until you get upstairs," Aaron explained, breathless from his race down the stairs.

"Then I guess I'd better get upstairs," Charles said. He squeezed Maddie's hand. "I hate to impose so soon, but we need to get a meal ready for the whip and his guard. Would you mind seeing to it? I'm certain Jesse already has something cooking. You'll probably need to do little more than set the table."

Maddie felt the disappointment reel through her because he had not invited her upstairs. She'd helped him select the gifts, had wanted to be present when the children first saw them. She forced herself to remember that she was here to help Charles. He had no real feelings for her, nor she for him. She was to be his helpmate, not the love of his life. Shoving her disappointment aside, she responded in the only way a woman of her circumstance could. "I'll be happy to."

"Wonderful. We won't be long."

She watched as he took the girls by the hand and walked out of the room. Aaron followed, begging for hints. Gradually, his elated voice faded away.

Loneliness crept through her as she glanced around the dining room. A long oak table with several chairs surrounding it dominated the room. If more than one stagecoach arrived, ample seating would be available for all the guests. She walked toward the wooden hutch where china dishes were visible through the glass molded into the doors.

Opening the door, she studied the tiny blue flowers adorning the delicate dishes. She touched the china and smiled at the smooth, cool texture. She lifted a delicate cup from the shelf.

"We don't use the good dishes."

The deep, unexpected voice caused her to jump back, the cup slipping from her hand. She reached out, capturing the cup inches from the floor. But it wasn't the knowledge that she'd saved the cup that caused her heart to skip a beat. It was the fact that a large, warm hand was cradling hers as she cradled the cup.

As slowly as he'd helped her down from the stage, Jesse unfolded his body, straightening her stance with no more than a movement of his hand beneath hers. His eyes held hers, and she found herself swimming in a black ocean, an ocean beckoning to her, drawing her farther from shore, into deeper waters, waters she'd never before swum.

"We only use the good dishes when we have guests," he said, removing his hand from beneath hers.

His words caused the ocean to recede, leaving her standing unsteadily upon the shore. "I thought we were having guests. The stage driver—"

"The whip and his guard work for the stage company. They aren't considered guests. They'll eat in the kitchen with us, just regular dishes."

He took the cup from her palm, set it back into the hutch, and clicked the door into place. "I'll show you the kitchen."

She followed him through the room into the east ell of the house. The kitchen had a high-beamed ceiling. Copper pans and iron pots hung from one wall. A spicy aroma teased her nostrils.

"It smells good," she offered.

"It's just son of a—" He glanced over at her. "Son of a gun stew. We'll use the bowls in that cabinet there."

She repressed her smile. She'd often fixed the same stew, but the men who'd been in her company didn't refer to it as son of a gun. She didn't think this man normally called it that, either. The stew wasn't fancy, but it stuck to a man's ribs. The tender strips of beef were surrounded by tomatoes, onions, potatoes, and anything else within easy reach. It simmered until the aromas blended and became indistinguishable from one another. Her father had taught her that if she could detect the smell of an ingredient, the stew wasn't fit to eat.

She removed several bowls from the cabinet and placed them one by one on the scarred wooden table. From the corner of her eye, she watched as he lifted the lid on the heavy iron pot and stirred the contents within.

"So you and Charles are brothers," she said, trying to fill the void of silence. His hand stilled as he glanced at her, and she wished she'd kept silent.

"You didn't know he had a brother?"

She moved her head slowly from side to side, once again swimming within the black depths of his eyes, eyes she was certain scrutinized every aspect of her being, eyes she feared could look far beneath the surface of a person to uncover the hidden truths. She adjusted the positioning of the last bowl as though it made a difference where it was placed on the table. "The little boy—"

"Aaron?"

She forced a small smile. "Yes, Aaron. He said Texas Rangers don't cheat. Was he implying you're a Texas Ranger?"

"Was. I'm not anymore. Gave it up a little over a year ago."

Little wonder he scrutinized her so closely. Resolutely, she convinced herself that what he was before had little bearing on what he was now. No badge decorated his chest; no gun was strapped to his thigh; no rifle rested in the crook of his arm. "What do you do now?"

"Work here."

"And where do you live?"

"I have a room upstairs."

Suddenly, she felt as though the house weren't nearly large enough. "Are all the bedrooms upstairs?"

"Yep, there's eight of them. Those on the east side are for the family, those on the west for guests."

"I see." Idly staring at the man who was staring at her, she wondered what was keeping Charles. Whenever her father had returned home and handed her a gift from his saddlebag, she'd barely taken time to say thank you before she'd run off to enjoy it. She'd expected to hear the children running down the stairs long before now. "Where would I find some spoons?"

Silently, with sleek movements she would have never expected of a man his size, he moved across the room to a wooden hutch and pulled open a drawer. "Spoons are in here."

He didn't take any out. He didn't move away. She didn't know if he was challenging or testing her, but she knew she had to establish her place in this family. She walked across the room and dipped her hand into the drawer. "Thank you."

"Have you known Charles long?" he asked.

She wrapped her fingers around some spoons. "Not long."

"Were you a friend of Alice?"

He stood so close that she could see her face mirrored in his black eyes. "Alice?"

"Charles's wife."

"No, no. I didn't know her."

"Are you from Fort Worth?"

"No."

The silence wove around them until she felt as though she was being wrapped in a shroud.

"Where are you from?" he finally asked.

"No place in particular. We moved around a lot."

"Like Gypsies?"

"I thought you said you were no longer a Texas Ranger."

"I took an oath to protect the welfare of this state when I joined the Rangers in seventy-four. I didn't turn in the oath with my resignation."

"And you think I'm a threat to the state of Texas?"

"Not to the state, but maybe to this family. I know a lot of women who would take advantage of Charles's situation to better themselves."

"That doesn't say much for the company you keep."

He narrowed his eyes, and she noticed a subtle tightening of the muscles in his jaw. Quite suddenly, she regretted the sharpness of her tongue. Generally, she kept it sheathed unless she was extremely nervous or feeling threatened. At this moment, she felt both.

"How did you say you and Charles met?" he asked.

"I didn't say."

A sound in the doorway caused Maddie to turn. Pride reflected in his eyes, Charles stood in the threshold, holding each daughter's hand. Both girls wore dresses, white stockings, and black shoes. Charles had brushed their blond tresses to a sheen and placed violet ribbons in their hair. He'd scrubbed the dirt and smudges from their faces to reveal a scattering of freckles across the bridge of Hannah's nose and the top of Taylor's cheeks.

A disgruntled Aaron stood beside Hannah. His white starched shirt was buttoned all the way to his throat and a black string tie circled his neck beneath the collar. He wore pants that showed no indication they were worn for play. His brown hair was slicked down, a few errant strands sticking up in the back. He glared not at Maddie, but at Jesse.

"Uncle Jesse didn't have to dress up," Aaron announced.

"Uncle Jesse doesn't need to impress a lady," Charles said as he brought the children into the kitchen.

Smiling at Charles, Maddie felt the tears sting her eyes.

"I don't want to impress one, either," Aaron grumbled.

Maddie jumped as Jesse purposefully cleared his throat behind her.

Aaron guffawed. "Uncle Jesse says only guilty people jump when he does that."

Hannah released her father's hand, walked over to Maddie, and wrapped her small hand around Maddie's fingers. "Don't worry. I jump, too, and I'm almost always good." Her brown eyes grew larger and rounder as she looked to her uncle for confirmation. Smiling warmly, he gave her a nod.

Maddie prayed the man would never smile at her like that. She could easily forget that he'd once been a man who enforced the law, and that could prove disastrous.

"Why don't we all work together to get this meal served up, and when we're finished eating, we'll go see what those presents are," Charles suggested.

"You haven't given them their presents?" Maddie asked.

"Of course not. You helped me select them. You should share in the joy of giving them."

The joy. And she did feel the joy, smiling at him, seeing the understanding reflected in his brown eyes. For the first time since she'd agreed to marry him, she reached out and squeezed his hand. She wondered if she'd ever feel happier than she did at this moment.

3

Whiskey. Her eyes reminded Jesse of a glass of good whiskey, the kind that went down smooth and warmed a man's insides. The kind of whiskey a man enjoyed getting drunk on. And standing there, lifting her down from the stagecoach, he'd found himself getting drunk.

His hands had spanned her tiny waist and ached for the privilege to span the rest of her. She was as light as a billowy cloud floating in the sky. He could have held her above the ground all day, well into the night before he would have felt the strain. He'd wanted to yank the hat from her head and give freedom to the honey colored hair he'd spotted beneath, to let the silken tresses pour over his hands the way he poured honey over biscuits.

Since he'd been working at his brother's inn, he'd helped a hundred women climb down from the stagecoach. Many had been more beautiful than the woman he'd assisted today. So why had he not wanted to take his hands off her?

Until he'd discovered she was married to his brother. Then he hadn't been able to release her fast enough. But throughout the afternoon, his eyes had taken liberties denied his hands, caressing, touching her at every opportunity. He'd only caught a glimpse of her smile, but it was enough to make him understand why Charles had married her. What he couldn't understand was why she'd married a man who could only promise her grief?

The questions he'd asked in the kitchen had been an

attempt to glean some insight into her motives. She'd been wary, uneasy, and he'd thought he was making progress until she'd shot him down with her opinion on the company he kept.

He snorted. The company he kept. He'd been speaking in generalizations, not specifics. So why did he feel like she'd gotten the better of him?

It was her damned whiskey eyes. They'd distracted him until he was searching for facts like a fresh recruit searched for outlaws: with absolutely no success.

Sitting on a bale of hay, he rubbed oil into the harnesses he'd gathered. He studied the way his hands moved over the leather and imagined them caressing a delicately shaped woman. His hands would slide slowly along her ribs until they gently palmed her small breasts.

"What do you think of Maddie?"

Jesse jerked his head up and wiped the sweat from his brow with the sleeve of his shirt. He was damn grateful his brother wasn't a mind reader. "I don't make it a habit to judge people before I know them."

"That puts you in the minority, doesn't it?"

Shrugging, he went back to work on the harnesses. "I never put much stock in what the majority thought. When will the cattle get here?"

"The cattle?"

Jesse stilled his hands and slowly lifted his gaze to his brother's. He wasn't at all pleased with the tone in which the question had been asked, as though Charles didn't even know what a cow was.

"Yes, the cattle. The cattle I gave you money to buy."

Clearing his throat, Charles stretched his neck as though someone had just dropped a rawhide noose around it. Jesse's trepidation increased. He'd spent years saving that money, risking his life more than once for a dream. "You did buy the cattle, didn't you? That was one of the things you were supposed to do when you were in Fort Worth seeing the doctor."

"Well, I saw the doctor."

"And the man I told you to see about the cattle?"

Charles shoved his hands into his pockets. "Hell." He met his brother's unflinching gaze. "I needed the money for something else."

"For something else? With the railroads crisscrossing this state, the stage lines are starting to disappear. What the hell are we going to do then? The cattle were something we could fall back on when your inn plays out."

In retrospect, Charles realized he probably could have gotten by with a lesser bid, but all he had thought about at the time was the expression on Maddie's face, as though with each passing moment, she was dying a little bit inside. He had wanted to ensure no one else would bid. He had wanted her off that table without her trembling fingers slipping beneath the other strap of that gown. "I needed the money for Maddie."

"You spent my six hundred dollars on your wife?" Jesse roared, throwing the harnesses to the ground and rising to his feet.

"She wasn't my wife at the time."

"I'm listening," Jesse ground out.

"You ever been to Bev's when she's found a virgin to start working for her?"

"A whore? You spent *my* money on a *whore?*"

"No, I spent *our* money on *Maddie*. I paid a thousand dollars to get her off that damn table. I took her back to my hotel room and asked her to marry me."

"She must have been hell in bed."

Jesse was totally unprepared for the balled fist that slammed into his jaw and sent him sprawling over the bale of hay. Years of fighting to earn his place in the world had caused him to develop rapid-fire reflexes. Quickly, he recovered and jumped to his feet, his own fists balled at his sides. He stood there with his chest heaving. Any other man would have already felt his fist plowed into his face, but Jesse knew he couldn't hit Charles. He'd defend himself if his brother threw another punch, but he wouldn't hit him back.

"She's my wife, Jesse. You'll give her the respect she deserves as my wife or, by God, you'll stay the hell out of my house."

Jesse watched Charles storm out of the barn. Rubbing the spot he was certain would bruise, he gingerly moved his mouth. Well, he'd wondered what kind of woman would marry a man with Charles's affliction. Now he knew.

He dropped onto the bale of hay and buried his face in his hands. Raising cattle had been his father's dream, a dream that had moved them to travel from Tennessee, not knowing what lay ahead. He'd wrapped both his childish hands around his father's dream, felt like a man when his father discussed the ranch they'd build, the land they'd gaze out on, the cattle they'd raise. Upon his death, his father had handed his dream down to Jesse.

When Jesse had shared his dream of raising cattle with Charles, he thought Charles had embraced the dream as well. He groaned in frustration. Charles had traded his hard-earned money for a whore.

His options were limited. He could return to the honest labor of working for the Texas Rangers, occasionally risking his life. He could go back to endless nights before a campfire, the camaraderie of men, the absence of decent women and children.

Or he could take up bounty hunting. The thought curdled his stomach. As a Ranger, he'd hunted men because of the things they'd done, not because of the reward offered for them. As much as he tried to convince himself bounty hunting was no different, he couldn't. It was different.

Or he could scrape and pinch and hope the inn had a few more good years in it.

He lifted his head and looked out the open barn door into the blackness of night.

He knew Charles hadn't meant to betray his dream. It was the woman who was responsible. She'd no doubt swayed her hips, batted her eyes, and smiled at him. She'd convinced him to marry her and, like a silent thief, had stolen Jesse's dream.

Well, he had plenty of experience in dealing with thieves. In the farthest regions of West Texas, a Ranger served as judge, jury, and hangman when the situation warranted it, and this situation warranted his serving as all three.

Before he was finished, she'd regret taking his brother for a fool and robbing Jesse of his dream.

Not wanting to intrude, Maddie stood just inside the doorway and watched as Charles, resting on his knees with nightgowns draped over his thigh, prepared his daughters for bed.

Patiently, he removed their shoes, stockings, and dresses. Then he glanced over his shoulder. "Perhaps you wouldn't mind helping Hannah. She's not quite the wiggle worm Taylor is."

Maddie felt a tingle of gratitude, and the feeling of belonging touched her heart as she walked across the room and knelt beside Charles. He handed her a nightgown.

"Touch the stars," he said. Both girls lifted their arms and stretched their fingers toward the ceiling. He slipped a muslin nightgown over Taylor's head.

Smiling, Maddie imitated his actions and slipped the nightgown over Hannah's head, working her arms through the sleeves, drawing the gown over her body. She was finished before Taylor giggled and collapsed onto her father's lap. Charles carried her to a small bed. Each side had a wooden rail extending one foot above the mattress with wooden slats positioned at one inch intervals.

"Will those rails keep her in?" Maddie asked.

"No, they're just designed to stop her from falling out."

"Uncle Jesse made 'em," Hannah announced proudly as she crawled into her own bed. "Only I don't need 'em cuz I'm a big girl."

Charles walked to the dresser, picked up two brushes, and handed one to Maddie. "We'd better braid their hair. Otherwise, we'll spend half the morning untangling it."

"Uncle Jesse didn't braid our hair," Hannah said.

"Uncle Jesse didn't bathe you, either, did he?"

Hannah and Taylor shook their heads vigorously as grins filled their faces.

"Yeah, I think he forgot you were ladies."

Maddie sat on the bed and brushed Hannah's silky fine tresses. Watching Charles braid Taylor's hair, she was surprised he had the skills and wondered if he'd braided his wife's hair. When the task was complete, he kissed Taylor on the cheek.

"Give your ma some sugar, too."

Maddie kissed Hannah, then bent over Taylor. Taylor's chubby arms wrapped around her neck, wrapped around her heart. Then she stepped away as Charles brought the quilts over each girl's shoulders before placing a kiss on their cheeks. Swallowed by the bedding, they looked extremely tiny and vulnerable.

Charles dimmed the lamp resting on the night table that stood between the beds. "We leave it burning a little to keep the nightmares away. 'Night, girls."

Hannah sat up. "We didn't say 'night 'night to Uncle Jesse."

Charles returned to her side, eased her onto the bed, and covered her back up. "Uncle Jesse had some chores he needed to take care of. He'll be in later."

"But I wanna kiss him."

"Tell you what. Why don't you put a kiss in your hand and keep it under your pillow? You can give it to him in the morning."

Hannah looked doubtful, but she kissed her palm, balled her fist, and stuck it beneath her pillow. Taylor imitated her sister's actions. Charles gave each girl one last kiss before escorting Maddie out of their room.

Once in the hallway, he placed his hand on the small of her back. "We'll say good night to Aaron, but don't be disappointed if he doesn't give you a kiss. When he was four, he told Alice that he'd used up all his kisses."

"Used up all his kisses?"

Smiling, he nodded. "Yep, but I figure in about five years, he'll discover some he hoarded away."

Charles tapped on Aaron's door. When Aaron answered, he took Maddie's hand and stepped into the room. Aaron lay in the bed with the covers drawn over him.

"Thought we'd say good night."

" 'Night."

Charles sat on the edge of the bed. "I missed you while

I was in Fort Worth. Thought you might give me a hug."

Aaron cast a furtive glance Maddie's way. "Ain't gonna hug her."

"Did I ask you to?"

Shaking his head, Aaron sat up and slung his arms around his father's neck. Charles hugged him tightly. "I love your mother, Aaron. My marriage to Maddie doesn't change that." Feeling Aaron's arms tighten around him, he knew he'd tapped into some of the boy's fears.

"I miss Ma," Aaron whispered hoarsely against Charles's neck.

"I miss her, too. I think about her every night before I go to sleep, but a man needs more than memories to hold onto at night, he needs more than memories in his life. Someday you'll understand that a man likes to have a woman he can hold."

Aaron released his father. "Uncle Jesse doesn't have a woman to hold."

"He has his dreams, and I imagine buried somewhere within those dreams is a woman. He just hasn't taken the time to find her."

"How come Uncle Jesse didn't come home tonight?"

"He had some things he had to take care of."

Aaron scrunched his face in distaste. "Is he gonna bring a wife home tomorrow?"

Charles smiled. "I don't think so."

Aaron buried himself within the mattress as Charles rearranged the displaced quilts. "Don't suppose you'd just say good night to Miss Maddie."

Aaron looked past his father to the silent woman standing within his room. " 'Night."

"Good night, Aaron."

He nodded before rolling over. Shaking his head, Charles stood.

They stepped out into the hallway. "Give him time," Charles said quietly.

"He seems to think the world of your brother."

Charles nodded. "Jesse came to live here shortly after Alice died. I had a baby and a three-year-old I was trying to care for. What little time I had for Aaron wasn't enough. And the time I did find for him . . ." He shook his head. "We were in the barn, and I was yelling at him about something he'd done wrong. I can't even remember what it was now. Suddenly, Jesse cleared his throat, and I jumped clear out of my skin."

Maddie smiled, and he touched the curved tip of her mouth. "See, you're not the only one he makes jump. Anyway, there he stood, looking for a place to call home. He gave Aaron the time and attention I couldn't. Which is good. I'm glad they're close."

They strolled the hall until they stood before the first bedroom. "Why don't you get ready for bed?" Charles suggested. "I'm going to check downstairs. I'll be back shortly."

"Why hasn't Jesse come back to the house?"

Charles averted his gaze. "He had some chores—"

She slipped her hand into his and brushed her thumb lightly across his discolored knuckles. "You told him, didn't you?" she asked quietly. "Told him how you met me?"

"It doesn't matter, Maddie. Jesse just doesn't understand. He sees everything as though it's been painted in black and white. I view things as though they've been painted in varying shades of gray. When the light shines on them, you see something different."

"I don't want to come between you two. Family is too important, Charles."

"You're family now, Maddie. Like Aaron, he'll come to realize that in time. Now, get ready for bed, and I'll be back in a few minutes."

She watched her husband descend the stairs before she opened the door to her new bedroom. She'd first seen it that afternoon when they'd brought the children upstairs to receive their gifts. The room spoke eloquently of Charles's relationship with his first wife.

Solid walnut furniture was an expression of his masculinity, but the frilled curtains adorning the windows and the handmade quilt covering the bed were evidence of her femininity. Nothing in the room overshadowed anything else, but each item had been specifically chosen to complement the other. The walnut washstand where he would shave in the morning, her delicate mirrored dresser where she would prepare herself for bed at night. Glancing around the room, she knew her husband had indeed shared something special with his wife. She felt a measure of relief knowing she was not competing with the woman for a place in Charles's heart.

She changed into her nightgown and wrapper before sitting in the plush velvet-covered chair in front of the mirrored dresser. As she worked the brush vigorously through her hair, she heard the door to her bedroom open. She closed her eyes, dreading what she might see when she opened them, afraid Charles's trip downstairs to check on things had included whiskey. She felt his hands come to rest on her shoulders and opened her eyes.

In the reflection of the mirror, he smiled softly. Relief coursed through her, and she smiled back. Reaching around her, he took the brush from her hand and brought it gently down through her honey tresses. Not since her mother had died had anyone brushed her hair. She'd forgotten how nice it felt to be pampered. The brush stilled, and Charles caught her gaze in the mirror.

"I'd like to hold you tonight," he said quietly.

Nervously, she nodded in agreement to his request. He handed the brush back to her. "I'll leave the braiding to you."

She took the brush and parted her hair as he walked away. She wondered how she would manage to braid her hair with her fingers trembling so badly.

Charles looked around the room, trying to decide the best way to prepare himself for bed. This room had no screen behind which he could discreetly change his clothes. And even if it did, he had nothing into which he could change. He'd always slept without a stitch of clothing on and owned no nightshirts. He thought about looking through Jesse's belongings, but he knew he'd find nothing appropriate there. He eased his shirt out of his pants and slowly undid the buttons.

Standing, Maddie studied the door. "I think I'll check on the children," she said, her voice quivering.

"That's a fine idea."

She rushed out of the room, clicking the door closed. Charles released a deep breath before quickly stripping down to his underdrawers and burying himself beneath the covers of the bed.

Quietly walking the hallway, Maddie opened the first door and peered into the girls' room. They were both lying on their sides asleep, their hands still holding kisses beneath their pillows.

She closed the door and walked to Aaron's room. She didn't have the courage to open his door, to chance disturbing him and making him dislike her any more than he already did. She walked to the end of the hallway and gazed out the window into the black night.

She thought of all the nights she and her mother had left a lantern burning in the front window so her father and brother could find their way back to them. She and her mother had dreamed of the life they'd have when things worked out for her father, when he had a job that paid off big. She touched her fingertips to the window. Her mother had died never touching her dreams. Now Maddie lived in a house larger than any she'd ever seen, married to a man kinder than any she'd ever known. She made a silent vow that Charles would never regret taking her out of Bev's.

She returned to her bedroom, opened the door, and peered in timidly. Charles lay in bed, one arm beneath his head.

Slowly, she walked across the room. She dimmed the flame burning in the lamp before removing her wrapper. This room contained no settee, and her husband had kept his promise. He hadn't passed out this night. She smiled shyly as he lifted the covers inviting her into his bed.

She eased beneath the sheets and lay stiffly on her back, her arms pressed against her sides. She wasn't certain how a woman went about letting a man hold her.

"Have you ever slept with a man holding you?" Charles asked.

"No," Maddie whispered to the ceiling.

"Does the thought frighten you?"

"No."

"Does it make you nervous?"

She shifted her gaze toward him. He was cast in shadows, but she thought she could make out the barest of smiles on his face. "Yes."

"I want you to roll over to your side."

Maddie did as instructed. Charles placed his arm around her and gently guided her into his embrace. She rested her head in the crook of his shoulder as his hand idly rubbed her arm. She released a nervous laugh. "I can hear your heart beating."

"And I can hear yours."

She stiffened. It was one thing to hear his heart, another to think he could hear hers. Somehow, it made her acutely aware that she was, for the first time in her life, lying in bed with a man. "Can you?"

"No, not really. I just thought if I teased you a bit, you might begin to feel more comfortable. You have nothing to fear in my bed, Maddie."

Then she relaxed a little and placed her arm over the quilt, her fingers threading through the hairs on his chest. An image of thick black hairs peeking through the opened collar of a chambray shirt came to her mind. She had, of course, seen other men without their shirts. Yet, she'd never had a urge to reach up and touch the curling hairs as she had this afternoon when she'd stepped down from the stagecoach.

"I see similarities between you and Jesse . . . and yet, you seem so different."

"Probably because we were raised differently. We were traveling from Tennessee, part of a wagon train, when our parents took the fever and died. We were farmed out to different families. When we hit Texas, the family that took Jesse kept heading west. The family that took me settled in Carthage."

"How old were you?"

"I was eight. Jesse was twelve."

"That must have been hard for you."

Charles stopped rubbing her arm. "It was damn hard. When I was nineteen, I decided to try and find him. Just started walking with no earthly idea where I was bound, where to look for him. Whenever I could, I traveled by stagecoach. One day, the stagecoach stopped here. I stepped out of the coach and tilted my hat to the owner's daughter. She smiled. The next morning when the stagecoach moved on, I didn't. Three months later, we got married."

"She must have been beautiful."

"She was beautiful to me."

She remembered his saying he never expected to love again and wondered at the type of woman who could so captivate a man. She felt more than heard him chuckling. "What is it?"

He cleared his throat. "I was just thinking. I asked both my wives to marry me an hour after I met them."

"Did you really?"

"Yep. Course, it took Alice a little longer to appreciate me and say yes."

"But eventually she came around," she stated softly.

"Yeah, eventually."

A comfortable silence eased in around them. "Charles, I really am sorry my presence has caused hard feelings between you and Jesse."

"Don't worry about it. Jesse's temper blazes, then dies quickly. He's just aggravated because he thinks I do things without thinking them through. He, on the other hand, doesn't do anything without thinking it to death. It's damn irritating sometimes."

"He doesn't seem to think it to death before he clears his throat."

He chuckled. "I guess I should have warned you about that."

Warned her about that? She just wished he'd warned her that he had a brother. A brother with eyes as black as sin. A brother who no longer wore the outer trappings of a Texas Ranger, but still carried the oath within his heart.

❧ 4 ❧

Leaning against the oak tree, Maddie watched the girls gather eggs from the hens. She wasn't certain a game had been created that could so captivate a child. The girls fearlessly searched every nook and cranny for the hidden wonders.

Earlier, Maddie had suggested that Charles spend some time alone with Aaron. He'd welcomed the idea. Since school was not in session, he'd decided to take Aaron fishing. She smiled at the memory of them ambling off with poles dangling over their shoulders, father and son, so alike in appearance. She hoped that some additional attention from Charles might lessen Aaron's animosity, but regardless, she thought the boy needed his father's guidance. She wasn't at all certain it was wise of Charles to allow his brother to have so much influence over his son.

"Never before knew a woman worth a thousand dollars."

Maddie jerked back and banged her head against the rough bark of the tree as Jesse stepped in front of her, effectively blocking off the early morning sun. The shadows falling across his face failed to cover the harshness of his features, or the cold disdain swimming in the murky depths of his eyes. She felt an icy shiver race up her spine. "I'm hardly worth a thousand dollars."

He braced his arms on either side of her. "Apparently, my brother feels differently. Did Charles happen to mention that six hundred dollars of that money he spent on you was mine?"

She shook her head, dreading any further words he might discharge.

Slowly, he grazed his knuckles along her cheek. "I'd say that sort of means you belong to me as well."

"I don't belong to you," she forced out, her breathing labored. Fear was something with which she'd grown accustomed to living, but the fear she faced in the past was trivial compared to that she faced now. "I married Charles. I'm his wife."

He trailed his finger down her throat. "I don't know why you're objecting. You were willing in Fort Worth to take any man into your bed, and I'm not greedy. I'd settle for you coming to me every other night even though I'm the one who had to give up the most to get you."

"I won't give myself to you willingly."

"You don't have to pretend with me." He lowered his mouth to her throat and blazed a path toward her ear. "I'm not Charles who's easily fooled. I know the kind of woman you are. He may think you're sweet and innocent, but I know the truth." Lifting his head, his eyes impaled her. "You're no better than dirt. You promised to spread your legs to the highest bidder. Well, lady, whether you knew it at the time or not, I was the highest bidder. You'll damn well spread them for me."

Each word had been fired with deadly accuracy, and she felt them slam into her heart. "I'll die first."

"You weren't willing to die in Fort Worth. Your body wasn't so precious to you then."

"It's still not," she hissed. "But the vows I exchanged with your brother are."

She didn't know whether her words or her vehemence caused him to ease back a little, and she didn't care. She took advantage of his confusion, pounded her fists against his chest, and slipped through the small crevice her actions had created. Lifting her skirt, she ran to the house.

She rushed into the kitchen, slammed the door shut, and pressed her back against it. Not that it would keep him out.

She didn't think he'd slept in the house last night. She

knew he hadn't come to the table for breakfast. She now had a clearer understanding of the argument that might have erupted between the brothers last night. Charles had spent Jesse's money on her. Whatever had possessed him to do such an irresponsible thing? His actions had constituted robbery, and Jesse was unjustly blaming her.

"Ma! Ma!"

The piping sounds reminded her of baby birds in a nest waiting impatiently for their mother to bring them food. Her hands trembled uncontrollably as she opened the door. The girls walked into the kitchen, carrying a pail filled with eggs between them. She took the pail, hearing the delicate eggs clatter as she carried it to the sideboard. She set the pail down, took a deep breath, and pressed her hands against the hardwood counter. She needed something to occupy her mind and her hands.

Turning around, she looked into the brown eyes looking at her expectantly. How easily children accepted what adults couldn't. She ventured a smile that she hoped hid her fear. "How would you like to help me bake a cake?"

Their eyes lit up, and she was reminded of shiny brown buttons. "What kind would you like to make?"

"Ponge," Taylor said.

"Ponge?"

"She means sponge," Hannah explained. "It's Uncle Jesse's favorite."

Maddie wanted to shriek. What was it about that man that made these children adore him? If she made a cake for him, she'd use salt in place of sugar—and lots of it. "What is your father's favorite cake?"

Taylor stuck her finger in her mouth. Hannah drew her brows together in thought, then shrugged her tiny shoulders. Maddie sighed in defeat. "Then I guess we'll make sponge cake."

She began gathering the ingredients from the pantry, turning when she felt a tug on her skirt. With a secretive smile, Hannah said, "You'll be glad."

"Oh, I'm sure I will. There's nothing I want more than I want to make your Uncle Jesse happy."

Hannah's smile grew. "He can't make his warning sound when he's eating sponge cake."

Maddie dropped to her knees and hugged the child close. "Then maybe we'll make two."

Coming out of the tack room, Jesse halted abruptly and watched Hannah walk through the barn. She was holding something in her palms, taking tiny steps and great care not to drop whatever it was. At the rate she was traveling, she'd reach him by the end of the week. With long, sure strides, he crossed the expanse separating them.

A big smile graced her face when she lifted her eyes and hands up to him. "For you."

Lowering himself to the ground, Jesse took the offering, returning her smile in kind. He took a bite of the cake, closed his eyes, and gave his approval with a gentle purring in his throat. He opened his eyes and touched a finger to the flour resting on her cheek. "Did you make it?"

"Me and Taylor and Ma."

He looked at the cake. It was still warm. He wondered why he'd thought Charles had made it when Charles had only returned a short time ago. He wondered why Maddie had sent Hannah out with the cake, and he wondered when his brother was going to come to the barn and beat the living hell out of him. He'd been doing as much hard manual labor as he could find so when Charles lit into him he'd be too tired to fight back.

"Eat some more," Hannah prodded. "Ma made it so you'd be happy. She said so."

He unfurled his body. The cake suddenly felt like a lead weight resting in his hand. "I'll finish it while I'm working back here." He headed for the tack room, then stopped and turned back around. "Tell everyone who made the cake that I appreciate it."

Delight raced across the child's features before she raced out of the barn. Jesse walked into the tack room and set the cake on a ledge against the wall.

*　　　*　　　*

Maddie stepped out onto the back porch and glanced around the yard. She'd spent the day avoiding Jesse, and it became obvious when he didn't join them for the noon meal that he was avoiding her as well. She wondered briefly where and what he was eating. It seemed unfair that he should starve to death because Charles had spent his money. If she could, she'd find a way repay him, but not in the manner he'd suggested this morning.

She stepped off the porch and walked toward a small fenced-in area where Aaron knelt before granite markers.

The girls had accepted her as easily as a new day accepts the first rays of the sun. She didn't expect Aaron to ever call her Ma, but she did want him to at least look at her without distrust marring his features. Taking a deep breath, she stopped beside the fence.

"This is my ma's resting place. You ain't welcome here."

Maddie studied the defiant set of his mouth and wondered what she could do to make sure this child didn't grow into a hard man, filled with bitterness.

"I noticed all the flowers growing at the front of the house. Did your mother like flowers?"

"She loves flowers."

"Perhaps you'd like to pick a few and bring them here."

"You pick 'em, they die. Then they're no good," he said as though she wasn't much smarter than a mule.

Determined not to lose her patience, Maddie sighed. "There are just so many flowers. What if we planted a few of them here beside the fence?"

"What do you mean?"

Excitement grew inside Maddie as she heard Aaron's voice for the first time with no anger in it. "Well, we could, *you* could decide which flowers were your mother's favorites, and we could dig them up and plant them here. Of course, it would all depend on whether or not you knew how to dig up a plant carefully so you don't damage the roots."

"Course I know how! I'm the one who helped Ma plant all her flowers." He twisted his mouth. "Probably ought to check with Pa."

"He's taking a nap with Hannah and Taylor."

"He takes a lot of naps. Could ask Uncle Jesse."

She wanted to scream. Her permission was all he should need. She was his mother now, although she thought she'd lose whatever she'd gained if she told him what she thought. "If you think you need someone's permission, go ask your uncle, although people seldom need permission to do something good."

He pondered her words with great seriousness. "I guess we don't need to ask Uncle Jesse." He came outside the fence. "We got some little shovels. We could use the wagon Pa pulls Hannah and Taylor in when we go for picnics. They're just babies so they get tired easy."

"Why don't you get everything, and I'll meet you in front of the house?"

He darted off toward the barn, and Maddie ambled toward the front of the house.

They worked together in silence. Aaron favored the begonias which flourished in varying shades of red and pink. He carefully dug them up and handed them gingerly to Maddie to set in the wagon. When he had a dozen flowers gathered, he pulled the wagon to the fence that surrounded the small family resting place.

Maddie knelt beside Aaron and worked the ground, preparing the soil to receive the begonias, tunneling the dirt over, discarding the grass and weeds. "When my mother died," she said quietly, "I was alone. My father and brother were out on a job."

Aaron worked more vigorously.

"I tied two sticks together so they formed a cross and used that to mark her place."

He stopped working. "When did she die?"

"Long ago."

"How old was you?"

"Ten. I still miss her."

He said no more, but worked diligently to create a new garden. Not until all the flowers were returned to the earth, did he again speak. "S'pose if you wanted, you could step inside the fence." He stood and put the small shovels into the wagon. "Seein's as how you helped. I don't think Ma would mind."

She stepped inside the fence, whispered a few words, then left quietly.

"What'd you say?"

She picked up the handle on the wagon. "I thanked her for bringing such wonderful children into the world."

He came up beside her and slipped his hand around the handle. Half his hand covered hers. "I'll pull it."

"Why don't we pull it together to the house? Then you can pull it alone to the barn."

She breathed a sigh of relief when he didn't object to her suggestion.

Feeling an abundance of guilt, Charles walked into the barn. Night had fallen, supper had been served, and Jesse's absence had been keenly felt by all. He hadn't expected his brother to hold onto his anger for so long. "Maddie left some food out on the back porch for you."

Jesse glanced over his shoulder before returning to the task of grooming his stallion. Midnight had served him well over the years, and he never missed an opportunity to show his appreciation. "I saw it."

"So why didn't you take it? She's a hell of a cook."

"Is that the reason you married her?"

"I married her because I want my children to grow up knowing a mother's love."

"I don't know why the hell no one thinks I can take care of children." Jesse spun around and pounded a tightened fist to his chest. "I promised I'd take care of them. I'd see to it they stayed a family."

Charles heard twenty years of pain erupt in his brother's voice. "Is that what this is about?" he asked quietly. "You think I don't trust you to look after my children?"

"Why the hell else would you take a wife on such short notice?"

Charles sighed heavily. "Do you know what I remember most about our mother? I remember the way she smelled— like honeysuckle laced with flour. I remember the feel of

her fingers as she moved the hair off my brow, the lilt of
her voice as she sang us to sleep. My children have no such
memories, Jesse. They have none of that softness in their
lives."

"But why marry a woman you had to buy? What the hell
kind of a woman do you think works in a brothel?"

"A desperate one."

"And you want a woman like that, a woman who'd sell
her body, to raise your children? She'll have your daughters
dressed in red gowns and your son's virginity before he's
twelve."

Charles laughed, a sad, sorrow-filled laugh. "Dear God,
Jesse, how wonderful it must be to have never in your life
been desperate. To have always been in control of your
destiny. To have never once traveled a path not of your
choosing."

"A person always has a choice."

"When Mother and Father died and different families
took us in, were we choosing then? Did you want to—"
Closing his eyes tightly, he pressed a tightened fist to his
forehead. "Did you want to travel that road, Jesse? Is that
why they had to tie you up to keep you in that wagon?"
Opening his eyes, he glared at Jesse. "Two nights ago, you
told me you didn't judge a person before you knew them,
and here you are judging and hanging Maddie—" Groaning,
he brought another fist up and pressed the heels of both
hands against his brow.

Jesse took a few steps toward him. "Are the pains back?"

"They seldom leave anymore." He staggered before falling to his knees.

Jesse rushed across the space separating them, dropped
beside Charles, and dug his fingers into his hard thighs.
"What'd the doctor in Fort Worth say?"

"Same thing as old Doc Murdoch. Only he offered to
cut open my head and make sure. I wasn't interested."
A small cry escaped his lips as he collapsed into a piti-
ful heap.

Jesse edged toward him, slipped his arms beneath him,
and lifted him. He placed Charles's head in his lap and ran

his roughened fingers back and forth across his brother's furrowed brow.

"And what the hell does your wife think about all this?" he asked.

"She doesn't know," Charles ground out through the pain. He released a short laugh. "She thinks I'm a drunkard."

"You didn't tell her?"

He rolled his head slightly from side to side. It was becoming too difficult to concentrate on the words. "Wanted to wait . . . wait until she came to love the children."

"Jesus, Charles, you had no right."

Charles tried to wade through the pain, to explain, but all his thoughts remained trapped inside his head. He wanted Jesse to understand the complete look of despair that had marred Maddie's features that night in the brothel, to understand what it felt like to bear witness to the sight of a soul as it was slowly dying.

The pain continued to wash over him like the waves of the sea stirred up by a hurricane, harsh, unforgiving, drowning out his thoughts, his feelings, until eventually they'd drown out his life. He heard the roaring increase, felt the pain riding the crest of the wave until it took him under.

Charles's tortured face relaxed, and Jesse knew he hadn't heard a solitary word he'd uttered about the injustice of his actions. He stopped applying pressure to Charles's temples and lifted him into his arms, cradling him in the same way he had when Charles was a small boy and traveling across the country in a covered wagon had frightened him so much.

"You had no right, Charles, no right to marry her and not tell her she could be a widow before the year is out."

❧ 5 ❧

Standing in the doorway of the barn, his arm braced against the beam, Jesse watched the graceful display as lightning illuminated the blackened night sky and outlined the clouds. A thick drop of water bounced off his nose. The thunder challenged the lightning. The ground reverberated. Then the sky went black, and more drops of rain fell.

He stepped back into the barn, but his gaze remained riveted on the sky. Half of it flashed silver, then dissipated into blackness.

It had taken him an hour to rouse Charles from his stupor, something that was becoming increasingly difficult to do. As soon as Charles was fully lucid again, Jesse had begun his tirade on Charles taking a wife under the circumstances.

Charles had looked at him as though he was an idiot. "She's a whore for Christ's sake, Jesse. Surely, you don't think I should treat her like she has feelings?"

Feelings? The woman definitely had feelings, and Jesse had trampled all over them that morning. Pain, anger, conviction, and determination had swum within the amber pool of her eyes, but pain had been by far the greatest of what she'd been feeling. He wondered why he hadn't just taken a knife and stabbed it through her heart, or better yet, stabbed it through his own. He'd never been so disgusted with himself in his entire life. He'd treated known murderers and desperadoes with more respect than he'd treated her, had shown them more mercy than he'd shown her.

Yet she'd kept silent. The fact that he was standing there with only the bruise on his chin that he'd received the night before was proof of that.

He slammed his fist into the beam, wishing he could pound it into his brother's face. Damn! He thought the woman knew! He was certain she'd married Charles for any inheritance she'd receive upon his death. He squeezed his eyes shut, trying to erase the memory of the happiness reflected in her face yesterday afternoon when Charles had brought the children into the kitchen.

He cursed the heavens, then cursed his brother. The woman didn't know the happiness was fleeting, and it wasn't his place to tell her.

After his confrontation with her that morning, he'd stayed out of her sight for the remainder of the day, but still he'd managed to watch her from afar. In the cool morning hours, she'd sat on the back steps and churned butter while the girls played at her feet.

Late in the morning, she'd hauled hot water to the wooden tub outside, scrubbed the clothes, and hung them on the line to dry. It had been over two weeks since he'd been able to find time to wash clothes. The shirt clinging to his body could sit in a saddle without assistance. He knew that she had to have noticed his larger clothes mixed in with the others she was washing. Yet she'd scrubbed them to death and slung them over the line anyway.

He didn't think the sponge cake had been a peace offering. He couldn't remember ever seeing so much pride reflected in Hannah's angelic face. He never thought to let the girls help him cook. Cooking was a chore, and the sooner he got it done, the sooner they could eat. He couldn't fathom the amount of patience it would take to let those two little girls help bake a cake. He could only imagine the mess they would have created. It had to have taken them twice as long. Yet Hannah had thoroughly enjoyed whatever her role had been, the joy clearly reflected in her eyes.

The rain increased and fell in torrents. Jesse watched the puddles quickly take shape. The rain was good. It would help the flowers Aaron had transplanted take root in their new home. Aaron had come into the barn, pulling that wagon, contentment evident in his face. Why hadn't he or Charles realized what it would mean to Aaron to plant flowers beside his mother's grave?

The lightning illuminated the house. Even in darkness, the house was inviting. Charles had laid out the conditions under which Jesse would again be welcomed into his home. He hadn't expected to willingly call a truce so soon, but there was nothing to be gained with his misplaced anger, and he was beginning to realize there was much to be lost.

He turned up the collar on his shirt and dashed through the rain toward the house. He leapt up the steps, grabbed the plate being protected by the eaves of the porch, and rushed into the kitchen. It smelled like cinnamon. A lamp was burning dimly on the table as though someone was hoping to quietly welcome him home.

Beads of moisture dribbled down his face as he sat and lifted the warm layers of cloth away from the plate. The spicy aroma of chicken and dumplings wafted up, tempting him. He studied the food for some time, knowing he shouldn't eat her offering until he'd apologized, but the house was still and quiet. He knew everyone had gone to bed. He picked up a fork and pierced a piece of chicken. It almost melted in his mouth. Charles was right; the woman was one hell of a cook. He should be eating crow instead of something this delicious.

In the morning, first thing, he'd make amends.

Maddie didn't think it was the harsh thunder that woke her. She'd always had the ability to sleep through storms. She peered through her lashes. A little pixie stood beside the bed, hands clasped before her chest, eyes wide, lips set in a frown. Opening her eyes fully, Maddie smiled at Taylor.

Thunder spoke out against the night. Taylor jerked her head toward the window, then threw her tiny body against the bed. Maddie drew the covers aside before placing her hand gently on the trembling child's shoulders. "Come on.

Get into bed with us." With Charles's arm draped over her stomach, she helped Taylor as much as she could. The little girl snuggled down into the bed, and Maddie drew her nearer.

As the thunder again resounded, Maddie whispered, "Sounds like your Uncle Jesse's warning sound, doesn't it?"

Taylor giggled and nuzzled her nose against Maddie's shoulder. Maddie felt the child's tremors subside. She touched a soft lock of her hair. Children were so different from adults. Their skin carried the scent of innocence, a softness not yet jaded by the reality of the world. They trusted and loved completely.

She tucked the blankets more securely around Taylor. Lightning flashed, filling the room with a momentary brilliance. Her breath caught and her heart pounded furiously against her breast at the sight of Jesse standing within the open doorway.

Jesse didn't know how long he had been staring at the intimate scene before the lightning revealed his presence. He expected anger to flare in the woman's eyes, but there was no anger, no annoyance, just a need to understand— to understand something he couldn't explain. He reached into the room, grabbed onto the glass handle, and pulled the door until it clicked into place. He pressed his forehead against the oak door and listened to the silent tranquillity within. Emblazoned within his mind was the sight of Taylor snuggled against Maddie as her arm protectively circled the child, and Charles sleeping peacefully as he held his wife.

He felt an unaccountable ache in his chest for things he'd never experienced. The women he'd taken to bed during his life weren't the kind a man held in his arms afterward, weren't the kind a man took with him into his dreams or his future. And they certainly weren't the kind of women who'd ever allow a child to crawl into their bed.

He walked to his own room. He closed the door, crossed the room, and braced both hands on the window. Gazing out, he watched the storm send down torrents of rain. Like the lightning flashing across the tempestuous sky, it suddenly occurred to him that when Charles had been talking about choosing paths to walk, his brother had been talking about his own path, a path Charles hadn't chosen, a short path whose final destination was certain death.

Jesse stripped off his clothes and fell into bed. He shoved an arm beneath his head and stared at the beamed ceiling, the play of shadows as the thunder chased the lightning across the sky.

Charles hadn't chosen his path, but he was traversing it with more courage than Jesse knew he, himself, would. He had little doubt that during the day there was enough activity going on to keep Charles's mind off the future, but at night when it was dark and quiet and the desire for things that could never be crept into a man's mind, what did a man do? He wrapped his arms around a woman and became lost in her scent, her softness.

Perhaps Charles had married Maddie as much for his sake as for the children's. No man wanted to walk the path toward Death alone, and Jesse knew he was a poor substitute for the compassion and understanding a woman could provide.

He rolled to his side and pounded his fist into his pillow. He'd never before realized how lonely a bed could be when only one person lay in it in the dark of night.

The early morning sun filtered in through the window, creating a hazy light within the kitchen. Jesse slid his gaze from his reflection in the small mirror above the sink to that of the woman standing in the doorway behind him. His gaze holding hers in the mirror, he reached for a towel and slowly wiped the last remnants of his shave from his face.

"I'm sorry. I didn't know you were in here," Maddie said.

Straightening, he turned, tossed the towel onto the counter, and reached for his shirt. "That's all right."

She took a step back. "I'll leave you—"

"I'm done." He shrugged on his shirt. She remained standing in the doorway as though afraid if she came into the room, he'd attack her. He knew he should apologize, but after spying her curled up in bed last night, he thought any apology he could have uttered would seem insignificant.

She glanced around the room as though seeking permission to enter. "I thought I'd take a cup of coffee to Charles. He's somewhat irritable before he's had his coffee in the morning."

"It's a family trait."

Raising an eyebrow, she curved up her mouth almost imperceptibly. "So you haven't had any coffee since I've been here?"

She was offering an honorable surrender, and he wondered why his defeat felt like a victory. "It would appear not."

She smiled fully then, a smile more intoxicating than the shade of her amber eyes. Her bare toes, peering out from beneath her wrapper, wiggled up and down. Such tiny toes attached to tiny bare feet. Bare feet attached to bare ankles. He couldn't see past the bare ankles, but he wondered how far up she went before she was no longer bare. As though following the course of his thoughts, she pulled on the sash of her wrapper. The gesture, if intended to ward off his thoughts, failed; it only emphasized the narrowness of her waist. Jesse flexed his fingers as he remembered the feel of that tiny waist as he'd held it in his hands.

"That was quite a storm we had last night," she said, her voice uncertain as she shifted her weight from one foot to the other.

"Yeah, it was. May have done some damage."

"The thunder and lightning frightened Taylor. That's why she crawled into bed with us."

"Thunder always frightened Cassie, too."

"Cassie?"

"Our sister. She'd crawl into bed with us whenever there was a storm."

A hint of loss echoed within his voice. She decided against pursuing the subject, not wanting to lose whatever she'd gained this morning, not certain how she'd managed to gain it. "Will you be joining us for breakfast?"

"Depends."

"On what?"

Jesse dropped his gaze to his boots. Now was the time to apologize formally, to say all those words that had been circling around in his head all night like the rain circling on the winds of the storm. He lifted his eyes to hers and saw her as he'd first seen her when he'd lifted her down from the stagecoach—young, innocent, sweet. The apology clogged his throat. "On whether or not I'm welcome."

"You are."

He knew he should show some sign of appreciation for her forgiveness. He wanted to tell her the sponge cake was the most delicious he'd ever had the pleasure of tasting. What little bit he'd had. The ants had devoured it as it sat upon the shelf. Instead, he asked a question that had been preying on his mind. "Why didn't you tell Charles how I treated you yesterday?"

"He can't force you to accept me, although judging from the bruise on his knuckles and the bruise on your chin, I'd say he tried."

Self-consciously, he grazed his finger along his tender flesh. "I'd better go see what's keeping Aaron and the milk."

He headed out the door. Maddie walked to the sink and glanced out the window. He'd stopped in his tracks and was watching her. He made a motion as though to come back into the house. Then he apparently changed his mind and walked briskly toward the barn.

With trembling fingers, she picked up a cup, poured black coffee into it, and headed back to her bedroom where her husband waited for her.

Charles dipped his fork into one of the fried eggs Maddie had set before him. They weren't as hard as the ones Jesse usually cooked. She placed some buttered bread on the table, took her seat, and smiled at him. He returned her smile. As she filled her plate, he noted the way she ignored Jesse, the way Jesse watched her.

"The storm seems to have passed," he said.

Jesse snapped his eyes to his brother's and knew Charles wasn't talking about Mother Nature's storms. "Appears it has."

"Good. Then you shouldn't mind taking Maddie into town today."

"What?" Jesse asked harshly, his brows drawing together.

Charles had the impression Jesse was sorely tempted to give his throat a sound clearing. Maddie came to attention, her eyes no longer studying the food on her plate, but nervously watching him. "I'm sure, now that Maddie's been here a couple of days, she's come to realize there are things she needs."

"You take her," Jesse barked.

"I've been gone a week. I'd like to spend today with the children."

"Take them with you."

"It's two hours into town, two hours back. It's tiring for them. I want a relaxed day. Besides, there's other supplies we need. You're more familiar with what we've run out of since I've been gone."

"Charles, I really don't need anything," Maddie said.

"A woman always needs something," Jesse growled as he scraped his chair across the floor and stood. "Be ready in twenty minutes."

Quite accurately imitating the storm that had barreled through the night before, he stomped out of the kitchen.

Maddie slumped forward and looked at Charles. "Why did you do that?"

He placed his hand over hers and squeezed gently. "Because I want him to care for you as much as I do, and that won't happen if you ignore him."

"I wasn't ignoring him. As a matter of fact, I spoke with him this morning when I came to get your coffee."

"Well, then, if you're friends already, it should be a very pleasant day."

A very pleasant day. It was an exceedingly pleasant day. The cold weather that had whipped through earlier in the week had dissipated, and the last remnants of spring were giving way to the fullness of summer.

The company, however, was unpleasant. Maddie sat, hugging her side of the bench seat, her back stiff and straight, her eyes on the canopy of leaves passing by overhead. Jesse was hunched forward, his elbows digging into his knees, his eyes trained, she was certain, on one of the horse's rumps. In contrast to the mood, the wagon swayed gently from side to side.

"Does the town have a name?" she asked brightly.

"Raeburn," he replied brusquely.

"Is that a family name?" she asked less brightly.

"Probably," he replied more brusquely.

She nodded as though he would care whether or not she acknowledged his inadequate answer and his desire not to engage in further conversation. She watched the horses flick their tails. She adjusted the positioning of her small hat, the one that matched her serge traveling dress. She felt the sweat trickle between her breasts and settle around her waist. Nothing she ever could, should, or would need was worth traveling with this man. The horses plodded along, and she began to wonder if they would ever reach the town.

"I have an idea," she said at last.

He grunted, and she was tempted to bury her knuckles in his arm. "You can stop the wagon and let me out here."

He jerked his head around, his dark eyes darkening further beneath the brim of his dark brown hat.

"You can leave me here, go into town, then pick me up on the way back so you don't have to endure my company for the day."

"You're going to sit out here for five hours?"

She shrugged lightly as though his concern was of little consequence. "There is plenty of shade. I ate a hearty breakfast. I should be fine."

His eyes narrowed. "I know the truth. It's my company you don't want to have to put up with."

"I have decided there isn't enough coffee in the entire world to improve your disposition."

"I don't like to be manipulated, and Charles did just that this morning."

"So you're taking it out on me?"

"I'm not taking it out on you."

"What do you call it when you'd rather stare at the back end of a horse than talk to me?"

His gaze went forward, and his expression darkened. "Hell."

She wasn't certain if her words or something he'd spotted on the back end of the horses had so aggravated him. She looked toward the road, realizing it was neither. Three-fourths of a tree, charred where lightning had severed it from the trunk, blocked the road. The horses halted. Jesse vaulted over the side of the wagon and stalked toward the tree, jerked his hat off his head, and wiped his brow with the sleeve of his shirt.

"I suppose we could just turn around and go home," she offered.

"Hell no! We need supplies! You need something from town!"

Scrambling down from the wagon, she walked to where he stood. "I don't need anything from town."

He plopped his hat back on his head and walked around the tree, studying it from all angles. "It's going to have to be moved eventually. Might as well do it now. You go stand over there beneath that tree."

"Are you hoping there's a loose branch somewhere that might fall on my head?"

He squatted. "Won't happen. Not with the luck I've been having."

Forcefully, she kicked the tree, rustling the branches. Jerking back, he landed on his backside. She smiled triumphantly as he scowled at her.

"It's not so funny to be startled into making a fool of yourself, is it?" she remarked.

"Get in the shade before the sun burns your nose." He got to his feet and walked toward the wagon.

She scurried over and blocked his path. "You didn't answer my question."

Towering over her, he glowered at her. She tilted her head back, refusing to be cowed. He tugged his shirt out of his pants and shoved the buttons through the holes. "Get in the shade."

"And if I don't?"

Shaking his head, he walked away, took off his shirt, and tossed it onto the seat of the wagon. He reached into the back of the wagon, hefted out a rope, and draped it over his shoulders.

Reluctantly, Maddie moved into the shade and watched him work. In the sunlight, she could see what she'd been unable to see in the gloom of the kitchen. The back she had so admired that morning carried a thin diagonal scar across it that began at the tip of one shoulder and raced toward his hip, disappearing somewhere beneath the waist of his pants. It was an ancient scar, blending in with the coloring of his body.

"How did you come by that scar on your back?" she asked.

"War."

She moved out of the shade. "The War Between the States?"

He tied the rope to the harness. "That's the one."

"You're a lot older than I thought."

He stopped working and stared at her. "How old did you think I was?"

"Thirty-three, thirty-four."

He nodded. "Thirty-four."

"You would have been a boy during the war."

He led the horses to the other side of the tree. "Old enough to beat a drum for the Union when it started, old enough to tote a rifle when it ended."

"But Texas stood with the Confederacy."

He studied her a moment. "You don't look old enough to know what slavery looked like. I couldn't defend it." He anchored the rope to the charred trunk and guided the horses toward the side of the road, the fallen tree trailing easily behind. He loosened the rope, pulled it out, and wrapped it around his crooked arm, bringing it over his shoulder.

"War is no place for a child," she said, watching the manner in which he worked, concise, wasting not a solitary movement.

"War's no place for anyone. Brings out the worst in men." Grabbing onto the harness, he led the horses back to the wagon. "Brings out the best, too," he threw over his shoulder as he tossed the rope into the back of the wagon before hitching the horses back into place.

He grabbed his shirt, slipped it on, buttoning it as he went around the wagon, and came to stand before her.

"And which did it bring out in you?" she asked.

"The best, of course."

He gave her a smile, the same warm smile he'd given Hannah that first day. Maddie wished he hadn't. Charles smiled all the time, but none of his smiles ever made her wonder what it would feel like to press her lips against that smile. She knew she shouldn't have those thoughts now.

He placed his hands on her waist, and she prayed he couldn't feel the rapid thudding of her heart that his nearness caused. The smile eased off his face as he stared into her eyes. His Adam's apple slowly slid up and down, and she felt his fingers tighten their hold. Then he scowled and lifted her into the wagon, leaving her with the uneasy feeling that he'd been privy to her thoughts. He climbed onto the wagon, took the reins, and set the horses into motion with a flick of his wrist.

In silence, Maddie watched the scenery roll by. Charles had been wrong. The storm hadn't passed.

The brass bell above the door clanked as Jesse opened the door. Maddie preceded him into the store, stiffening slightly when he took her elbow and led her toward the counter.

"McGuire, this is Mrs. Lawson. Whatever she wants, you just put on our account."

Angus McGuire's bushy white eyebrows shot straight up. "Mrs. Lawson, is it? And how long have you been that, lass?"

Blushing, Maddie wished Jesse hadn't drawn attention to her. "A few days."

"Ah, she's a pretty one, Jesse."

Jesse scowled at her. She lifted her chin. He snorted and laid a list of needed supplies on the counter. "Just get my supplies, will you, McGuire?"

"Marital bliss didn't last long," McGuire mumbled under his breath as he headed to the back room.

Jesse walked to the back of the store where a huge barrel was filled with nails. He grabbed an empty box and dropped nails into it. Then he returned to the front and set the box on the counter. Maddie was still standing where he'd left her.

"I don't want to spend all day in here. Get whatever it is you need so we can get going."

"I told you I don't need anything."

"You must have said something to Charles to make him think you needed something."

She drew her brows together. "No, I don't think so."

He expelled his breath. "All right. So there's nothing you need. There must be something you want."

"I want to make Charles happy." She glanced around the overly stocked store. "But I don't suppose there's anything in here I could buy that would do that."

Astounded and bemused at the same time, Jesse studied her. Some moments she appeared to be a woman of the world, and others she seemed as young as Hannah. He wanted to believe her words were declared to catch him off guard, and they did because within her voice, he'd heard the absolute truth. "Come here."

Hesitantly, Maddie followed as he threaded his way toward a distant corner. He stopped and waved his hand over a shelf laden with bottles. His hand seemed that much larger and more masculine next to the small, delicately shaped glass.

"Pick out some sweet smelling bath salts you can use."

Maddie stepped back, flinging her hands to her hips. "Are you saying I stink?"

He looked toward the ceiling and released a quick burst of air. "No, I'm not saying that. You more than anyone ought to know that I say what I mean."

"You didn't this time. You tell me how bath salts are going to make Charles happy."

"A man likes for his woman to smell sweet." He picked up a bottle and held it up to the window. "When he curls up next to her in bed, it's nice if she doesn't smell like the wood he's been chopping all day or the sweating horses he's been caring for." He set the bottle down. "Hell, do what you want." He started to walk off.

"Wait." He stopped, and Maddie cautiously approached the shelf. "There's so many. Which one would Charles like?"

"Hell, I don't know. Buy whatever you usually buy."

"I've never had bath salts."

"Never?" Jesse asked as he moved in behind her.

"Never. If we were fortunate, we had lye soap."

"Lye? It gets the dirt off, but no man wants to lie next to a woman who smells like him. Take the tops off the bottles and find one that smells like you should."

Self-consciously, Maddie reached for a bottle, pulled out the stopper, and sniffed. "I don't know what I should smell like. Like this?" She held the bottle out to Jesse.

"No, rose is too common. You need something different." He studied the bottles while Maddie continued to remove the stoppers and sniff.

"I never knew there were so many different smells."

"Scents. They're called scents," he informed her.

"So what should I scent like?"

Jesse stopped his hand halfway to its destination and glanced back over his shoulder. She had that challenging glint in her eyes, the one she'd worn that morning when she'd questioned him about his avoidance of coffee since her arrival. What should she smell like, this woman who the more he came to know was nothing at all what he'd expected? "Unusual, something unusual." He picked up a small bottle. "Here, try this."

She removed the stopper, and a soft, delicate fragrance wafted out of the bottle.

"Forget-me-not," Jesse said, "you should smell like forget-me-not."

"Do you think Charles will like it?"

"He'll like it."

"I wish there was some way I could surprise him."

"I could set up the bathtub in the Princess room."

"The Princess room?"

"Yeah, the one with the brass bed and all the frills. The one that looks like a fairy princess ought to be sleeping in it. You could bathe in there just before bedtime, and he wouldn't know until you got into bed."

"You'd do that for me?"

He looked away. "I want Charles to be happy, too."

She clutched the small bottle to her breast. "I guess I did need something after all."

They walked back to the front of the store, and she set the bottle on the counter beside the box of nails. Then she studied the jars of candy arranged on the counter.

"Do you want some?" Jesse asked.

"I was thinking of the children. Could we take them some cinnamon balls?"

"I don't see why not." He watched her pick up a small sack and carefully place six cinnamon balls inside. He suddenly wished she did want something. "You sure there's nothing you want?"

"I'm sure." She set the sack on the counter as McGuire came out of the back.

"I'll have my boy load your wagon," McGuire said.

"Fine," Jesse said. "Add these items in, and I might as well pick up the mail while I'm here. We'll have a stage coming through in a day or so. Save you a trip."

He followed McGuire to a little cubicle area with iron bars in the window. McGuire began gathering the pieces of mail and dumping them in a bag.

With nothing else to do, Maddie trailed behind Jesse. She glanced at the wall. Her knees wobbled, her lungs refused to draw in air, and she feared at any moment she'd hear the ricochet of bullets echoing around her.

"You all right?"

She jumped back, her hand to her throat, her gaze falling on Jesse. "I'm just fine." But her high-pitched voice sounded too nervous even to her own ears.

Jesse cast his glance to the reward posters covering the wall, and a look of pure disgust crossed his face. "You shouldn't concern yourself with animals like those." He studied her for a moment, then added, "You look a little pale. Why don't we get something to eat before we head home?"

Nodding, Maddie fought back the tears, the panic. She had never again expected to see those faces.

❧ 6 ❧

Acutely aware of Jesse scrutinizing her, Maddie stared out the window of the small restaurant. She thought if she lived to be a hundred, she'd never forget the look on his face when he'd confronted those images on the wall. Black and white Charles had said. Everything to Jesse was black and white. How could he possibly understand how everything in Maddie's world was gray? And if he learned the truth, what would he do then? And if he told Charles, would Charles's gray shadows suddenly become a stark black and white?

"You need to eat so we can get going."

"Are you always in such a hurry?" she asked, directing her attention to the man sitting across from her.

"If I was in a hurry, we wouldn't be in here now."

She stuck the tines of her fork into a bean, then pressed the bean against the side of the plate and worked it free, a thought niggling at the back of her mind. "Why did you leave the Texas Rangers?"

Jesse shoved his empty plate to the side and planted his elbows on the table. "My reason for wanting to be a Ranger no longer existed. I found what I was looking for."

"And what was that?"

"Family. Being a Ranger gave me a monthly stipend and the freedom to look for Charles and Cassie while I pursued the outlaws and troublemakers. When I found Charles, I felt like I'd come home."

"Did you ever find Cassie?" she asked quietly.

He glanced toward the street. "Family that took her in left without a trace when a smallpox epidemic struck their community. I have my doubts that she's even still alive. Every lead I get takes me nowhere."

"I'm sorry."

He glanced over at her, her eyes a reflection of his sorrow. Only a handful of people had understood his need to find the brother and sister who'd been torn from his life at such a tender age. He wondered why it didn't surprise him that she understood. He shrugged off-handedly. "At least I found Charles."

"I would imagine your life as a Ranger was exciting."

"It had its moments. Saw a lot of the state, worked alongside some fine men."

"Do you miss it?"

He shook his head. "I kept working as a Ranger for a while after I found Charles, but I began to feel like a tumbleweed in the wind. A Ranger is always searching for an outlaw, a renegade, someone. His life can't be worth more to him than the lives of the people he's supposed to protect. When I found Charles, met his family, I grew tired of the chances I was taking. After Alice died, he needed some help running the place, so I resigned."

"Charles loves Alice very much."

"They seemed to share something special, but now he has you."

Forcing a small smile, Maddie shook her head. "He told me he still loves her, that he'll never love anyone else."

"He has to have some feelings for you, or he wouldn't have married you."

"Whatever his feelings, love isn't one of them."

She watched the sunlight stream in through the window, caressing his profile as he studied her in silence. When at last he spoke, his voice was as gentle as the lowing of a lone steer in the dead of night. "A marriage without love seems like a hell of a sacrifice for a woman to make."

"I made the decision to accept a life without love when I walked through Bev's door. I'm not a fool. Men don't fall in love with soiled doves."

Jesse leaned forward. "No, you're not a fool. You strike me as being an extremely intelligent and well-educated woman . . . not at all the kind of woman a man would expect to find in Bev's parlor. Why the hell couldn't you have survived another way?"

She tilted her chin. "And how would you suggest I earn my keep? I grew up beneath the stars, a campfire burning brightly into the night the only permanence I ever knew, the only thing I could count on always being there. My father was an educated man. He taught me and my brother to appreciate the written word. I know Shakespeare and Dickens and have just discovered the wonder of Mark Twain. I enjoy reading poetry. I can write and decipher." She leaned forward. "I know. I could be a schoolteacher."

He narrowed his eyes.

"What? Don't you think a community would hire me to teach their children?"

"Maybe. If you had tried."

"Don't you think I did? My education is excellent, but informal. I never sat in a schoolhouse. I don't know what goes on in a classroom. And I have no references. No school can attest to my abilities. I can count the number of people who knew me on one hand, and two of those are now dead. The other two can't write their names and can usually be found in saloons."

Jesse leaned further across the table. "Damn it, Maddie, you could have found something if you'd tried harder. You didn't have to resort to selling your body like some cheap—"

She slammed her hands on the table. "Damn you!" she hissed through clenched teeth. "Damn you and your damn self-righteous judgment. One day I'm laughing with my brother, Andrew, and the next day I'm holding him in my arms while he dies. All I ever had that I could call mine was my father and my brother. And then they were dead. And all the things they'd promised, all the grand plans they'd made for me died with them. I was alone and scared and hungry. I traded everything I had to trade until I had nothing left to trade but my body. It may not have been a fine, upstanding occupation, but at least it was an honest one. I would have given something in exchange for what I got. And if that thought sickens you, Mr. Lawson, allow me to let you in on a little secret. It sickened me as well."

Abruptly, she stood. "Just go to hell. Just go to bleedin' hell."

Jesse watched her storm out of the building before he buried his face in his hands. Sighing heavily, he rubbed his roughened fingers up and down his face.

"You and Mrs. Lawson have a little spat?"

He peered through his fingers at Jean Lambourne, the elderly woman who owned the restaurant. Slowly, he brought his hands down. People were staring at him, but he didn't think any of them had been seated close enough to hear any of the conversation.

"Nothing I can't undo. How much do I owe you?"

Smiling, she patted his shoulder. "This one's on the house. Married life just ain't always what some women think it oughta be."

Standing, Jesse placed his hat on his head and brought the brim down low. " 'Preciate it. It was a good meal."

Once outside, he searched the boardwalks for a petite woman with a fiery temper and the slightest of English accents that emerged when she was angry. He swore under his breath when he finally caught sight of her, on the outskirts of town, trudging toward home.

Maddie heard the rumble of wagon wheels, the clip-clop of horses' hooves, but she kept her gaze focused straight ahead, her step determined. Then she smelled the sweat of horses as they neared, and one nudged her shoulder.

"Get in the wagon, Maddie."

"Go to hell!"

"Thought it was bleedin' hell."

"Bleedin' hell, then. Go to bleedin' hell." She jerked away from the horse and quickened her pace.

"Was your father English by chance?"

Maddie spun around. "What?"

Jesse drew the horses to a halt. "When you get angry, you talk with a slight accent. Thought maybe you'd picked it up from your father."

She felt the blood drain from her face. How could she have been so careless in her anger to forget that this man had made a living searching for outlaws, and would easily detect the small clues that would give away a man's identity—or a woman's?

"My family is none of your damn business." Turning, she walked briskly away.

Jesse set the brake on the wagon and wrapped the reins around the brake handle before jumping from the wagon and walking quickly to catch up with her. He placed a hand on her shoulder. She shrugged it off.

"Come on, Maddie."

"Leave me alone."

"I can't do that. I know who you are now."

She froze, everything within her screaming at another one of life's injustices. She lived in a home at last and had a family with children. His knowledge would strip her bare of both.

Gently, he turned her around, cupped her chin, and tilted her face, wondering at the tears filling her eyes. "You're my brother's wife, the poor woman who's been burdened with a jackass for a brother-in-law."

A mischievous glint she'd never before seen sparkled within the black depths of his eyes. Relief washed over her, and she couldn't contain the hysterical laughter that erupted from her throat. Then the laughter died and brought to life tears, flowing freely down her cheeks.

Jesse wrapped his arms around her, drawing her against his chest. "Maddie," he whispered against her hair.

Sobs wracked her body. "I didn't want to be a whore. I didn't. I wanted honest work. I offered to scrub floors, to clean out stalls. No one would hire me." A shudder coursed through her, and he pulled her more closely into his embrace. "I was cold and hungry and alone. I didn't want to go into Bev's. I didn't."

He tilted her face, his thumbs caressing her dampened

cheeks, his eyes holding hers. "I know."

"I'll be a good wife to Charles. I'll do whatever it takes. You'll see. I'll make him happy."

Lightly, he touched his thumb to her trembling lower lip. "I know you will. Now, come on. We're gonna be lucky to get home before nightfall."

He hoisted her into the wagon. Wiping away the last of her tears, she watched as he moved around to the other side of the wagon and vaulted up, unwrapped the reins, and flicked his wrists to set the horses into motion.

"Need to take your hat off," he said. "Something's wrong with it."

Reaching up, Maddie pulled out the hatpin. Then she placed the hat in her lap, studying it from all angles. "What's wrong with it?"

Jesse dropped his hat on top of her head. "It's not shading your face. You'll have more freckles than Hannah before we get home."

She smiled. The sweat from his brow had soaked into the brim of his hat and now cooled her as a warm breeze wafted across the land. It somehow seemed exceedingly familiar and intimate to be wearing his hat. She discovered she wanted to know everything about him, about his childhood, the life he'd led as a young man. Clutching her hat, she knew it wasn't *his* life she should be curious about. "Tell me about Charles as a boy."

He leaned back and smiled in fond remembrance. "He was a lot like Aaron."

"Was he really?"

He nodded. "Everything was funny. He smiled all the time, laughed at everything. It was damned irritating sometimes."

Her laughter took Jesse by surprise. It was soft like a flower unfurling its petals. For a moment, he didn't mind that she was laughing at him. But only for a moment. Then he glared at her, his eyes little more than slits challenging her to admit the truth. "What's so funny?"

"Charles said the same thing about you."

He was taken aback by her answer, confusion clearly

etched on his features. "He said I laughed all the time?"

Her laughter increased, revealing the flower in full bloom, and he wondered how he could have ever thought of this woman as a whore.

She tilted her head to peer at him past the wide brim of his hat. "No, he said you think things to death before you ever do anything. He said it was irritating."

"A man makes a mistake if he doesn't think things through."

"So you think Charles made a mistake when he married me?"

He tore his gaze from hers and studied the road ahead. "I don't know what to think anymore," he admitted reluctantly.

She tamped down the joy growing within her. Once before, she'd misjudged his mood and been thrown back into the middle of the storm. This time she decided to tread more carefully.

She studied his sharp profile, beginning to understand the life that had brought it about. His facial features had been chiseled away over the years; determination and survival had been Fate's tools, turning the soft face of a boy into the rugged visage of a man. A boy separated from those he loved, a boy going off to war, a boy trying to be a man. A man whose goal in life had not been a search for wealth or fame, but simply a search for those he loved.

"What was Charles supposed to have bought with your six hundred dollars?"

"Nothing important."

"I didn't think Texas Rangers were supposed to lie."

He glanced over at her, a smile easing onto his face. "Cheat. We're not supposed to cheat."

"Lying is a form of cheating."

His smile increased. "You've been spending too much time with Aaron." His Adam's apple bobbed. "That was real nice what you did yesterday, helping him plant the flowers by his mother's grave."

Embarrassed, she did little more than shrug off his praise. "I'd like to know what you had planned for your money."

He turned his attention to the horses. "Cattle. I wanted some cattle."

She glanced around at the trees growing in abundance around her. "Here? You thought you could raise cattle here?"

"It was my father's dream . . . to raise cattle. It's what brought us to Texas. He passed his dream on to me as easily as he passed on his black hair and eyes."

"I'm sorry, then," she said quietly. "Sorry Charles didn't buy your cattle."

"It doesn't matter anymore. As long as you make Charles happy, I'll consider it money well spent."

The day before, she would have taken offense at his statement, but now she was beginning to understand his gruff demeanor. Part of her wished she didn't. As odd as it seemed, it was much easier being in his presence when she didn't like him.

Within the small parlor, Maddie sat in a wing chair beside the barren hearth, reading aloud. Charles sat at a right angle to her, his gaze occasionally shifting from her to the children gathered on the floor at her feet.

Jesse sat on the settee on the opposite side of the room, his nose buried in *Farm and Fireside,* a semimonthly journal. He listened to the melodic lilt of Maddie's voice. He'd been lost for some time now in the varying moods she created as she brought the story to life for the children. He thought if one of his old prim schoolteachers had dared to reveal the emotions of the story with the subtle changes in voice inflections that Maddie used, he might have been an avid reader of books. Instead he'd been content to read wanted posters, memorizing the characteristics of outlaws and desperadoes. He'd learned to recognize what was written in a man's face, his eyes, the stories he harbored within his soul that made him do the dastardly deeds for which a rope would one day bring his life to an end. Yet, as skilled as he'd become at reading a person, he'd failed completely where Maddie was concerned.

He lifted his eyes from the page and studied the tranquil

scene before him, regretting for a moment that a fire wasn't needed in the hearth. How cozy it would be in the winter to hear the snap of burning logs, smell the smoke rising up the chimney, feel the warmth permeating the room. He wondered if Charles would be here then, to enjoy the family he'd created.

Yawning, Taylor struggled to her feet and toddled over to Charles. He lifted her onto his lap and pressed her head into the crook of his arm. Hannah scooted across the floor, placing herself against Maddie's skirt. Maddie stopped reading in the middle of a sentence, placed the book on the table beside the chair, and reached for the child. Hannah eagerly took her place on Maddie's lap and curled against her side. Maddie lifted the book and once more brought Tom Sawyer's adventures to life.

Aaron was stretched out on his stomach, his chin digging into his palms, his elbows pressed against the hardwood floor. He glanced over his shoulder at Jesse. Smiling, Jesse flicked his head back and dropped the journal onto the floor. Aaron scrambled up and sat on the settee beside him. Jesse resisted the urge to pull the boy against him, to hold him as securely as Charles and Maddie held the girls. Aaron had definite ideas about how a boy his age should be treated, and his ideas didn't include cuddling or affectionate hugs from his uncle. Jesse stretched his arm across the back of the settee.

Aaron chewed on his bottom lip as his gaze darted between Maddie and Jesse. When his gaze returned to him, Jesse raised a brow. Aaron squirmed before revealing in a hushed whisper, "I'm thinking I like her, Uncle Jesse. Jest a little. You reckon that's all right? You think Ma would understand?"

Jesse looked across the room at the contentment on Charles's face, the daughter who had fallen asleep in his arms, the woman who from time to time lifted her gaze from the pages of the book and smiled at Charles. Then he looked at Aaron. "Yes, I think she would. I happen to like her, too."

"You do?"

Jesse nodded.

Aaron chewed on his lip once more. "A little or a lot?"

"A lot."

Aaron bobbed his head once before settling in against Jesse's side and turning his attention back to Maddie and the story. "Yeah. I'm thinking I might come to like her a lot, too."

The grandfather clock in the parlor rang the first of eight chimes. Maddie read the final words of the chapter and quietly closed the book. She glanced at the sleeping bundle of joy nestled within her arms.

"I guess it is about time for bed," Charles said as he stood, careful not to waken Taylor.

Maddie set the book on the table, then shifted her body and scooted to the edge of the chair.

"I'll get Hannah," Jesse said as both he and Aaron got to their feet. He crossed the room in sure, long strides and dipped down to take the sleeping child from Maddie's arms. He was slow in taking her, waiting until Charles left the room. "I'll get your bath ready," he finally said quietly as he lifted Hannah into his arms and strode out of the room.

Maddie had just finished braiding her hair when Charles returned from making sure everything was secure. She had changed into her nightgown and pulled her wrapper snugly around her. She was certain he wouldn't suspect anything when she made her nightly ritual of checking on the children one last time. She thought he probably appreciated the few minutes alone when he got ready for bed.

He sat on the bed and heaved a sigh as he removed his boots. "Lord, I feel like a herd of horses trampled me today."

Turning slightly in her chair, she studied him. He looked worn, as though his burdens had increased. She was suddenly very glad that she had a surprise to give him. Anxious to share it with him, she stood and walked to the door. "I'm going to check on the children one more time."

Charles smiled at her as she slipped out the door.

Maddie tiptoed across the hall and quietly opened the door of the bedroom across from the one she shared with Charles. She peered inside. A low fire burned in the hearth, not enough to heat the room, but enough to keep her from shivering when she finished her bath. A wooden tub sat before the fire, the misty water emanating a flowery fragrance. Glancing quickly around the room, she noted that it had indeed been decorated for a fairy princess. She stepped inside, closed the door behind her, and walked to the tub. She dipped her fingers into the warm water.

"Is it warm enough?"

She twirled around, only now seeing Jesse's silhouette in the shadows. "Do you have to do that?"

He stepped out into the light. "Do what?"

"Sneak up on me."

"I'm clear across the room."

She eyed him suspiciously. "I think you just enjoy watching me jump."

His smile was as warm as the water as he ignored her rightful conclusion and approached her. "Is it warm enough?"

"Yes, it'll do nicely. Thank you."

Reaching out, he took the hand she'd dangled in the water and brought it near his lips. She felt his breath fan her fingertips.

"You should always smell like this," he said quietly before releasing her hand. "Enjoy your bath."

He strode across the room, opened the door slightly, and halted. "You should wear your hair down."

Maddie watched him slip out of the room and heard his steps fade as he descended the stairs. She crossed the room and quietly opened the door. The hallway was empty. She heard a distant door downstairs open and close. She hurried across the hallway and stepped into the girls' room, then crossed over to their window. She slipped her fingers between the curtains and peered through the tiny opening she'd created, gazing into the yard that surrounded the back of the house. She watched Jesse walk slowly across the yard, his head bent, his hands shoved deep into the pockets of his trousers. He stopped, glanced back at the house, then disappeared into the thick grove of trees.

She stood for long moments thinking about him: the way he had looked sharing a confidence with Aaron on the settee when he thought no one was looking; the warmth, the gladness she'd felt when she'd realized he'd been waiting for her in the Princess room. The loss she'd felt when he'd left the room. The greater loss now that she knew he'd left the house as well.

She retreated to the Princess room. She slipped off her clothes and lowered her body into the tepid water, only then realizing how long she must have lingered across the hall. She eased into the water until it lapped at her chin and the delicate scent surrounded her, reminding her of her quest to make her husband happy, a quest shared by one equally anxious to make Charles happy.

When the water grew cold, she rose, stepped from the tub, and dried off with the warm towel that had been set on a chair before the fire. She put her nightgown on and, carrying her wrapper, walked back across the hall to her own room.

Disappointment assaulted her when she saw that Charles had fallen asleep. She eased into bed, trying not to disturb him. Her surprise suddenly seemed insignificant. She remembered Jesse saying to wear her hair down and slipped out of bed. She loosened her braid and brushed her hair until it flowed smoothly down her back. Perhaps the surprise would be as nice for Charles when he awoke in the morning.

She returned to bed, lying on her back, her fingers intertwined across her stomach, her eyes focused on the ceiling. She did not want to lie in bed with her husband and think of his brother, but her mind seemed intent on traveling its own journey.

She remembered the sight of him as she'd stood watching the play of his muscles as he'd moved the tree from their path, the width of his shoulders, the way his back tapered down to meet his narrow hips. She remembered the strength of his embrace, tempered with gentleness, as he'd held

her. The tenderness of his smile as he'd reminisced about
Charles.

In the hotel room, Maddie had only vaguely understood
when Charles had explained about giving other women
nothing of equal value in return for their sacrifice. But this
afternoon when she'd watched Jesse's powerful body tamed,
when she'd felt his comforting embrace, she'd glimpsed the
magnitude of her sacrifice.

❧ 7 ❧

Taking a deep breath, Maddie stepped off the back porch. The coffee sloshed over the side of the cup she held in her hand. She halted, steadying her hand, steadying her nerves. She heard the resounding thud and crack as Jesse chopped the wood. Regaining her composure, she walked to the side of the barn and stopped when Jesse came into view.

His back was to her, his shirt hanging loosely over a nearby bush, his hat resting on top of it. His bronzed back glistened with the sweat of his labors as he swung the ax into a hunk of wood, brought the wood to the stump, worked the ax free, and with one deliberate swing, split the log into two pieces. Bending over, exposing a narrow band of white flesh as his pants strained with his movement, he picked up the pieces and tossed them onto a large pile of split logs before swinging his arm yet again and claiming more wood.

His actions were fluid, purposeful. Maddie had always thought poetry was restricted to words written upon a page, flowing smoothly, but watching Jesse work, she realized poetry existed in many forms. The rhythm of a man's body, the rippling of his corded muscles as he labored could be as poetic, as pleasing as a well-written poem, could evoke emotions that touched one's heart.

"I brought—" She stepped back as he spun around, his chest heaving with his exertions, his arm hanging loosely by his side, the ax held with the grip of his strong hand. With his free hand, he combed the damp hair back from his brow, his expression unreadable. She extended the tin cup. "I brought you some coffee." She took a small step forward. "Since the coffee wasn't made this morning when I went to the kitchen, I assumed you hadn't had any." She advanced another step. "I didn't want you—"

"To spend the day in a foul mood?" he asked, raising a brow and one corner of his mouth.

She nodded, grateful for the slight teasing tone in his voice.

Jesse took the coffee, his fingers brushing against hers, taking note of the trembling cup, not certain if it was caused by her or him. He gulped some coffee, regretting that action as the steaming dark brew burned his tongue and scorched his throat. But the brief moment of pain served to take his mind off things he didn't want to be thinking about: the reason for the pale blue half moons resting beneath her eyes, the reason she looked as though she hadn't slept much during the night.

He didn't want to acknowledge the envy coiling around his insides like a rattler preparing to strike whenever he thought about his brother lying in bed with this woman. He'd spent most of the night standing by the creek, watching the muddy waters, alone with his thoughts. He hadn't wanted to be sleeping in his bed where the sounds of passion might ease out of one room, whisper along the hallway, and enter unwelcomed into his dreams.

He lifted the cup. " 'Preciate it."

Maddie's gaze strayed to the damp hairs on his chest, the sweat visible beneath. How could she find something like sweat so appealing on this man? She lifted her gaze back to his. "I wanted to thank you for preparing the bath."

A slight breeze rose up and brought the scent of forget-me-nots hovering around Jesse. He wondered how she could smell so fresh after a night of what was certain to have been unbridled passion. If she had come to him, smelling so sweet, her hair cascading around her . . .

He downed the remainder of the coffee, wishing it would burn his thoughts away as easily as it burned his tongue. Holding the cup out to her, he watched her small, delicate hand take the cup from his larger, coarse one.

"Yeah, well . . ." He turned back to the pile of wood he'd decided to tackle that morning in hopes of relieving the frustration that had haunted his night. "Any time you want a bath, just let me know, and I'll haul the water up for you."

"The surprise is over. I'm sure in the future, Charles won't mind doing it."

He slammed the ax into a piece of wood. "Charles doesn't need to be hauling stuff around."

"But Charles is my husband. He should—"

"He's the owner," Jesse said, turning on her. "I do the labor around here. He takes care of the books. If you need something lifted or some work done, you tell me." He set the wood on the stump, worked the ax free, and brought the ax down.

Maddie watched the manner in which he worked, as though he was trying to drive something away. Probably her. "I don't want to ask things of you. I don't want you to resent my presence."

"I don't resent your presence," he said as he buried the ax into another log.

"Did you stay away at night before I came?"

He glanced over his shoulder, his grip on the ax tightening.

"I heard the clock downstairs chime four times before you came to bed."

Sweet Lord. Had Charles kept her awake all night making love to her? He plowed his hand through his hair knowing he would have done the same thing. If a man could get easily drunk just gazing into her eyes, what in God's name would he feel buried deep within her? "I had something on my mind and couldn't sleep. I walked down by the creek. Time got away from me. It had nothing to do with you."

She lowered her gaze and then peered at him through her thick, golden lashes. "Texas Rangers aren't supposed to lie."

And this Ranger couldn't very well tell her the truth, either: that he'd wanted to stay in that damn room and watch her bathe; had wanted to sponge the scented water over her body, lift her, smelling of forget-me-nots, from the water, carry her to the bed, and sip the glistening drops from her body.

He gave her what he hoped was a teasing grin. "I'm not telling a lie."

Her eyes widened. "Oh! My biscuits!"

Jesse watched her run off, yelling something about a meal and his need to hurry and finish his chore. He buried the ax in the log. She was his brother's wife, had exchanged vows with Charles that she intended to honor. He'd better make damn sure he stayed clear of her.

"Maddie suggested we take the day off and go on a picnic," Charles announced to everyone sitting at the table.

The children squealed and clapped their hands.

After wolfing down the biscuits, Jesse had been concentrating on shoveling the syrup-drenched flapjacks into his mouth so he could fill his stomach and get out before his eyes betrayed him and strayed over to watch Maddie. As he slowly lifted his gaze, his eyes lit upon her and branded into his memory the image of her sitting with her hands in her lap and her eyes fastened on her plate. He shifted his gaze to Charles.

"We hoped you'd join us," Charles said.

Jesse looked at his brother's smiling face, the children anxiously awaiting his answer. He didn't want to disappoint the children, but better to disappoint them than to do something he might later regret. "I think a picnic is a fine idea, but I'll have to pass today. I have a lot of work I need to get done."

"Surely, the work can wait. After all, it's Saturday," Charles said.

Jesse eyed his brother. "I didn't get anything done yesterday because you sent me into town. I'll take my day of rest tomorrow like everybody else." His fork clattered as it hit the plate, and he stood. "Now, if you'll excuse me, I have things that need to be done." He stalked across the room, grabbed his hat from the peg on the wall, and shoved it down low over his brow before pushing open the door.

He walked to the shed, picked up his hammer and bucket of nails, and walked away from the house. Whenever time allowed, he'd been erecting a wooden fence that would separate some of Charles's land from the land Jesse had planned to graze his cattle on. He'd wanted a safe place for the children to play so he wouldn't have to worry about them getting hurt by an angry bull.

He reached the unfinished fence and glanced down the length of it. He hadn't made much progress on it, and he probably had no reason to finish it now that he no longer had the means to purchase the cattle. Still, he dropped the bucket among the weeds. Then he took off his shirt and hung it on a post. He clenched some nails between his teeth, picked up his hammer, and hefted one of the boards he'd brought to this spot months before.

And he began hammering. Hammering hard and fast while the sun beat down on him.

As the day wore on, Mother Nature became a cruel mistress. She made him sweat and then teased him with the gentlest of breezes that carried the laughter of children.

It didn't seem to matter how hard he pounded the nails into the wood, the wind and the laughter drifted around him, calling to him, tempting him.

Yesterday, he'd listened to Maddie's laughter, enjoyed her company, her smile, but she wasn't his to enjoy. Her eyes weren't his to get drunk on, her waist wasn't his to put his hands around, her hair wasn't his to run his fingers through. Her secrets weren't his to share.

He had no right to wonder what it was about the aging posters on the wall that had taken the color from her face, to wonder what had happened in her past to put fear in her eyes at the oddest moments. She wasn't his to protect, his to cherish. She belonged solely and exclusively to his brother, and when he was with her, he felt as though he was trespassing on sacred ground, wanting things he had no right to want.

Mother Nature was relentless, bringing a stronger wind that carried the children's laughter before it had time to fade. He heard Charles's deep laughter mingle with that of his children. He leaned on the top rail he'd just hammered into place. How long had it been since he'd heard Charles laugh?

He dropped the hammer into the bucket with the nails, jerked his shirt off the post, and started walking. He had no idea where they'd gone for their picnic, but their laughter carried on the wind was a map as accurate as any that had been charted by man.

He came upon them near a bend in the creek where the trees lined the banks and the water captured the sunlight.

"Jesse!" Charles waved from where he sat beneath a towering oak tree.

Maddie spun around, lost her footing, and slid down the muddy creek bank on her backside, hitting the cold water at the creek's edge.

Bending at the waist, Aaron released a raucous laugh. "Uncle Jesse didn't even clear his throat, Miss Maddie!" Imitating an otter, he lunged for the steep creek bank, sliding on his stomach, headfirst into the water. He came up spluttering and tossing his head around, his thick hair sending out droplets of water.

Maddie was struggling to climb the muddy bank when Aaron cupped his hands together and splashed her.

"Aaron Lawson!" She slid back into the water and advanced on Aaron, splashing him until he yelled for mercy.

Jesse dropped down beside Charles. Charles chuckled. "They've been doing that most of the afternoon, ever since they dug the rocks out of that area so they could slide without getting bruised or cut."

Jesse watched Aaron and Maddie plop down on the creek bed, their laughter subsiding as they regained their breaths. She wore a pair of Charles's pants, the legs rolled up to her knees, a rope keeping the pants around her waist. An old shirt was plastered to her body. Her bare toes stuck out of the water and her ankles were covered by the murky brown water.

Where the creek bank eased gradually to the water, the girls played in the mud with tin plates, cups, and tarnished spoons. Taylor stood, holding a plate, and waddled over to Charles. "Eat pie, Pa."

Leaning back, Charles pushed out his stomach and scratched it. "I've had four already, Taylor. Think you'd best share this one with your Uncle Jesse."

Jesse bestowed upon his brother a menacing glare as Taylor offered her creation to him. Gingerly, he took it, held it beneath his nose, and sniffed. "Smells good. Why don't you run on and make me another one while I eat this one?"

Taylor's brown eyes flashed with delight as she scurried to the muddy bank. Jesse scooped the mud out and flung it aside. Then he looked at the black mess coating his fingers.

Charles leaned forward. "Hannah! Don't go in the water!"

Jesse quickly wiped his hand on the back of Charles's shirt and smiled triumphantly as Charles voiced his objections to being used as a towel.

Drawing up a knee, Jesse rested his forearm on it as his fingers toyed with a tall weed. "You know those reward posters that McGuire keeps tacked on his wall near that corner he uses as a post office?"

"Yeah."

"The sight of those posters seemed to upset Maddie yesterday."

"I'm not surprised."

Jesse stilled his fingers, his dark eyes scrutinizing his brother. "You're not?"

"No. Her father and brother were killed during a stagecoach holdup. Maybe she recognized the men who did it."

Jesse jerked up the weed and tossed it aside. "She mentioned that her brother died in her arms. Do you know when this happened?"

"A couple of weeks before I met her. Their deaths apparently left her with no means to provide for herself."

Jesse winced under the flaying Charles delivered with his direct gaze, a gaze that provided redemption for Maddie's presence in a brothel, a gaze that stated clearly that Jesse would have known had he bothered to ask why she had lowered herself to seek refuge at Bev's.

"You think they were passengers on the stage?"

Disbelief washed over Charles's face. "Well, hell yes. What else would they have been?"

Noncommittally, Jesse shrugged a shoulder. "She just seemed unusually frightened, that's all."

"I would imagine so. Wouldn't you be if you saw a likeness of the man who killed your father and brother? Maybe she's afraid he'll come after her." Charles bolted upright. "Do you think he would?"

Jesse shook his head. "If he'd had concerns about her causing him trouble, he'd have taken care of her when he killed her brother and father. On the other hand, if he's not already wanted for murder, she could serve as a witness."

Charles slumped back against the tree. "That's the Ranger in you talking now."

Smiling, Jesse stretched out on his side and rested up on an elbow. "Maybe."

"Uncle Jesse!" Aaron cried. "Come slide with us!"

With exaggerated emphasis, he swept his head from side to side.

"Come on! It's safe!"

Charles punched his shoulder. "Go on. Spend this afternoon being a young boy again."

"You do it."

"I would, but I got a pain brewing in my head."

Jesse studied his brother. He hated the slight furrow between Charles's brows that had recently taken on a permanence, a constant reminder of his discomfort. "You gonna be all right?"

Charles nodded slightly. "As long as I don't do too much I should be fine. It just feels like a late summer squall. It's when it starts turning into a storm that I have to worry. I'll just sit here and watch the girls, but you should go play."

"It's not seemly." Jesse pulled up the shorter weeds with-in his vicinity and tossed them aside.

Charles laughed. "Seemly?"

"It's not seemly for me to be around your wife when she's dressed like that."

"What's wrong with the way she's dressed? I think it's kinda cute."

Jesse scowled. It was damn cute. That's what was wrong with it.

"Ah, Jesse, you spent so much time being a big brother, even when I wasn't around, that you never learned how to enjoy life. Father had no right to place that burden on your back, to make you promise to take care of me and Cassie."

"He had every right. I was the oldest."

"You were twelve years old. A child. He asked you to become a man." Charles placed his hand on his brother's shoulder. "So go back to being a boy for the day. Go play with them. Who's going to see? We're family. We ought to feel free to enjoy each other's company."

Jesse contemplated his decision, then gave in to his desires. He sat up. Tugging off his boots, he glanced over his shoulder at Charles. "Just remember it was your idea."

He pulled off his socks and shoved them into his boots before pulling his shirt over his head.

He brought himself to his feet. Slowly, quietly, he crept toward the two people standing at the top of the incline. Aaron saw him, and his eyes widened. Jesse quickly held up a hand, then pressed his finger to his lips. Aaron nod-ded in understanding, then turned Maddie's attention to an imaginary blue jay perched in a tree.

Hearing a twig snap, Maddie jerked around and found herself lifted off the ground, held firmly in Jesse's arms. Before she could protest, Aaron rammed his shoulder into Jesse's thigh. Jesse hollered as his legs slid out from beneath him. Gallantly twisting so his back hit the mud, he careened down the slope with Maddie angled across his chest. They hit the water. She flew off him and landed facedown in the creek.

She came up spluttering, tossing her wet hair out of her eyes. "You bleedin' idiot!"

Struggling to stand, Jesse dropped down and stretched out against the cool mud, flinging his arms out, sending his laughter to the thick branches overhead.

Stunned, Maddie listened to the deep rich timbre of his voice and watched the way his chest rumbled.

He lifted his head and looked at her. "Lord, I love your accent when you're angry."

She could not have been more surprised if he'd told her he loved her. His generous mouth had formed a broad smile. His onyx eyes latched onto hers, holding her captive. Even with mud on the tip of his nose, he was devastatingly handsome.

He fought the cloying mud clinging to his body, stood, and waded out to her. "Are you all right?"

"No, I'm not all right. What in the world did you think you were doing?"

The smile slowly disappeared from his face, and he extended his hand. "Here, let me help you."

"I can get up by myself." With the mud squishing between her toes, she struggled to her feet. The mud sucked at her foot as she tried to lift it, and she tumbled back into the water.

He moved in behind her as quickly as the thick mud allowed and slipped his hands beneath her arms. Twisting, she shoved him. He lost his balance and fell into the water. She fought back her smile. "Not much fun being tossed into the water, is it?"

He flicked his wet hair off his brow. "Oh, I don't know about that."

"What were you thinking?" she asked softly.

"I don't know. Charles told me to play, so I thought I'd give it a try."

He stood and extended his hand to her. She wrapped her hands around his, and he pulled her up. As they waded toward the shore, Aaron's laughter echoed around them. Jesse tipped his head back to stare at the urchin sitting at the top of the bank, slapping his knees. "Aaron, what were you thinking, pushing me like that? You're supposed to be on my side!"

"Ain't no sides, Uncle Jesse!"

"You're gonna wish there were when I'm done with you!" Jesse started climbing the embankment. Aaron jumped to his feet, threw a hasty taunt out to the man coming after him, then hightailed it toward the trees as fast as his legs could carry him.

When Jesse finally caught up with Aaron and pulled him out of the tree, he took him fishing as punishment for the prank he'd pulled. While they fished, Maddie, Charles, and the girls sat beneath a nearby tree, laughing and eating the blackberries they'd gathered. As the late afternoon shadows blanketed the creek bank, they began the trek home.

Trudging along, the adults lost sight of Aaron as he ran ahead through the trees. The girls squealed. Pulling the wagon, Jesse glanced back to make sure they hadn't fallen out. He wasn't paying much attention to the ruts and rocks that made for a bumpy ride. Instead, he discreetly watched the woman walking along beside him. Charles walked on the other side of her, and Jesse couldn't understand how his brother could walk beside her and not touch her. If she was his wife, he'd at least want to put his arm around her and feel her pressed against his side.

She'd slipped a skirt over the pants, leaving her mud-caked feet visible. Her hair dangled in a braid over her shoulder, but some strands had gained their freedom and hung in disarray around her face. If he had the right, he'd give all her hair its freedom for a brief moment before capturing it and imprisoning it in the palm of his hand.

A dark blue stain outlined one corner of her mouth. A tiny splatter of mud had dried on one ear, a larger splatter had claimed her cheek, a cheek the sun had caressed and burned, a cheek rounded with joy as a smile filled her face. She was lost in her youth, carefree, and happy.

Aaron came thrashing back through the trees. "We got company!"

Charles looked across Maddie's head at Jesse. "We don't have a stagecoach scheduled to stop today."

"Lots of company! Hurry!" Aaron yelled before darting back through the trees.

Everyone increased their pace, which left Maddie gasping for air once they made their way to the backyard, and the inn was in sight. At least two dozen adults and a host of children were gathered in the yard. Jesse released his hold on the wagon as Hannah and Taylor scrambled out.

"Well, the newly married couple have finally returned!" McGuire yelled as the townsfolk surrounded them.

Jesse caught the surprise and confusion on Charles's face, but it was the fear in Maddie's eyes as people pulled her away that caused him to shove people aside to get to her. He wrapped his hand around her arm. "It's all right, Maddie. They're just here to make you feel welcome."

Then his hold on her slipped, and a group of women led her across the yard to the back porch. Jesse was hoisted precariously upon shoulders and carted across the yard as though he was a sack of grain. Amid the confusion, he was unceremoniously dumped at Maddie's feet. Momentarily disoriented, he struggled to stand and placed his hand on the small of Maddie's back, hoping to reassure her, knowing any words he could have offered would have been drowned out by the madness surrounding them.

"Go on, man!" McGuire prodded. "Kiss your wife. You can't go off getting married in private and not paying a price for it."

Jesse stared at McGuire as though the man had lost his mind. They thought Maddie was *his* wife? He tried to remember what he'd said in town to give them that impression and couldn't remember a single thing he'd said to any of them. He'd introduced her.

He issued a silent curse. He'd introduced her as Mrs. Lawson, but he hadn't bothered to explain it was Mrs. Charles Lawson. Looking across the sea of faces, he wondered why Charles hadn't worked his way to the porch to claim his bride.

Panic struck him with the force of a stampeding bull when he saw Charles bend over and brace his arms on his knees. He stepped off the porch, his goal to get to Charles before he was staggering with the pain. His mission of mercy was halted, and he was shoved back beneath the eaves of the porch as the chorus of "Kiss her!" resounded around him. He was on the verge of explaining that Charles was in pain, and he needed to help him when Charles threw his head back and released his laughter.

Laughing! Charles was laughing because these people thought Maddie was married to him! Stunned, Jesse could do little more than feel the irritation swell deep within him. He narrowed his eyes. So Charles was enjoying this embarrassing misunderstanding, was he? Well, Jesse could enjoy it as well. And if Charles wanted something to laugh about, then by God, he'd give the man something to laugh about.

He turned to Maddie. The confusion and worry in her eyes almost stopped him, but when she reached out and clutched his shirt, he took her in his arms and lowered his mouth to hers.

It was a mistake.

He knew it the moment his lips lighted upon hers, and he felt her response: a slight fluttering like a butterfly touching its first petal.

Perhaps it was the surprise of his actions that caused her mouth to open slightly. He didn't care. He settled his mouth more solidly against hers, taking advantage of the opportunity to slip his tongue inside her mouth and taste her fully. She tasted of blackberries and carried the scent of the creek mingled with the shadow of forget-me-nots.

Then the mistake intensified. For she responded not in the manner he'd expected, but in the way he'd dreamed, mating her tongue with his, imitating an ancient ritual with an innocent abandon. It was all he could do not to groan aloud.

He wanted to tell her to place her arms around his neck so he could feel her breasts pressed against his chest instead of her balled fists clutching his shirt. He wanted to tell her to breathe so he could feel her warm breath fan his face. He wanted to tell her she tasted better than sponge cake, but he knew once he lifted his lips from hers, he'd never again be allowed to touch them.

He cupped the back of her head with one strong hand and leaned her over dramatically in hopes when the kiss ended, when Charles claimed her, laughter would greet his audacity. But until that moment, he savored the kiss, drawing it out, plundering that to which he had no right.

He felt a hand grip his arm. Reluctantly, he lifted his mouth from hers. She stared at him, her eyes unblinking, her breathing labored. He shifted his gaze to Charles.

"What the hell do you think you're doing?" Charles demanded.

"Kissing your wife."

"Wait a minute, man!" McGuire bellowed. "Thought she was married to you, Jesse."

"No, she's married to Charles."

Murmurs echoed among the gathered neighbors.

"Then it shoulda been Charles what kissed her!" McGuire announced.

"And I appreciate all of you giving me the opportunity to officially welcome her into the family."

Riotous, good-humored laughter surrounded them as he eased Maddie into Charles's arms. "Maybe next time you'll claim her a bit quicker."

Charles felt Maddie tremble. He kissed her lightly on the forehead before drawing her closer and glancing at his neighbors. "If you'll excuse us for a few moments, we'd like to make ourselves presentable. Then we'll welcome you all into our house."

He shot a harsh glance Jesse's way before leading Maddie inside.

Peering discreetly through the bedroom window, Maddie watched the shadows lengthening as twilight drew near. Charles had taken the children down the hall to make them presentable, leaving her alone. She knew she should be washing the mud off her feet, brushing her hair, deciding which dress to wear, but she felt as though her ability to think, to function had been stolen away by Jesse's kiss.

She pressed her fingers to her lips. They were a poor substitute for his mouth. His mouth had been as hot as a midsummer day. Yet for those few precious moments, cradled within his arms, she'd felt as though she was a dew-kissed rose, awakened in the cool dawn, little more than a tiny bud slowly unfolding. It had never crossed her mind to push him away or to stop him.

Only when his lips left hers did the truth taunt her. She did not belong in Jesse's embrace. He was not hers to kiss or to hold. He was not the one to whom she should carry cups of coffee in the morning. He was not the one whose movements should remind her of poetry.

She reprimanded herself with a litany of vows tumbling through her mind. It must never happen again. She must never again forget she was married to Charles. She was his wife.

She heard a soft tapping on her door and walked across the room. Opening the door slightly, she peered out, and her heart thumped wildly within her breast as Jesse stood before her.

"I drew you a bath. It's in the Princess room." His voice was low, his manner subdued.

"You shouldn't have kissed me like that . . . out there . . . in front of everyone. I'm married to Charles."

"I know that. I thought I'd tease him. It didn't work out the way I expected."

"Those people—"

"Think it was a practical joke."

"But it wasn't."

Jesse allowed his gaze to drift to her lips, still swollen from his kiss. He shoved his hands into his pockets to stop himself from drawing her back into his arms. "No, it wasn't. But only you and I know that. And it won't happen again."

"But Charles—"

"I'll make sure he understands it was all my doing. Now you'd best get across the hall. We've got people waiting."

Tearing his gaze from hers, he walked down the hallway. Quietly, he stepped into the girls' room and took a moment to watch Charles pull Taylor's coveralls off. Then he took a deep breath, hoping to mask the raw emotions rumbling around within his chest. "I drew a bath for Maddie. Why don't you dip the girls in the water?"

Spinning around, Charles advanced on his brother. "What the hell did you think you were doing out there?"

"Why the hell didn't you rush up and claim her once you understood what they all thought?"

Their eyes clashed, black against brown, challenging, questioning, slowly easing into forgiving. Shaking his head, Charles grinned heartily. "The expression of horror on your face once *you* realized what they thought—" He laughed. "Oh, Jesse, if only you could have seen yourself. I'll never forget the look on your face as long as I live."

The words, a careless reminder, sobered Charles and took the anger from Jesse.

"It didn't mean anything," Jesse said. "What happened out there."

"Means something," Charles said as he turned around and helped Hannah step out of her coveralls. "Means my good habits are starting to rub off on you, and you're not thinking things to death before you do them."

Jesse expelled the breath he'd been holding. "I'll help Aaron get ready."

Walking out of the room, he wished to God he *had* thought it through before he'd kissed her.

❧ 8 ❧

Throwing open the wide double doors of the parlor, Jesse invited everyone inside. The majority of the people had known Charles for years and felt comfortable making themselves at home. Someone hauled in a large table, and the women spread an assortment of cakes and pies along its length.

The men helped themselves to the cabinet stocked with liquor. In between pouring themselves a drink, they tossed good-natured jibes Jesse's way. Easing his way across the room, he smiled and accepted the ribbing that was his due. When he reached the barren fireplace, he perched his elbow on the mantel and had a clear view of the stairs.

Tromping down the stairs, Aaron smiled as his best friend, Billy Turner, broke free of the crowd and rushed toward him. The towheaded boy grabbed Aaron's arm and whispered in his ear. Aaron's face lit up like an autumn bonfire. In unison, the boys raced toward the door. Jesse forcefully cleared his throat, and a heavy silence descended over the room. Aaron and Billy froze.

"You need to wait until your pa and Miss Maddie come down before you run off," Jesse said.

"Ah, Uncle Jesse, Billy says he's got puppies in his wagon. Do we hafta wait?"

Jesse gave a curt nod. Aaron trudged over and leaned against one of the doors. Billy took his place beside him. Both boys glared at the man who was punishing them for no apparent reason. People who had turned into human statues released their breaths and once again filled the room with laughter and conversation.

Jesse smiled as the girls worked their way to the bottom of the stairs where the women smothered them with attention. Then he lifted his gaze to the top of the stairs and felt as though someone had delivered a good solid blow to the center of his chest.

It was difficult to believe the woman gracefully descending the stairs with her arm linked through Charles's was the same one who'd been wallowing in the mud all afternoon. She'd swept up her hair and left a few strands loose to frame her face. The sleek dress hugged her slim waist and narrow hips. The emerald green silk enhanced her amber eyes, accentuated her sun-kissed cheeks, and brought out the highlights in her honeyed hair.

Compared to the other women, dressed in their homespun and calico, she was a rose blossoming among dandelions.

In spite of the people crowded within the room, Maddie knew exactly where Jesse stood as she walked down the stairs, her fingers clutching Charles's arm. She hoped to disguise her awareness of him by glancing around the room, but when her gaze completed half its journey, it fell on him. His dark features were more prominent against the stark white of his pressed shirt, and she felt as though he'd reached out and touched her. Her step faltered, and her pretended indifference made a mockery of her true feelings. Charles steadied her. Gratefully, she smiled at him and hoped he'd blame her clumsiness on her nervousness at meeting his friends and not on the unfamiliar emotions flittering through her heart.

Walking beside him into the parlor, she was surrounded by faces that had weathered the harsher aspects of life, people who knew the joys to be found in the simplest of things because often it was all they had. Their faces were not the type into which she was accustomed to looking. Their roughness was limited to the outer surface and did not extend inward to their hearts. She didn't know how to react to these people who were so eager to welcome her into their midst.

Knowing she'd remember few names, she smiled hesitantly as introductions were made. As she strolled through the room, she was acutely aware of Jesse's gaze following her, almost like a caress.

Her smile became genuine when she recognized the woman who'd served them at the restaurant. Jean Lambourne ushered them to the table laden with food.

"Now, before we start to eating and celebrating, we have a small gift for you." She reached behind a chair and set a large box wrapped in brown paper on the table. A triumphant smile graced her features as she stood with her fingers intertwined across her stomach.

Leaning down, Charles whispered in Maddie's ear, "Open it."

She glanced at him. "You should open it. They're your friends."

"But they want to be yours. Besides, I think it's customary for the bride to open the wedding gift."

She gave him a tremulous smile. The only time she'd ever been in a room with this many people had been the night she'd stepped into Bev's parlor.

With trembling fingers, she pulled the string holding the paper around the box. The paper fell away. She lifted the lid on the box and touched a block of cotton scraps in various shades of blue pieced together into a log cabin design.

"We give all the new brides a quilt when they get married," Jean said. "That one was supposed to go to Mary, but she ain't getting married for two more months so we decided to give it to you. We'll just make her another one. Course, we all thought this was going to you and Jesse, which is why men shouldn't take on the women's job of gossiping." She gave Angus McGuire a hard look. "But truth be told, we're all right fond of Charles here. Glad to see him take a wife."

Maddie wanted to die when the sob escaped her throat. Charles put his arms around her. "They're just trying to make you feel welcome," he assured her.

She shook her head. "They don't understand," she whispered. "They think our marriage—"

"Is a happy occasion."

She could hear the murmurs and wished she was anywhere but where she was. "I don't deserve their gift, Charles. Please tell them—"

Jesse cleared his throat. Her eyes swimming with tears, Maddie jerked her head up and glared at him.

From across the room, he held her gaze, and she felt as though he was standing right beside her. He gave her a warm smile and lifted his glass. "I'd like to make a toast. To my brother, Charles, and the woman who can make him happy."

He touched the glass to his lips amid approval and applause, and Maddie realized she'd been given a gift more precious than the quilt. And she couldn't accept one without accepting the other.

Charles handed her a glass. Smiling shyly, she sipped the fruit flavored drink. He sipped from the same glass before inviting people to help themselves to the food spread before them. Then he turned slightly and lifted his glass in a silent salute to Jesse. Jesse returned the gesture and downed the liquid remaining in his glass.

Aaron charged across the room, Billy close on his heels. "Uncle Jesse, can we go now?"

Jesse gazed at the expectant faces. "Yeah, but don't get any notion you can keep one of those dogs." He watched the boys run off before turning his attention back to the newly wedded couple.

The girls worked their way free of the admiring ladies. Charles hefted Hannah into his arms. Maddie lifted Taylor and settled her on her hip.

Slipping his free arm around Maddie, Charles escorted her through the room, stopping occasionally to exchange pleasantries with one person or another.

Standing by his side, almost a silent shadow, Maddie was amazed at the ease with which he carried on conversations with different people, discussing crops with one man, a new foal with another. She had never known a man such as Charles, with a gift for putting people at ease, an ability to offer friendship unconditionally. As she came to understand the deep affection the townspeople held for her husband, she reaffirmed her vow to make certain he never regretted the night he'd asked her to marry him.

Excusing himself, Charles walked to the liquor cabinet where an elderly, stoop-shouldered man captured his attention and prolonged his stay.

With Charles no longer at her side, Maddie felt the loneliness weave around her even though she was surrounded by people. Taylor squirmed. She set the child on the floor and watched her walk to the table, where an elderly woman promptly filled a plate for her. Maddie made her way over to the doorway. She had often dreamed of a life that included other people, had somehow expected it to ease the loneliness with which she'd grown up. Glancing across the room, she saw Charles laugh. Then she slipped away into the night.

Maddie had come outside seeking a few moments of solitude. Instead, she'd discovered shadows from her past lurking behind the barn. Rushing across the backyard in a vain attempt to outrun her conscience, she came up short at the sight of Jesse sitting on the porch steps.

"What are you doing out here?" she asked, her tone clipped, her breathing labored.

"Needed some fresh air. Too many people inside. What are you doing out here?"

Forcing her fists to unclench, her body to relax, she took a deep breath, then spoke with a calmness she didn't feel. "Same thing."

"You're not used to being around many people, are you?"

She glanced quickly around the yard, then up at the blackened sky. "No."

Stretching out his long legs, he leaned back and propped his elbows up on the porch. "Neither am I."

She looked at his sprawled body, the length of which had been pressed against hers earlier. She felt the alarm she'd experienced behind the barn dissipate in his commanding presence and wondered at his ability to allay her old fears while stirring to life her new ones. She intertwined her fingers and pressed her sweating palms together. "I would have thought you'd spent a great deal of time around people."

He shook his head. "For too long, the only company I had was a campfire burning brightly into the night." He shrugged. "Or something like that."

The moon was but a gleaming sliver in the sky, yet it cast enough light that within the shadows of his face, she could see the barest of smiles. Remembering their conversation in the restaurant when she'd described her life in similar terms, she eyed him warily. "Are you making fun of me?"

"No." He drew himself into a sitting position, planting his elbows on his thighs and dangling his hands between his knees. "Why don't you sit down?"

She glanced longingly at the steps. She wanted to prolong her time outside, but wasn't certain she wanted to prolong her time in his company. The crickets chirped with a resonant cadence. A bullfrog croaked in the distance, and she was reminded of Jesse's warning sound. "Why do you clear your throat when the children misbehave?"

"Because I tend to look a lot meaner than I am when I yell. If I clear my throat, will it make you sit down?"

She forced back her smile. "I'm not certain it's a good idea for me to sit out here with you."

He waved his hand over the porch. "Plenty of room. We won't even be touching."

The crickets fell into silence as she walked over and sat on the porch. Taking a deep breath, she listened as the creatures became comfortable again and resumed their nightly sounds. She wished she could adjust as easily when things around her changed.

She heard the warmth of laughter and glanced over her shoulder. "I can hear Charles laughing."

"Yeah, he's been laughing a lot more since he brought you home."

She slipped her hands between her knees and pressed them together. "You don't laugh very much. Your laughter at the creek this afternoon surprised me."

"Yeah. Surprised me, too."

They sat in companionable silence for long moments, the scent of honeysuckle wafting through the air. She peered over at him. "Did you explain to Charles—"

"Yes."

"Do you think he understood?"

"Seemed to."

Thoughtfully, she nodded, wondering if she should ask him to explain it to her so she'd understand why he'd even wanted to kiss her—as a practical joke or otherwise. The woman she'd seen standing before the cheval mirror as she prepared to take her bath had mud caked on almost every exposed surface of her body. Strands of her hair were sticking out like the prickles on a cactus. Her clothes were soiled, her feet bare. She certainly understood why Charles hadn't charged forward to claim her. But why Jesse had taken her in his arms to begin with baffled her. There had been nothing attractive or appealing about the woman standing on the back porch. As for the reason why she hadn't shoved him away and the feelings that had surfaced during the kiss, it was best not to contemplate those. She had made her choice in Fort Worth. If she could not have fulfillment as a woman married to Charles, she would at least find fulfillment as a mother and a dutiful wife.

Shifting onto one hip, Jesse rested back on an elbow. "Was your father English?"

His voice, though low, startled her from her reverie. His question was safer than the ones she'd been asking herself. She offered him a small smile. "And my mother. She was the firstborn daughter of a duke. My father was the seventh son of an earl."

He said nothing, simply watched her.

"Do you know what that means?" she asked.

"That if your mother had been a guest here, she would have wanted to sleep in the Princess room?"

She laughed, and Jesse wished he understood the secret that caused her laughter to flow.

"It means she wasn't supposed to marry him."

"Why not?"

"Because he had no title, and she was destined to be a duchess."

"But she did marry him."

She brought her feet to the top step and wrapped her arms around her knees. "She loved him that much. They ran away, got married, and left England. Then he brought her to Texas. She believed his promises, accepted his dreams." Gazing out, she rested her chin on her knees and sighed wistfully. "In spite of everything, she never stopped loving him."

"What was *everything?*" he asked, his voice blending in with the sounds of the night.

She lifted a shoulder. "Loneliness. Disappointment. My father's occupation kept him away a great deal of the time. Mother was always happiest when he was home telling her how we'd live once things worked out for him. He had such grand plans. Mother taught me all the things a lady should know so I'd be comfortable in our new life when it arrived. Father would hold me on his lap and tell me some day I'd marry a fine man."

"And you did."

Smiling, Maddie glanced over at Jesse. "And I did. I've never known anyone like Charles. He has a good heart."

"He's definitely one of your better people."

Reaching out, she touched the bruise on his jaw. "He didn't strike me as the kind of man who would hit another."

Wrapping his hand around her fingers, he returned her hand to her lap, returned his hand to his side. "He's not. That's why his fist was able to get as close to my jaw as it did. I wasn't expecting it."

She turned slightly so she could watch him more closely. "You strike me as the kind of man who would hit someone."

"I am."

"But you didn't hit Charles back."

"I'm not going to hit my baby brother."

She studied him. They were brothers, only four years separating them, and yet Fate had chosen to give them different lives, to shape them into different men. "Have you fought many men?"

"Fought my share."

One side of her mouth curved up, mockingly. "And I suppose you always won."

He gave her a small smile. "Not always."

His honesty and refusal to be a braggart surprised her. The men she'd known would not have hesitated to puff out their chests, claim countless victories, and inflate the truth with lies. "Aaron would be disappointed to hear that. He worships you."

"I know." Disgust marred his voice. "I've tried to explain to him . . ." His voice drifted away.

"What have you tried to explain?"

"That I'm not a hero. I had a job to do, and I did it. That's all."

She tilted her head. "Maybe that's all any hero is. Someone who didn't turn back until the job was done."

"Was your father a hero?"

Turning her face away, she hugged her knees. "I don't deserve Charles, you know."

"That's for him to decide."

She peered over at him. "Is it?"

He nodded.

"And if you discovered that I didn't deserve him?"

Sitting up, he leaned toward her. "Am I going to discover that, Maddie? Is that what you're afraid of?"

She released a small scream and jumped to her feet. A small black shadow had scampered across the short space and pounced on her shoe. She hopped back. The shadow yelped and attacked again.

Jesse scooped up the writhing puppy and held him up in the pale moonlight. "Now, I wonder where you came from?"

Inching forward, Maddie tentatively reached out and tried to touch the puppy's head, but the dog tipped his wet nose up toward her palm, his tongue darting out to lick her. She giggled. "Where *did* he come from?"

"Billy brought some puppies to show Aaron. This one must have gotten away."

"Can I hold him?"

"Sure." Jesse transferred the wiggling dog into Maddie's care. She lowered herself to the ground, held the dog in her lap, and ran her hands over his body. She laughed as the puppy rolled off her lap and jumped back into the pool of her skirt.

Jesse dropped to one knee. "He's going to grow into a big dog."

"How do you know?" she asked, her voice filled with wonder.

He palmed one of the puppy's paws. "Because he's got big feet."

"Can we keep him?"

She lifted her gaze to his, hope replacing the wariness he so often saw in her eyes. He felt an unaccustomed need to have her look upon him with the unfettered faith of a child, not the apprehension of an adult who has learned the harsh lessons of misplaced trust. He wanted to keep the smile on her face and the laughter in her voice. He wanted to bring about the dreams of happiness her father had only promised. "I don't see why not. If Billy's not opposed to giving him up."

She laughed as the puppy licked her chin. "Will you ask?"

Charles opened the back door and stepped out onto the porch. "What are you two doing out here?"

"Oh, Charles, look!" Maddie held the puppy out for him to see as he approached. "Jesse said we could keep him."

Charles bent down and admired the radiant smile on her face. "Oh, he did?"

"Yes, that's all right, isn't it?"

"It's fine with me." He glanced over at Jesse, who'd suddenly become engrossed in pulling up handfuls of grass. "People are getting ready to leave. We need to thank them for coming." Slipping his hand beneath Maddie's elbow, he helped her to her feet. Jesse stood. Charles leaned toward him and whispered with laughter laced through his voice, "Didn't think you liked dogs."

Quickly, he moved away from Jesse and placed his arm around Maddie, chuckling as they walked toward the front of the house where their neighbors had left their wagons and horses.

With the puppy nestled within her arms distracting her, Maddie found it easier to thank everyone for their kindness and wish them a pleasant journey home.

"Ah, heck!"

She looked at Aaron's disgruntled face as he trudged toward her with his small hands balled into fists by his side. The puppy licked her ear, and she smiled.

Aaron glared at her. "You weren't supposed to find him till everyone left."

"Told you he wouldn't stay in that little box," Billy said.

Aaron held his hands up to Maddie. "Will you give him to me, please?"

She handed the puppy down. Aaron hugged the puppy fiercely. "Bye, Ranger." Then he passed the black dog off to Billy.

"You want to explain exactly what's going on here?" Charles asked.

Guiltily, Aaron fidgeted and mumbled, "Uncle Jesse said we couldn't have a dog, so me and Billy figured if one got left behind, maybe Uncle Jesse would like it once he got to know it, and we could keep it."

"I see. Do you know where Uncle Jesse is right now?"

"No, sir."

"It's my understanding he's looking for Billy so he can ask him if it's all right if we keep that dog."

Aaron's eyes widened. "Honest?"

Charles smiled. "Honest."

Aaron snatched the puppy out of Billy's arms. "See, I told you my uncle was the best that ever lived." He raced away. Billy followed close on his heels.

Charles pulled Maddie closer to his side. "Guess I should have mentioned to him the puppy was for you."

Smiling, she slipped her arms around him and pressed her cheek against his shoulder. "Doesn't matter. As long as we keep him."

"Ranger." He sighed. "Jesse's going to love that."

"Why didn't he want Aaron to have a dog?"

Watching as the wagons filled with contented people rolled off into the night, Charles said quietly, "Because dogs are something else to love that die."

Closing her eyes, Maddie relished the feel of the brush traveling the length of her hair. Unable to sleep, she'd squirmed until Charles had likened her to Taylor. Then he'd ordered her out of the bed and told her to unbraid her hair.

"Nice?"

She opened her eyes and caught her husband's gaze in the mirror. She smiled. "Very nice."

"Did something happen tonight? Did Jesse—"

"No, Jesse didn't do anything. We only talked." She wished she could blame her restlessness on the excitement of the evening, but she knew its cause ran much deeper, was steeped in something that had happened when she'd walked out of the house, something she had no desire for her husband to know about. "After all we did today, I expected to fall asleep as soon as my head hit the pillow. I don't know why I didn't."

He continued to brush her hair. "That happens to me sometimes, too. A walk outside usually helps me settle down."

She shook head. A walk outside was the last thing she wanted tonight. "I think you've got the cure in your hands right now. Did you brush Alice's hair?"

"Every night. She wanted it brushed a hundred strokes." He grinned. "But I don't recall ever getting that far."

"Did she fall asleep while you were brushing her hair?"

Blushing, he cleared his throat. "Uh, no, we'd just get distracted."

As the meaning of his words dawned on her, she issued a small "Oh," and studied her hands folded tightly in her lap. "What was Alice like?"

The brush stilled, and Maddie peered at Charles's reflection in the mirror. His expression held a tenderness, his eyes filled with love in the remembrance of another woman. "She was quiet and gentle. She loved to watch butterflies in the spring. That's why she planted so many flowers. She hoped to draw them near the house. She had a strength deep within her that I could always rely upon to see me through the hard times.

"Ah, Maddie, I wish I could explain what I felt for her. It went beyond love. I felt as though she was part of me. Perhaps I didn't mourn properly, but even upon her death, I never felt that she truly left me. I still feel as though she's here with me, guiding me, walking along beside me. Sometimes, I hear her voice in the wind, feel her caress in the sunshine. I believe what we shared is rare. Perhaps that's why I hold onto it so tenaciously. Perhaps that's why I won't make room in my heart for another." He ran his finger along her cheek. "Even though I like you immensely and find you a joy to be around. Do you regret marrying me?"

She held his gaze in the mirror. "No, I'm happier here than I've ever been in my entire life."

He smiled gently. "Good." Then he returned to brushing her hair. "Jesse said you were upset yesterday."

Inwardly, she smiled. She hadn't expected Jesse to confess his rude behavior during their meal.

"Did you know the men whose likeness you saw on the reward posters?"

She stiffened. Charles stopped brushing her hair. "Jesse thought you recognized someone."

Shaking her head vehemently, she struggled to draw air into her lungs. Turning her slightly, Charles knelt before her and cupped her face in his hands. "You don't have to be frightened. We won't let anyone hurt you. Do you know who killed your father and brother?"

If he hadn't been gazing at her with such earnest concern, perhaps she could have lied. Instead, she forced out a whispered truth. "Yes."

"Did you see their likeness yesterday?"

"No."

He combed his fingers through her hair. "Are you afraid they'll come after you?"

Fear kept her silent.

"Maddie, if you're afraid of these men, talk to Jesse. As a Ranger, he tracked the worst men that ever dared commit a crime; he saw they were justly punished. Do you want him to find the men who killed your father and brother?"

"No," she whispered hoarsely.

He closed his arms around her. "You don't have to be afraid."

But she was. The thought of Jesse searching for the men who'd killed her father and Andrew terrified her.

The scream of terror shattered Jesse's dream. He jerked awake, his body bathed in sweat. Then the scream came again, and he realized it hadn't been part of his dream.

He bolted out of bed, struggling into his pants as he ran out into the hall. He buttoned only enough buttons to keep his pants anchored to his hips before bursting into his brother's room.

Tangled in the sheets, Maddie writhed and flailed her arms about her face as though warding off demons. Charles was nowhere to be seen. Crossing the room, Jesse sat on the bed and drew Maddie up against him. Wrapping his arms around her trembling body, he held her close as her sobs subsided into whimpers that tore at his heart. "Shh, Maddie. It's only a dream."

Cradling her with one hand, he awkwardly worked the tangle of blankets loose until she was free of their hold and only her nightgown separated them.

Tenderly, he brushed away the stray strands of hair that had worked free of her braid and clung to her damp cheeks. Pressing her face against his bare chest, he felt the slow trickle of warm, silent tears. "Where's Charles?" he asked quietly.

She shook her head.

"Do you want to tell me what made you scream?"

Again, she shook her head. Bowing his head, he pressed a kiss against her temple. "I'd never let anything hurt you."

Maddie felt his late-night beard graze her cheek and thought how often something rough protected something soft. His work-roughened fingers caught on the muslin of her nightgown as his hands glided gently along her spine. She could hear the strong, steady pounding of his heart, feel the warmth of his flesh, the softness of the hair covering his chest against her cheek. She heard the deep timbre of his voice as he whispered reassurance and promises of protection. How desperately she wanted to accept those promises, to trust him, to confess all, to stop living with the fear.

Jesse felt every curve the woman possessed pressed against his body. Her hair was soft against his cheek. Her tremors eased away. Her tears cooled upon his chest. No fresh tears surfaced. It was as though her body trusted him and knew he wouldn't take advantage of this moment. He wished her heart would trust him as easily.

He didn't know how long he sat holding her, how long he comforted her. Nor did he know how long Charles had been standing beside him, watching. He loosened his hold. "She had a bad dream."

Charles nodded. "I couldn't sleep. I was walking outside when I heard her screams."

Jesse didn't think he could have been holding Maddie as long as he thought he had if Charles had heard the screams and come rushing in. He glanced at his brother's bare feet, and then he understood why he hadn't heard him come into the room.

He eased Maddie down to the pillow, got up, and watched Charles stretch out beside his wife because it was his right to do so. A right Jesse didn't have. He'd almost overstepped his bounds by sitting on the bed, holding her as closely against his body as he had.

Turning from the intimate scene, he came up short. Aaron stood in the doorway, his wide eyes reminiscent of full moons. Jesse turned the boy around, placed his hand on his shoulder, and led him out, closing the door quietly behind them.

In the hallway, two little waifs stood, their eyes big and frightened. The limp rag doll was caught in the crook of Taylor's arm as she pressed her fists to her mouth. Taylor's eyes filled with unshed tears and her chin quivered. Jesse dropped to one knee and took both girls in his arms.

"It's all right now. Your ma just had a bad dream. Anyone want some cocoa?" He didn't wait for an answer, but unfolded his body, lifted both girls in his arms, and carried them toward the stairs. Aaron picked up the lamp his father had left on a table in the hallway and darted ahead of his uncle so he could light the way.

In the kitchen, Jesse deposited the girls in their chairs, then set about warming some milk. An unnatural silence hovered over the room as Jesse melted the cocoa in the warm milk. He poured the concoction into four cups, set the cups on the table, and stepped around the dog at Aaron's feet.

"Drink up," he ordered before taking his own seat. His mind drifted as the silence gave way to the slurping sounds created by small mouths and the dragging of cups back and forth across the table.

"What do you think she was dreaming about, Uncle Jesse?"

Brought out of his lengthy reverie, Jesse glanced at his nephew. His hands were wrapped around the cup, his concerned expression striving to appear grown-up. Shaking his head, he gazed at his own hands wrapped around the cup. The cocoa had cooled long ago. He'd never brought the cup to his lips. "I don't know. Been a lot of changes in her life. Her father and brother died. She got married. Found herself with three children—"

"You don't think we'd give her nightmares!" Indignation resounded from the small male voice.

He looked down the table. Taylor closed her eyes. Her head bobbed, then her eyes sprang open. Hannah waited expectantly for his answer as her tongue darted out to pick up any lingering traces of cocoa on her lips. He smiled.

"No, you wouldn't give her nightmares."

"Maybe she was dreaming 'bout that kiss you give her. Billy said you was sticking your tongue down her throat. Maybe she was dreaming you was trying to choke her."

Jesse bit back a retort on Billy's description of the kiss. "I did not stick my tongue down her throat. And my kisses aren't known to give women nightmares." He shoved the cup away.

Grabbing the discarded cup, Aaron poured its contents into the bowl on the floor beside his chair. He smiled as Ranger lapped greedily at the offering. "Maybe it was that man she was talking to out behind the barn."

Jesse's gaze snapped over to Aaron. "What man?"

Aaron lifted both bony shoulders until they nearly touched his ears.

"What'd he look like?"

"Like he was friends with the devil."

❧ 9 ❧

Standing on the wooden chair, Aaron scrutinized each likeness tacked to the wall. Looking at these stark faces, etched in black and white, made him feel as though some critter that lived in mud was crawling over his skin.

"Well?"

He turned to his uncle. "I don't see him."

Heaving a frustrated sigh, Jesse jerked his hat off his head and tunneled his callused fingers through his hair. It had been a long shot, but ever since Maddie had screamed in her sleep, he'd been more than curious about her past and the man with whom Aaron had seen her talking. Buying a birthday present for Hannah had provided him with the perfect excuse to bring Aaron into town to see if he recognized the man.

It was possible a description of the man was on the wall, but the descriptions were so vague, he thought it unlikely an eight-year-old boy would recognize the man if he read the descriptions to him.

"All right." He lifted Aaron out of the chair and set him on the floor. "Run and find Hannah a present so we can get back."

Placing his foot on the broad seat of the chair, he rested his forearm across his raised thigh. Studying the images, he wondered which one was the cause of Maddie's fears. He yanked a yellowing sheet of paper from the wall. "McGuire, you need to keep current on these posters. Sam Bass has been dead four years."

"Hell, man, I imagine half those desperadoes are dead or in prison. I only put the posters up because the sheriff makes me, and he don't make me take them down, so I don't bother. Don't imagine anyone pays much attention to those things, anyway."

Someone had paid a lot of attention to them, however. Maddie had seen something here that had put the fear of God into her. Not the kind of abstract fear one experiences when danger is in the air, but the kind of concrete fear that only comes from personal knowledge. Somewhere on this wall was at least one man who had touched her life in some way, who might be touching it still.

Impatiently, he glanced at the child tugging on his sleeve.

"Uncle Jesse, I been calling you. I found a present for Hannah. Come see."

Reluctantly, Jesse scraped the chair across the floor and deposited it before the black potbellied stove. Then he followed his nephew through the store.

"You ever seen anything like it?" His face beaming, Aaron held up a tiny white teacup with dainty hand-painted red roses adorning its edge. "It's got everything. Tiny plates and bowls. And a pot for making tea. Well, not really for making tea. Just for pretending, but she'd love it, don't you think?"

"Reckon she would."

"Does that mean we'll get it for her?"

His answer came in the form of a broad smile and a ruffling of the young boy's hair.

Hannah's tiny fingers plucked at the string. Then she slowly peeled the brown paper back. Birthdays didn't come very often, and she enjoyed feeling like a princess on her day. They'd eaten supper in the grand dining room with the pretty dishes with the blue flowers. Everyone was wearing their best clothes and talking to her like she was special. And when she finished opening her present, they'd eat her cake. A big chocolate cake with chocolate icing.

Lifting the lid on the box, she peered inside, but it was too dark to see anything. She flipped the lid off. Her mouth formed a perfect circle as she released a pleased sigh. Carefully, she picked up a tiny plate.

Taylor scooted over toward the box and looked inside. "I see?"

While the girls examined the delicate contents of the box, Aaron boasted, "I picked it out."

"You did a fine job, son," Charles said, his smile as bright as Hannah's.

"Wish I'd done as good with the wanted posters."

Jesse stopped himself from clearing his throat. To do so now would only draw attention to Aaron's remark, and he hoped everyone would overlook it.

"What wanted posters?" Maddie asked quietly, fear reflected in her eyes.

Hoping to minimize the damage, Jesse leaned forward. "It's not important—"

"Uncle Jesse wanted me to see if I could point out the man you was talking to out behind the barn."

Jesse dropped back into his chair. Why in the hell hadn't he explained to Aaron this was a secret?

"What man?" Charles asked.

"You're sneaking around spying on me?" Maddie asked, disbelief and hurt mirrored in her voice.

"I wasn't sneaking around," Aaron answered even though she was glaring at Uncle Jesse. "Me and Billy just went off to talk, and we seen you."

"What man?" Charles asked again.

"Ask your brother. He knows so bleedin' much." She strode to the table. "Come on. It's time to have some cake."

She began cutting off huge ragged pieces, dropping them on plates, and slinging the plates into place at the table. She walked over, picked up Taylor, and set her in her chair. Then she picked up Hannah, who writhed and shrieked because she didn't want to leave her dishes. Bending down, Maddie picked up a tiny plate and a cup. Then she carted Hannah over to the table, set her on a chair, and placed her precious dishes beside her. Hannah stuck her fingers into her piece of cake and scooted it onto the smaller plate, where it hung over the sides, the icing oozing onto the table. She stuck her sticky finger into Taylor's mouth.

The male members of the family trudged over to the table like convicted criminals and sat quietly.

"Happy birthday, Hannah," Maddie said, forcing a bright smile as she sliced into her piece of cake with a fork and shoved the piece into her mouth. She wasn't certain she'd be able to swallow past the lump growing in her throat.

A round of happy birthdays followed, and everyone began to eat silently.

Jesse leaned over the table. "Maddie."

"Don't 'Maddie' me. You had no right."

"Maddie, the sight of those wanted posters scared the hell out of you, and don't deny it. Fear was clearly written all over your face. Then Aaron sees you talking to a man we don't know, and you wake up in the middle of the night screaming. I just wanted to know why."

"Then why didn't you ask me?"

He leaned back in his chair. "All right. I'm asking. Who was the man you were talking to?"

"None of your damn business."

Jesse threw his hands up in the air. "Do you know who he is, Charles?"

"No, but I agree with Maddie. You had no right to do all this prying behind her back, and I don't appreciate it one bit that you used my son to do it."

"Somebody needs to do it, because you sure as hell didn't before you married her. What do you know about her?"

Charles bristled. "I know all I need to know."

"A person is made up of their past, Charles. You know absolutely nothing about Maddie's."

"Marriage is supposed to be based on trust!" Maddie threw out, her cheeks a fiery red, her eyes daring Jesse to deny it.

Charles was about to explain that the trust was supposed to be between a wife and her husband, not a woman and her brother-in-law, when Jesse leaned across the table and locked his gaze onto hers.

"All right. I'll stop making inquiries. I'll stop being curious if you'll answer one question."

She tilted up her chin.

"Is there any chance that man you talked to would harm these children?"

She glanced slowly around the table at the small children staring at her through brown eyes. She cherished their faces, anticipated their hugs, and adored the lilt of their childish voices. Her gaze finally shifted to Jesse's hard, unforgiving countenance. "No, he would not harm these children." And she prayed her lie would not come back to haunt her.

Jesse came menacingly out of his chair, leaned over the cake, and planted his hands firmly on the table. "I pray to God you're telling the truth because I promise you this: if you aren't and anything happens to these children, the nightmares your friend out behind the barn gives you will seem like pleasant dreams once I'm done with you."

Charles jumped to his feet. "Jesse, I won't tolerate you threatening my wife that way."

Maddie shoved herself away from the table and ran from the room, slamming the back door as she rushed outside.

Charles gave his brother an icy glare. "Can't you ever forget, for one moment, that you were a lawman?"

Jesse watched him stalk from the room and then glanced around the table. He'd been left with two little girls crying, their large teardrops falling into their cake.

"Uncle Jesse?"

He slid his gaze over to Aaron.

"Maybe we shoulda kept looking at the wanted posters a secret."

"Yeah, I was thinking the same thing."

Charles caught Maddie on the outskirts of the yard before she disappeared into the trees. He placed his hand on her shoulder, turned her around, and welcomed her into his embrace. Her sobs fell upon his chest. "Ah, Maddie."

"Charles, I swear to you, nothing in my past will hurt those children. It's filled with bitter memories, that's all.

It's got nothing to do with my life now, the happiness you've given me."

"I believe you." Leaning back, he tilted her chin until he gazed evenly into her eyes. "And I trust you. I don't know why, but the first time I set eyes on you, I knew you'd be a good mother to my children. That's all that's important to me. Jesse is a big brother who had twenty years of not having anyone to be a big brother to. Sometimes he gets carried away with his concern."

"Sometimes? Seems to me he's always getting carried away. I don't know how he does it, but he brings out the worst in me. He can make me so angry."

He smiled. "It's just part of his charm."

She issued a very unladylike snort. "He hasn't an ounce of charm in his entire body."

"Oh, he has some. You just have to look deep to see it." He wiped the tears from her cheeks. "Now, come on. Let's go see if we can undo the damage. I thought I heard the girls crying as I left."

Keeping his arm around her shoulder, he led her toward the house. She eased in closer against his side. She found his defense of her comforting, but woven through the comfort were threads of disquiet, for his trust was undeserved. She forced herself to ignore the darker threads. "I should have held my temper in check," she said, quietly. "It wasn't fair to ruin Hannah's birthday."

He opened the door, and they stepped into the kitchen. "Children recover quickly. I'm sure by tomorrow Hannah will have forgotten, and she'll think this was the best birthday she's ever had." He tilted his head. "Listen. I can't even hear them crying anymore."

They walked into the dining area, and Maddie felt her anger at Jesse slipping away. She managed to grab onto the tail end of it and rein it back in. She wasn't going to easily forgive him this time, but she found it difficult to remain angry at a man who was sitting on the floor, awkwardly holding the delicate handle of a tiny teacup.

"More tea, sir?" Hannah asked.

He held the cup out toward his hostess. "Yes, ma'am."

She tilted the teapot over his cup and watched the imaginary tea pour out.

"That's more than enough, Miss Hannah," Jesse said.

She set the teapot on the floor. What remained of the chocolate cake was sitting on a plate on the floor. Taylor spooned out some cake and flicked it onto a tiny plate. Face beaming, she handed it to Jesse.

"Thank you, Miss Taylor. I do believe this is the best cake I've ever eaten."

Charles moved away from Maddie. "Well, I hate to put an end to the party so soon, but Maddie and I need to put the children to bed now." He lifted Taylor and handed her to Maddie. Then he reached for Hannah, bringing her into his arms. "Jesse, why don't you see if you can clean up this little mess you made . . . that part of it that can be cleaned."

Jesse nodded, then glanced over at Maddie. She averted her gaze and walked out of the room. She stopped when she got to the stairs.

Aaron sat on the bottom step, holding Ranger close against his chest, his fingers buried in the puppy's thick fur. Solemnly, he lifted his gaze. "Didn't mean no harm."

Maddie sat on the steps. "I know, Aaron. I'm not upset with you."

"Uncle Jesse don't like to see you having nightmares. He was just gonna get that man and make him leave you be. You were the one that said a person didn't need to ask if he was doing something good."

Maddie sighed. "This is different, Aaron."

"How come?"

"It's hard to explain. You, Hannah, Taylor, your pa, and your Uncle Jesse are a family. I was beginning to feel like I was part of your family. Tonight made me feel like I wasn't."

"Why?"

"If your Uncle Jesse saw you playing with a boy he didn't know, do you think he'd go around town asking people who the boy was, or do you think he'd come and ask you?"

"He'd ask me," Aaron responded, no doubts echoed in his young voice.

"Why?"

He furrowed his young brow. "On account of I'm family?"

"That and he trusts you. Now, go put Ranger in his box in the kitchen, then come on to bed."

He stood as his father placed his hand beneath Maddie's elbow and helped her to her feet.

"Hurry," Charles commanded.

Aaron nodded. Hugging Ranger close, he rushed through the dining room into the kitchen. He placed the puppy in the box by the cast-iron stove. "Don't reckon I'd better sneak you into my room tonight. It's bad enough getting in trouble when it ain't my fault. Don't want to get into trouble when it is." He pulled the remains of a worn blanket over the dog's head. Then he walked back into the dining room. Jesse was stacking the dishes on the table.

"'Night, Uncle Jesse."

Jesse glanced over at him. "Sleep tight."

Aaron nodded and walked solemnly out of the room. Jesse decided then and there to sneak the puppy and his box to Aaron's room once everyone else had settled in for the night. He owed at least that much to the boy. He glanced over at the table. The mess could stay there until morning.

Picking up a lamp, he walked down the hallway to the study. With its shelves lined with books, the room smelled of must and knowledge. He wished he could garner some of that knowledge tonight.

He poured himself a drink, sat in the big leather chair, and stared into the glass. Just his luck, the only thing they'd have in the house was whiskey, and looking into it was like looking into her eyes. It seemed he'd been studying the whiskey in the glass an eternity before he heard Charles walk into the room.

"Don't you trust anyone?" Charles asked.

Jesse glanced up. "Trusted you."

Charles heaved a deep sigh and dropped into a chair across from his brother. "You can't blame Maddie because

I spent your money on her. She didn't ask me to."

"I don't blame her. I don't even care about the money anymore."

"Then what prompted your actions today?"

Jesse downed the whiskey, reached for the bottle, and refilled his glass. "Want some?"

"No."

He held the glass up to the lamp on the desk. "It's pretty with the light shining through it, don't you think?"

"You're drunk."

Jesse shook his head. "Sometimes, Maddie's eyes look like this. A light shining through them." He lowered the glass. "But most of the time, they look like this . . . dark. She's afraid of something." With his fingers crooked, he turned his hand. "If I could just grasp whatever it is she's afraid of, I could take the darkness away. Keep the light in her eyes all the time."

"You could just ask her, you know."

"I'm one of the things she fears."

"Can't image why. Promising her nightmares worse than the ones she already has."

"She was lying."

"You think—"

"I know," Jesse insisted, his voice hard, leaving no room for doubt. "That man's trouble, Charles. She was nervous that night we sat on the porch, but I thought it was because of all the people who were here. She's afraid he'll come back, and damn it, if I don't know who he is, how will I know him when he shows up?"

"Maybe she'd trust you if you'd stop thinking of her as a case—"

"Believe me, Charles, I'm not thinking of her as a case." He brought the glass to his lips and threw his head back.

"What are you thinking of her as?"

Jesse gave his brother a hard stare. "Your wife."

❧ 10 ❧

Proudly, Maddie gazed at the table. She'd ironed the white cloth until there wasn't a wrinkle in it. Then she'd set the china dishes and silver utensils in place. A duchess would be honored to eat here.

The stagecoach had arrived just after noon. The passengers had disembarked and were now relaxing in the parlor. The stagecoach that had come through before had only stopped long enough for a change of horses and to pick up the mail. But today, the whip was giving the passengers a two-hour rest before he drove them on to Austin.

She walked into the kitchen, picked up two folded towels, and wrapped them around the handles of a large pot. Jesse came up behind her.

"I can get that for you."

She elbowed him in the ribs, picked up the pot, shoved her way past him, and walked back to the dining room.

Charles's laughter filled the kitchen. "Remind me never to make her angry. I didn't know she had such a fiery temper and held a grudge so long."

"Hell, you didn't know *anything* about her."

Charles's smile faded. "I knew a hell of a lot more than you realize."

Maddie walked back into the room. "Charles, don't you think the hired hand ought to be seeing to the horses?"

Charles bit back his laughter at the thunderous expression crossing Jesse's face. Seemingly oblivious to it, Maddie placed a warm loaf of bread on a plate and walked back into the dining room.

"Maybe you ought to see to the horses," Charles suggested.

Jesse stormed across the room, yanked his hat off the peg on the wall, and slammed the door behind him. Utter contentment written across her face, Maddie walked into the kitchen. "You can tell our guests that the meal is ready."

She began to set the table for the family, adding additional places for the driver and his guards, neglecting to set a place at the end of the table where Jesse usually sat.

"Maddie, it's been three days. Don't you think you could forgive him just a little bit?"

"When he apologizes."

"He doesn't think he did anything wrong."

"Then it's time he learned that he did."

"I know he hurt your feelings—"

"He did not hurt my feelings. The food I set out for our guests is getting cold."

Sighing in defeat, Charles walked out of the room. Maddie stepped out onto the porch and called the children. She had just placed them at the table and filled their plates when Charles returned and took his seat. The door opened, and the driver and two guards walked in, Jesse following behind.

Jesse glanced at the table and retrieved a plate from the cabinet as everyone else took their places. He dug some utensils from the drawer. Scraping his chair across the floor, he dropped down and proceeded to heap food upon his plate.

"This is real good, ma'am."

Maddie glanced at the whip. He looked to be a man who spent a great deal of time sampling food. His red hair lay flat against his head but flared out at the sides so it appeared he was still wearing his hat. He flicked some crumbs from his scraggly beard. She forced a smile. "Thank you."

"So you're traveling with two guards now, Nate?" Jesse asked.

"Yep. We've had too dang many robberies lately. You'd think people'd forgotten what honest work was. Rangers have been setting up ambushes in areas where they think a robbery is likely to take place, but if they guess wrong, I got these two right here to cover my butt."

"How many times have you been attacked?" Jesse asked.

"Twice this month." Nate Webster eyed Jesse. "You thinking of going back to being a Texas Ranger?"

Jesse shook his head. "Nope, I like it right where I am."

"Even with the missus mad at you?" Nate guffawed, then nudged Jesse's elbow. "Wanna tell me what you did to get her all riled?"

Since his uncle was only glaring at the man, Aaron spoke. "She's mad at him cuz—"

Jesse cleared his throat with such force that one of the guards jerked back and nearly toppled over in his chair. Aaron would have laughed, but with his uncle's intense gaze concentrated on him, he wasn't even daring to breathe.

Nate stretched his arm across the table and tapped Aaron's hand. "Come on, boy, you can tell me."

Swallowing, Aaron shifted his glance over to the whip. "No, sir. I'd best not."

"Ah, come on, boy. Me and your uncle's old friends. We got no secrets from each other."

"I should have let those Comanche braves take your scalp," Jesse growled.

Aaron's eyes widened as Nate slapped his hands on the table, threw his head back, and howled out his laughter.

"Did Uncle Jesse save your life?"

Nate wiped the back of his hand across his mouth. "Sure did, boy. Course it was way back before he was a Ranger. He was still in the army, so he weren't much bigger than you when he did it. Indians had us surrounded. Then this skinny feller comes riding over the hill, guns a-blazing!" Nate held his hands in the air, his forefinger and thumb extended, his thumb bending back and forth, rapidly. "Bang! Bang! Bang! He chased 'em away!"

"Did he really?" Aaron hopped up, his excitement at hearing a tale about his uncle too great to keep him in his chair.

"Sure as hell did."

"More than likely it was the half-dozen men riding behind me that scared them off," Jesse said.

"Behind you is right. Hell, they was so far behind you, you was the only one who knew they was there."

Jesse scowled. "Don't be filling the boy's head with lies."

Nate leaned across the table, his dark eyes honing in on Aaron's. "Then I'll tell you the honest to God truth, boy. Your uncle is the best lawman that ever lived. Ain't a person who knows him will tell you different."

Maddie had become so caught up listening to Nate's rendition of the event that she forgot for a moment that she was angry with the hero of the tale. Instead, she found herself watching him, trying to imagine him as a young man, his beliefs then in the difference between right and wrong as strong as they were now.

His eyes captured hers for a brief moment before he shoved his chair back and walked out of the house.

"Why'd Uncle Jesse leave 'fore he was finished eating?" Aaron asked.

"Cuz, boy, he don't like being bragged on," Nate explained as he scraped the beans across his plate and shoved them into his mouth.

Alert to any sounds coming from the hallway, the intruder tiptoed through the room. The stagecoach had left but moments before, and he knew everyone would be returning to the house soon.

Cautiously, he pulled open the top drawer of the bedside table. Peering inside, he allowed a victorious smile to travel across his face before reaching for the tattered and worn book.

A journal. His uncle's journal in which he'd recorded his exploits as a Texas Ranger. The words that graced the pages were a mystery, for he had yet to learn how to read the writing with the fancy curves and curls that adults used, but he planned to learn someday. When he did, he'd read the journal and know all the things about being a Texas

Ranger that his uncle kept secret.

Leafing through the yellowing pages, Aaron halted when he came to the two pages between which the key rested. He took the key out and set the book on the bed.

He moved stealthily across the room to the huge trunk where his uncle kept the souvenirs of his life as a Ranger. He inserted the key and twisted it. Grunting, he lifted the heavy lid.

He moved aside the woven blanket that had been given to his uncle by an Indian chief. He shoved aside the commendation medals, the gun belt into which an outlaw had carved notches. He moved aside spurs and dug deeper until he felt the messenger of death. Slowly, he pulled it out to inspect as he had on numerous occasions when no one was around.

He ran a knobby-knuckled finger over the polished ivory handle. The sun pouring in through the window glinted off the silver metal of the barrel. He'd never seen anything so beautiful in his entire life. He folded worshipful hands around the Colt revolver.

"Whacha doing?" Hannah asked.

Crouching, Aaron spun around and clamped his fingers around the gun. "Don't you know better than to sneak up on people?"

Her eyes widened. "You ain't supposed to play with Uncle Jesse's gun. I'm gonna tell Pa."

He charged across the room and grabbed his sister's arm. "Ah, come on, Hannah. Did Uncle Jesse ever show you where he keeps the key to his chest?"

She shook her head.

"Well, he told me so I could use his gun whenever I needed it."

Hannah appeared doubtful despite the evidence.

"I ain't playing with it. I just wanted to have it with me when I went out to the woods in case that man I saw with Miss Maddie is still around."

"What you gonna do in the woods?"

"I was just gonna play Texas Ranger. I'll let you play if you won't tell Pa. Telling Pa'll get Uncle Jesse into a heap of trouble."

Thoughtfully, she chewed her bottom lip.

"You don't want to get Uncle Jesse into trouble, do you?"

She shook her head.

"Good." He wrapped his hand around hers and tugged her toward the door. He peered out into the hallway. Not a soul was in sight. He hurried down the hall, pulling Hannah along with him. He dashed into his father's room and scurried to the door that led out onto the veranda.

"Why are we sneaking if Uncle Jesse wants you to have the gun?"

"Shh!" Aaron scolded. "If you're going to be a Ranger, you got to be awfully quiet. I'm testing you now to see if I can let you into my outfit or not." He pushed open the door and eased out onto the veranda. Still no one was in sight. With Hannah close on his heels, he haltingly descended the stairs, keeping his eyes and ears alert. When his feet hit the dirt, he ran toward the woods.

He didn't stop running until he was hidden by the trees. Then he waited, listening for Hannah's small feet. Breathless and wide-eyed, she finally caught up to him.

"I reckon you'll make a pretty good Ranger. You can help me search for Sam Bass."

"But Uncle Jesse shot him."

"No, he didn't. Another Ranger did. But Uncle Jesse helped track him down. That's what we're going to play. We're in Round Rock, and we know Bass is gonna be here any time cuz one of his men sent us a telegram." Reaching down, he picked up a stick. "Here. You can be Uncle Jesse, and I'll be the Ranger that shot Bass."

Wrinkling her nose, Hannah studied the forked twig, trying to decide which end was the shooting end.

"Follow me," he whispered as though they were surrounded by outlaws.

"Aaron, you really think that man is still here?"

"Might be. That's why I got the gun."

"How will I know if I see him?"

"You'll know."

"How?"

Aaron moved closer to her and whispered as though the trees had ears, "He's bigger than Uncle Jesse, so big he blocks out the sun. And he's got scars running all over his face. His face looks like the creek when the water's low and the mud dries."

Her eyes grew round.

"And he stinks something fierce. Me and Billy thought it was a skunk behind the barn. That's what we went to see, but it wasn't. It was him."

Her eyes got wider, and Aaron couldn't help himself. He shouted, "Boo!"

Hannah shrieked, and Aaron laughed. "Come on, Hannah. If you see him, just holler and I'll save you." He headed into the woods.

Hannah bent down and cautiously moved forward. She heard the branches rustle and tightened her hold on the twig. She heard a field mouse scurry under the moss and squeezed the twig until her fingers ached. She heard leaves from previous winters crackle in the distance and felt her heart pounding against her chest.

They came to a clearing. She had no desire to be in the open. She wanted to stay hidden. She stopped on the outskirts, but Aaron trudged forward. "Aaron," she squeaked.

"Shh!" he commanded as he moved across the clearing.

She knew she should follow him, but she was hearing too many noises. Aaron disappeared into the brush on the other side of the clearing. The noises behind her increased. Not daring to breathe, Hannah glanced behind her as a large shadowy figure emerged from beyond the trees. She screamed at the top of her lungs.

Aaron came thrashing back through the trees. His boot caught on the gnarled root of a tree. He fell forward. His arms hit the hard ground, jarring his elbows as his fingers tightened on the trigger. The recoil from the gun momentarily lifted him and shoved him backward.

Upon hearing a child's terrified scream, Jesse rushed into the clearing. The sound of an explosion registered in his mind a split second before he felt something slam into him and ignite an invisible fire within his body. His knees buckled as he clutched his left side, vaguely aware of the sticky warmth flowing through his fingers.

Through a haze of pain, he saw Aaron dart away. On his knees, bracing himself upright with one arm, he called out to the boy, but the sounds coming from his throat were garbled and distant, unrecognizable.

Collapsing to the ground, he watched blackness ease in around the outer edge of the sky. Tiny fingers patted his cheek.

"Hannah, get your pa," he forced out through labored breaths.

"You gonna whup Aaron?"

He rolled his head from side to side, blinking the sweat from his eyes, fighting down the bile rising in his throat. "No, just get your pa."

"Promise you won't whup Aaron?"

"Promise." The last thing he saw before the blackness enveloped him was a little girl patiently watching him as though he was a wilting wildflower.

Far away through the dense fog hovering over him, he heard the pounding of the ground. Cattle. Cattle were coming, stampeding. He had to get out of the way, but he was so damned tired. He opened his eyes to the gray skies. Sweet Lord. He'd come awake too late. He already felt as though he'd been trampled. He tried to sit up, and the warmth flowed around him. The cattle were getting closer. He ceased his efforts as the stampeding grew louder. Then the pounding stopped, and the sky was obliterated by Charles's concerned face.

Whiskey. He needed whiskey. And then she was there, kneeling beside him. He drank of the whiskey in her eyes, strengthening his resolve not to die from a wound made by an eight-year-old boy.

"Aaron," he croaked. "My fault. Shouldn't have—"

"Doesn't matter right now," Maddie said as she quickly eased his shirt aside.

Charles felt his stomach lurch as the torn flesh in Jesse's side just below his ribs came into view. Breathing deeply, he bowed his head. "Dear Lord."

"You look worse than I feel," Jesse said.

"Damn you, don't you dare pick now to develop a sense of humor. I don't know the first thing about bullet wounds. It'll take me two to three hours to get Doc Murdoch here—if I can find him."

"I know how to tend a bullet wound," Maddie said quietly as she reached beneath her skirt, ripped off a portion of her petticoat, and pressed it to Jesse's side. Her gaze shifted between the two men. "When my father got shot, I tended him."

"Your father died," Charles harshly reminded her.

Considering the circumstances, she didn't take offense at his tone but merely reassured him calmly. "He didn't die from the wound I treated. This wound looks much worse than it is. The bullet went through, and it's far enough to the side that I don't think any serious damage was done."

Hope ignited within Charles's eyes. "He's too heavy for me to carry. Will you stay here with him while I get the wagon?"

She nodded. Charles leapt to his feet and ran toward the barn.

Gingerly, Maddie once again inspected the wound. The wounds she'd tended before had been worse. She was certain they had been, but they hadn't frightened her like this one did, and she couldn't explain her fear. She felt Jesse's unsettling gaze latch onto her. "Will you please stop staring at me?"

"If I die, I want the last thing I see to be your eyes."

She snapped her head around. "That's not funny."

"Wasn't meant to be."

Gazing down on him, she blinked back her tears. His voice sounded as though it came from far away, as though it was flowing away from him as easily as his blood, and he looked so much older with pain etched within the creases of his face. "You're not going to die. I just need to stop the bleeding and keep it from getting infected."

"Does this mean you've forgiven me?"

"No."

"Ah, Whiskey, I'm not the one who'll hurt you."

❧ 11 ❧

Jesse eased down onto the bed. Damn Maddie for being right. Climbing the stairs with his arm draped over Charles's shoulder had been a mistake, just as she'd promised it would be, but he'd wanted his hurting body in a soft bed. The Princess room was as far as he'd gotten, but he figured it was for the best. He'd need the brass headboard before everything was said and done.

He felt like the rag doll Taylor draped over her arm as Charles worked Jesse out of his shirt. One of the doll's embroidered eyes had lost most of its threads. He needed to talk to Maddie about fixing it. Maybe she could redo the doll's entire face. A little girl's doll should have a pretty face.

He heard his bloody shirt slap the floor. Charles had stripped off Jesse's remaining clothes and draped a sheet over his lower body, when Maddie walked into the room carrying a tray. Jesse reached up and wrapped his large hands around the frail brass spirals. Charles hurried out of the room. Jesse glanced over at Maddie. She was pouring whiskey over her hands. The glint of a steel edged knife resting on the bedside table caught his eye. "Are you going to cut on me?" he asked.

She kept her gaze averted as she replied, "You'll heal quicker and easier if I clean the wound and remove the flesh that's bound to die anyway." She cast him a furtive glance, the apology woven in her words. "It won't be pleasant. I'll do it as quickly as I can."

"Do whatever you have to. I won't scream or fight you."

"Got some laudanum Doc Murdoch gave me for an emergency," Charles said as he rushed back into the room. "I'd say this was an emergency. I'll give you a couple of spoonfuls, and with any luck you'll go to sleep before Maddie gets started."

Charles lifted Jesse's head and spooned the medicine into his mouth. Jesse grimaced and returned his head to the pillow. He gave Maddie a weak smile before clenching his teeth and nodding slightly. He tightened his hold on the railings.

Night was easing in around them. "Charles, will you hold the lamp so I can see better?"

Charles moved into position. "Are you sure you know what you're doing?"

Tentatively, Maddie touched the outer edges of the wound and felt Jesse tense. Glancing at his tortured face, she wished he wouldn't be so stoic. Somehow it made her task seem that much harder. "Please don't watch me while I do this."

Closing his eyes, Jesse took an image of her delicate features with him, preparing himself for the hell she was about to deliver. His body convulsed as she cleaned the wound, wasting good whiskey in the process. He wished he could keep quiet. He was certain listening to his grunts and groans wasn't making her job any easier. Then he felt her fingers leave his side and heard the knife scrape across the table. He'd lied. He thought he released a strangled scream just before he plunged into the black abyss of hell and lost consciousness.

Maddie didn't remember sewing up the wound or wrapping the bandages around it, and she didn't realize she was crying until Charles wrapped his unsteady arms around her. She turned her face into his chest, wishing it was Jesse's chest, Jesse's arms comforting her. Now she understood why the wound frightened her so much. It made her realize Jesse was vulnerable. His strength, his dedication to protecting them could be taken away as easily as a child plucked a flower from a meadow.

"Is he going to die?" Charles asked.

She tilted up her face. His brow was furrowed, the corners of his mouth no longer eager to form a smile. His eyes delved into hers, seeking the truth. "No, we were fortunate. The bullet went through without hitting anything but flesh and muscle. He's lost a lot of blood." She forced a smile of reassurance. "He's not going to be able to chop any wood for a while, but considering how much wood he's chopped lately, we probably won't need any for a couple of years, anyway."

He cupped her cheek. "Don't know what we would have done if you hadn't been here."

"You would have managed."

He shook his head. "I don't know how you stayed so calm. How'd you remember all that from treating one wound?"

Nervously, her gaze flickered around his face. "I have a good memory."

A sob caused them to snap their heads around. With a tear-streaked face, his lower lip quivering, his hands balled into fists, Aaron stood in the doorway.

Charles charged across the room, grabbed Aaron's arm, spun him around, and applied his hand soundly against Aaron's backside. Then he spun him back around. "What the hell did you think you were doing?"

Aaron moved his head slightly from side to side, his voice trapped somewhere deep within his terrified soul.

Charles shook him. "Get to your room, and don't you dare come out until I've said."

"Yes, sir," he forced out, his small voice wavering as he took one last look at the still figure lying on the bed before dashing out of the room.

Charles plowed trembling fingers through his hair and dropped his head back. "Christ!" He pounded a fist against the wall. "Christ Almighty!" He leaned his forehead against the wall.

Maddie crossed the room and placed the heel of her palm against his back. "Charles?"

"I've never hit him before, but, dear Lord, when I think of what might have happened—"

"But it didn't happen."

He gazed down on her. "What do we need to do now?"

"I want to watch Jesse tonight, to be near in case he needs anything."

"What can I do?"

"Fix the children some supper, tuck them into bed, then go to bed yourself."

"I'll get you something to eat as well."

"I don't think I could eat right now."

He nodded his understanding. He thought it'd be at least a week before he'd be able to keep any food down. "I'll bring you some warm water for the washbasin in our room."

"That would be nice."

They glanced over at Jesse's inert body before walking into the hallway. Aaron's muffled sobs eased out beneath the closed door to his room.

"I can use the water that's already in the washbasin," Maddie said. "Why don't you see after Aaron?"

Charles ran his hand through his hair. "I guess I'd better."

Maddie walked to the door of their bedroom and glanced over her shoulder. Her husband was seriously studying the floor. "Charles?"

He lifted his gaze. The weight of the spanking he'd given Aaron was clearly visible in his eyes.

"Don't think it to death," she said quietly.

He forced a small smile. "I won't." Then he headed for the stairs.

Aaron heard the door to his room open. He squeezed his eyes shut and balled his fists around the covers. He heard the door close and felt the light from a lamp touch his eyelids. He heard a tiny yelp and opened his eyes. His father was crouched beside his bed, holding a lamp in one hand and Ranger in the other.

Charles set the lamp on a table beside the bed. Meeting his son's distressed gaze, knowing he was the one responsible for putting the fear there, pained him more than anything in his life ever had. "Want to tell me what happened?"

Tears flooded Aaron's eyes. "I shot Uncle Jesse."

Charles dumped the dog onto the bed and took Aaron in his arms.

"I'm sorry, Pa." Aaron sobbed against his shoulder.

Sitting on the bed, Charles drew Aaron onto his lap. "I know. I'm sorry I hit you." He held Aaron's head against his shoulder. "I want you to tell me what happened."

Aaron sniffed. "I heard Hannah scream. I thought it was that man I saw out behind the barn. Guess she did, too, but it was Uncle Jesse. I was running to help her, and I tripped. The gun fired. I didn't mean for it to. Is he gonna die?"

Charles squeezed him. "No."

"Do you hate me, Pa?"

Charles held him tighter. "Oh, God, no. I love you, son. Always will, no matter what you do. What happened today scared the hell out of me. Guns aren't something to play with. That's why we keep the rifles locked in the closet downstairs."

"I won't never touch a gun again."

Easing Aaron back, Charles looked at him. "Guns have a purpose, Aaron, but playing isn't one of their purposes. Taking Uncle Jesse's gun this afternoon was wrong. That's why you're to stay in your room. Not because you shot Uncle Jesse, but because you took his gun. Do you understand the difference?"

Sniffing, Aaron ran his finger beneath his nose. "Think so. Want me to do Uncle Jesse's chores until he gets better?"

Charles squeezed his shoulder. "We'll do them together until he gets well."

Stepping into a room not filled with the presence of blood had made Maddie acutely aware of the odor emanating from her clothes and hands. Quickly, she'd stripped out of her clothes and washed Jesse's blood from her skin, but she continued to scrub at her hands. She'd forgotten how difficult it was to remove the feel of blood.

Her skin was pink and tingling by the time she finally dried off. She slipped into her nightgown and wrapper before walking across the hallway into the Princess room.

Jesse's fingers were still resting between the bent spirals

of the headboard. Gingerly, she moved his arms to his side. Thudding and bumping in the hallway caused her to look toward the door.

"How's he doing?" Charles asked as he pulled a rocking chair into the room and deposited it beside the bed.

"He hasn't come to yet. Probably won't for a while. His body needs the rest. How are the children?"

"Fed and in bed. Quickest meal I ever fixed."

"You should try and get some sleep."

"I will later. Have a seat."

Maddie sat in the rocking chair. His eyes steadfastly watching his brother, Charles stood by the bed. "You know, it's strange, but the day he showed up on my doorstep, it felt as though only twenty minutes had passed since we'd last seen each other . . . instead of twenty years. Still, I'd do almost anything to make sure my children would never be separated from each other."

Maddie took his hand and gave a gentle squeeze. "Well, you're not going to be separated from Jesse again for a good long time. Why don't you go on to bed? I'll wake you if anything changes."

He patted her hand. "Come and get me if you need me."

She watched him walk out, then turned her attention back to Jesse. She dipped the cloth into the cool water in the basin and wrung it out before sitting carefully on the bed. Gently, she wiped Jesse's face. The cloth caught on the beard stubble covering his chin. She'd shave his face when he felt stronger. The thought of tending to his manly needs caused warmth to sluice through her. He was stronger than Charles. Even as he lay there, his muscles were firm.

"He died?"

Maddie spun around. Aaron stood at the foot of the bed, his eyes glistening with tears. "Pa washed Ma like that when she died."

She rose from the bed and knelt before him. "No, no. He's not dead." With her fingers, she lightly combed the hair back from his furrowed brow. "He has a small fever, and I'm trying to cool him down. That's normal with a wound like his. His body's fighting to heal. Would you like to help me?"

The need to help his uncle was clearly written in Aaron's eyes. "I ain't supposed to be out of my room, but I was scared. I don't want him to die, Ma."

Maddie's heart overflowed with joy as she pulled Aaron into her embrace. Of all the times for her to feel such gladness. His arms went around her neck, holding on to her as though she was his salvation. "I didn't shoot him on purpose."

"We all know that." She leaned back. "I'm really tired. I think your father would understand if you helped me, and it would make your uncle feel better."

Relief evident in his features, Aaron nodded. He sat on one side of Jesse, Maddie on the other. She handed him a damp cloth, and he lightly touched his uncle's face.

"Your uncle's fairly tough. He won't crack if you touch him a little harder."

Nodding, Aaron moved the cloth down Jesse's neck. Maddie rinsed her own cloth out before wiping his damp chest. "Did your father talk with you?"

Aaron peered over at her. "He ain't so mad no more."

She took the cloth from his small hand, dipped it into the water, wrung it out, and handed it back to him. "I think he was always more scared than he was mad. He loves you very much and it frightened him to think you might have been the one to get hurt."

Aaron twisted his mouth and ran the cloth along Jesse's arm. "I'm glad Pa married you."

The words were spoken so quietly that she almost didn't hear them. She smiled softly as they continued to work together in silence.

Jesse opened his eyes. A lamp burned low on the table beside the bed. Maddie sat in the rocking chair, her head turned at an awkward angle, her eyes closed. Aaron, with his long legs dangling, was nestled against her shoulder, asleep. Despite the pain in his side, the heat of his body, he felt a strange yearning. He was the only person in this family who hadn't slept within her comforting arms.

Her braided hair was draped over her shoulder and across Aaron's hand. Above her closed eyes, her finely arched eyebrows were relaxed. She seemed younger, more innocent in sleep. He had a strong urge to protect her.

He almost laughed with that thought. Protect her? He wasn't capable of protecting himself. What had confounded him lying there, his life's blood flowing onto the ground, was the absolute certainty in her voice when she'd spoken. She'd dealt with bullet wounds before, was familiar with the dangers. Her fingers had been steady, her determination exact. She had the skills of a physician, but she wasn't a physician. A physician wouldn't have been forced to climb onto a table in Bev's parlor.

Aaron shifted in her lap, and she closed her arms more protectively around him. Slowly, she opened her eyes. There wasn't enough light for him to see the whiskey clearly, but just knowing it was there was enough for him. His eyes held hers. The only movement within the room occurred when she blinked. And that movement, simple as it was, broke the trance.

Sliding Aaron onto the seat, she eased out of the rocking chair and slipped a pillow beneath his head. She knelt beside the bed and drew her brows together as she studied his features closely. "Are you in pain? Do you want some laudanum?"

"Whiskey," he croaked.

"You want some whiskey?"

Shaking his head slightly, he cupped her cheek with his roughened hand, moving his thumb gently across her cheek. "Your eyes are like whiskey." His eyes drifted closed. "I'm sorry."

She resisted the urge to press a kiss against his palm as she sat on the edge of the bed. She took his hand and brought it to her lap, wrapping her hands around it. "I'm not exactly sure what you're apologizing for."

"All the times I made you cry."

"You've never made me cry."

He gave her a halfhearted smile. "Liar."

"Well, maybe once."

"Twice."

"Four times," she admitted.

Above his closed eyes, his brows drew together. "Four? Sorry."

"Uncle Jesse?"

He forced his eyes open.

"Uncle Jesse, I'm sorry."

Struggling, he lifted his hand from Maddie's lap and took hold of Aaron's hand, tugging weakly, but it was all Aaron needed to throw himself across Jesse's chest and wrap his arms around his neck. Jesse swallowed the grunt of pain that erupted with the boy's actions.

"I shouldn't have run off. I'm sorry."

The childish sobs tore at Jesse's heart. He worked his hand to Aaron's back, his fingers moving lightly, offering reassurance. "I ran off, too, first time I shot a man."

Aaron lifted his head, swiping the tears from his cheeks. "Did you really?"

He nodded slightly. Maddie touched Aaron's back. "You'd better get on to bed. Let your uncle get some more rest."

"I love you, Uncle Jesse," he whispered before releasing his hold and running silently from the room.

Jesse captured Maddie's gaze. "Don't let me die," he ordered before he fell back into painless oblivion.

Maddie brushed the hair back from his brow, knowing his request had little to do with his own desire to live but more to do with trying to spare Aaron's conscience.

For long moments, she watched him sleep. Then she picked up the lamp and left the room. Quietly, she walked into Aaron's room.

Looking down on the sleeping child, she felt her heart swell. It had taken a near tragedy, but Aaron had finally called her Ma. She hadn't expected the one word to touch her so deeply. She lifted the sheet over his back. There was a movement along Aaron's side and a wet, black nose poked out from beneath the sheet. Maddie smiled as she realized why Charles had headed down the stairs before talking to Aaron.

Holding the lamp, she slipped from the room, walked down the hall, and stepped into Jesse's room. She'd never been in this room, although she'd often wondered what it was like.

It carried his masculine scent, a scent far different from the one that wafted around the Princess room. Yet, she thought, the scents, though different, somehow complemented each other. The solid oak furniture would last his lifetime and beyond. He'd drawn the quilt neatly over the bedding. He'd left no clothing on the floor. The room reflected the life of a man for whom orderliness was a requirement. The only thing out of place was a journal resting on the bed.

Setting the lamp on the bedside table, she eased onto the bed and lifted the worn book into her hands. She turned back the cover and read the date and words that flowed freely on the first page. Her hands trembled with the realization that she was holding six years of Jesse's life, recorded in his handwriting. She had little doubt that within these pages she would find an honest accounting of his trials and tribulations, his feelings, and his thoughts. With his belief in honesty, he would have recorded nothing less. She knew she should close the book and quit the room, respect his privacy and his past in the same manner she was demanding he respect hers.

Leaning toward the lamp, she turned the page and continued reading.

Her eyes grew gritty, her back ached, and her heart knew a fear worse than any she'd ever known. She closed the book on the final page.

Charles had not exaggerated when he said Jesse was skilled at hunting men. Jesse had meticulously recorded the details of his assignments. She thought, if lawmen attended schools where they learned the tools of their trade, Jesse's journal could serve as the textbook.

Her thoughts drifted to the day he took her into town, and she glanced in innocence at the wall. The last thing she expected to see was a likeness of her father and Andrew. The three remaining members of her father's small gang were there as well, but they'd taken greater care in keeping their faces hidden and were nothing more than scant descriptions that could apply to anyone. But Jesse would be able to find them all if he set his mind to it.

Silas and Walsh were the ones she feared. She thought she'd evaded Silas until he'd appeared behind the barn. Ironically, he'd been in Waco scouting out the stagecoach he and Walsh were to rob, when he'd seen Maddie get in the coach. He'd altered his plans and followed her. He thought she knew where her father had buried a strongbox filled with money. She'd told him where to search, but knew he'd only find dirt. She prayed he wouldn't return. He threatened her dreams more than Jesse did.

Hearing a low moan, she laid the book on the bed as she'd found it, picked up the lamp, and walked swiftly to the Princess room.

Jesse was bathed in sweat, his hands clutching the covers. As she crossed the room and set the lamp on the bedside table, the pale light touched his face to reveal the deep lines along his brow and around his tightened mouth. As though weighted down, his eyes opened slowly.

Maddie laid her hand over his clenched fist. "Are you in much pain?"

"Tired." Closing his eyes, he wrapped his fingers around her hand. "Damn lucky."

She ran her free hand along the firm muscles of his arm. "Yes, we were."

"We?" He opened his eyes. "You're not mad at me anymore?"

His voice carried the lilt of a hopeful child and effectively melted away any anger lingering within her breast. She pressed her hand to his cheek. "I should be, but no, I'm not."

He ran his tongue over his dry lips. "Water."

"I'm sorry. I should have gotten you something to drink before now. Wait here."

He wanted to tell her there wasn't a whole hell of a

lot he could do but wait, but it wasn't worth the effort. Grabbing the lamp, she rushed out of the room, leaving him in darkness. A few minutes later, she returned with a tray.

Maddie set the tray down and moved the lamp onto the table. She picked up a glass and carefully lifted his head. "Don't drink too fast." She watched his mouth touch the glass and his throat work as he swallowed. She noted every small detail, wishing she could hate him, could use her anger as a shield, but as always, in his presence she felt her fears dwindle until they were little more than shadows lurking in a corner. She didn't fear the man, only the skills he'd acquired while he'd worked as a Texas Ranger. If he applied his skills, he could take away her dream. Unexpectedly, she realized she'd willingly give up her dream for his life.

He swallowed the last of the water. She set the glass down. "I brought you some soup as well. Do you feel up to letting me give you some?"

He gave a small nod. Maddie placed another pillow beneath Jesse's head. She eased down onto the bed and reached for the bowl, then lifted the spoon to her lips to test the warmth of the soup. She shifted her gaze to Jesse. He was watching her with a hunger that she feared had little to do with his stomach. "The soup was too hot when I put it in the bowl. I want to make sure it has cooled down enough."

"Has it?" he asked in a raspy voice.

She nodded and carefully moved the spoon to his mouth. She watched his lips light upon the silver, and he drew the soup from the spoon. She fed him in silence. He had drained half the bowl before he closed his eyes.

She set the bowl on the tray and gently removed the pillow from beneath his head to make him more comfortable. Then she dampened a cloth and gently wiped the last remnants of soup from around his mouth. Inadvertently, her finger brushed against the fullness of his lips, and she remembered how soft they'd felt when pressed against hers, how warm, how supple.

Tenderly, she wiped the glistening dew from his chest. Slowly, she glided the cloth over his ribs. How lucky they were that the bullet hadn't struck higher; how fortunate indeed. If he'd taken one step to his right, the bullet might have missed him completely; if he'd taken one step to his left, she might not have been able to help him at all.

The blanket was draped low over his hips, leaving bare a strip of flesh below the dressing she'd wrapped around him earlier. While she'd been tending him in the early evening, she'd given little thought to the fact that he was dressed as a newborn babe. His navel peeked out from beneath the bandages. She had a strong urge to press a kiss to the place where his life had begun.

"Will he hurt you?" Jesse asked quietly.

Maddie yanked the blanket up to his chest and jerked her head around. She thought he'd fallen asleep and wondered how long he'd been watching her.

"The man Aaron saw you talking to . . . will he hurt you?"

The temper within her ignited and died. He wasn't a Texas Ranger grilling her, but a friend concerned for her welfare. Perhaps it's what he'd been all along, but her guilt had prompted her to see him otherwise. She couldn't speak the truth, but neither could she lie. "Don't you think if he was going to harm me, he would have done so when he was here before?"

"Then what are you afraid of?"

Absently, she wiped the cloth over his chest. "It's not fear so much . . ." She squeezed her eyes shut and sighed as though someone had just dropped a heavier load upon her shoulders. "I don't know," she admitted raggedly. "Maybe it is fear." She opened her eyes. "I don't deserve all this— Charles, the house, the children. I did nothing to earn them. I feel as though at any moment someone will snatch them away. It's hard to explain, probably impossible for you to understand. Most people work hard to attain their dreams. All I did was stand on a table and pull the bodice of my gown down—"

"Don't!" he rasped. Jesse didn't want to see her on that table, didn't want to know all she'd endured before Charles had made his bid. Why the hell hadn't Charles bid on her sooner? The pain raging in his side was nothing compared to the one her quietly spoken words had started in his heart. He dropped his hand over hers where it had come to rest on his chest. "No one's going to take any of this away from you." He squeezed her hand as much as his dwindling strength would allow. "Give you my word."

Maddie squeezed her eyes to stay the tears. She was so very tired. The emotional ordeal of the day was taking its toll, and she didn't know how to react to his promise, knowing there might come a day when he'd have to break it, knowing he would resent her with every fiber of his being when he did. If Silas dared to return—

"What were you like as a little girl?" he asked.

Studying his haggard face, she remembered that she was supposed to comfort him, not have him comfort her. Dipping the cloth into the bowl, she squeezed it with one hand and wiped the sweat from his brow. "I was small, very thin. I spent a lot of time pretending."

"Cassie would pretend she was a princess. Is that what you did?"

She placed the cloth in the bowl. Tenderly, she combed her fingers through his hair, lifting it off his brow. "You still miss her, don't you?"

She watched the muscles in his throat work, but no words came forth. He closed his eyes. When he opened them, they were filled with a raw pain, an anguish greater than any she'd seen in his eyes that evening.

"She was so tiny," he said hoarsely. "What if they didn't take good care of her?"

It seemed a night designed for sharing fears. The house was quiet, the hour was late. She knew his slight fever and weakened state caused his fears and vulnerability to surface. Otherwise, he kept them imprisoned within his gruff exterior. She wished she could give him a promise as easily as he had given one to her. She pressed her palm against his bristled cheek. "I'm sure they did. They wouldn't have taken her if they didn't want her."

He laid his rough hand against her cheek. "Then why can't I find her?"

She was surprised by the strength he fostered to press her face against his chest. She felt more than heard his ragged sigh.

"Why can't I find her?"

❧ 12 ❧

Jesse eased his legs off the bed. Steadying himself against the twisted rails on the brass bed, he shoved his weight onto his shaking legs. Holding his tender side, he shuffled across the floor and slowly made his way to his room.

His room. After nearly a week, it was a welcome sight, even though he was breathing hard and his body had broken out in a cold sweat with his efforts. He walked stiffly over to the bed and eased himself down.

His journal lay in the center of the bed. He'd been a fool to share it with Aaron, an even greater fool to let him see the key. Well, he'd certainly paid for his foolishness. He picked it up and caressed the faded cover the way a man might caress a woman with whom he's spent a lifetime: lovingly, knowing every crease, every wrinkle; understanding and accepting the forces that had brought them about.

Sifting through the pages, he heaved a frustrated sigh. If he knew for certain that what was in Maddie's past would stay in her past, he'd leave it alone. But while he'd been confined to bed, he'd spent a lot of time wondering about the man behind the barn. She was afraid of him, whether she admitted it or not. If only she'd confide in him, he had the skills and the resources to put her fears to rest.

He heard Maddie's voice, followed by Aaron's laughter, filter through his window. Holding his side, he walked out of his room and worked his way down the stairs.

* * *

"Come here, Aaron Lawson!" Disgusted that she couldn't keep the smile from her face, Maddie stomped her foot.

"No, ma'am!"

She advanced on him, and he scampered away. Then he came to an abrupt halt, and his eyes widened. "Uncle Jesse!"

Maddie spun around. Leaving the back door open as though even the thought of closing it was too much, Jesse moved slowly onto the porch. She rushed forward, taking his arm and supporting him as he eased into a chair. He grimaced as he made contact with the hard wood.

"Aaron, close the door," Maddie ordered. "And you, what are you doing? You shouldn't be out of bed."

He squinted at her. "I need to start moving around. Besides, I've been in that bed so long, I'm getting sores on my butt."

Blushing, she looked toward the oak trees in the distance.

"Aaron, what are you not doing that Maddie wants you to do?"

"Ma wants me to sit in that chair out there so she can cut my hair, but I don't think it needs cutting. Do you?"

Jesse hadn't heard a word Aaron had uttered past the first one: Ma. When had the boy come to accept Maddie so thoroughly into his life? He felt as though he'd been living in a cave somewhere. Aaron scrutinized him. "What?" he growled.

"You need a haircut worse 'n me."

"I wouldn't be surprised. Maybe I'll go into town tomorrow and take care of it."

"Why don't you let Ma cut it? She cut Pa's hair before he took the girls to look for blackberries."

He shifted in his chair. "I think I've put Maddie out enough this week."

"I don't mind." She wiped her hands on her apron. "I'll even wash it for you."

"Come on, Uncle Jesse. If you let her cut your hair, I'll let her cut mine."

"Come sit out in the yard. You could use some sunshine," she urged.

"I feel like I'm being railroaded," he said as he sat in the chair in the middle of the yard. Deftly, she draped a towel over his shoulders and tugged the ends into the collar of his shirt.

"Tilt your head back a little," she ordered as she lifted a dipper filled with water.

He felt the water dribble over his head time and again, until his hair was soaking wet. She worked the soap through his hair and into his scalp. He almost groaned from the pure pleasure of it. Then she used the dipper filled with water to rinse out the soap. He'd almost fallen asleep by the time he felt the comb go through his hair and heard the first snip of the scissors.

"Well, well, what have we here?"

Jesse squinted at his brother holding a pail of blackberries. "At least I don't walk around with a blue ring around my mouth."

Quickly, Charles covered his mouth with his hand. He glanced at his giggling daughters, their mouths harboring shades of the evidence as well. "Guess we shouldn't have eaten so many, huh?"

A horn blast and the crack of a gunshot echoed in the distance and sent the giggles and smiles into hiding.

"Maddie, get the children inside," Jesse ordered as he shot out of the chair, bent over with pain, and struggled to catch his breath. Charles was already running for the house.

"What is it?" she asked as she took each girl's hand.

"Stage coming in with trouble in its wake."

He hobbled toward the porch.

"Where do you think you're going?" she asked.

"To help."

"Like hell." She grabbed his arm. "You're not strong enough yet."

"We've got no choice. Take the children to your room and bolt the door."

Maddie lifted Taylor onto a hip, tightened her hold on Hannah's hand, and rushed inside. She stopped by the stairs and watched Charles pull rifles out of the closet. "Do you really think those are necessary?"

Closing the door, he secured the lock and handed a rifle off to Jesse. Then he touched her cheek. "Let's pray they're not. Take the children upstairs. Aaron, your ma's never been through this before, so you help her."

"Yes, sir." Aaron tromped up the stairs. "Come on."

Maddie watched the men leave the house, then followed Aaron up the stairs. They went into her bedroom, closed the door, and bolted it. Aaron pressed his ear to the door.

"Stagecoach is here. Don't hear no more shooting." He cast a furtive glance toward Maddie as she sat on the bed, holding both girls close. "That's a good sign."

"It is?"

He nodded with a wisdom that belied his youth. "Means the robbers probably held back once they realized the stagecoach was nearing the inn." He pressed his ear back against the door.

"Robbers bad?" Taylor asked.

"Bad," Hannah acknowledged. "Uncle Jesse and Pa hate robbers."

"Shh. We should be quiet," Maddie said.

"Hear some voices, but they ain't loud," Aaron said. "That's a good sign."

"Why is that?" Maddie asked.

"Cuz if they was shouting, it would be cuz those robbers was attacking. I hate robbers." He moved away from the door and dropped to the floor. "It ain't right what they do, taking from people what's theirs and scaring people. I'm glad Uncle Jesse used to track 'em. When I grow up, I'm going to track 'em, too."

There was a soft tapping on the door. Aaron jumped to his feet and unbolted the door. Charles came into the room, and both girls leapt off Maddie's lap and ran to him. He knelt, hugged them close, and glanced over their heads at Maddie. "It seems the trouble's passed, but with darkness coming, the passengers will stay here tonight. Jesse and I'll keep watch. Why don't you see to our guests' comfort?"

Nodding, Maddie walked out of the room. She found it

disheartening to realize Jesse wasn't the only one who saw everything in black and white.

Stepping out onto the veranda, Maddie peered through the darkness. "Jesse?"

"Over by the steps," came his low voice.

She walked quickly to the other side of the veranda and knelt, only then able to see his shadowed form. "Brought you some coffee."

She felt his hand wrap around hers momentarily before he extracted the cup from her grasp.

" 'Preciate it."

She sat on the top step. Her leg bumped into his. "How are you feeling?" she asked.

"Tired."

"It's after midnight. Do you think they'll come?"

"No."

"Then why don't you go to bed?"

"Because when a man owns no soul, you can never be sure. Just because I don't think they'd be stupid enough to attack doesn't mean they won't."

She pulled her legs against her chest and rested her chin on her upturned knees. "Did you really run away the first time you shot a man, or were you just trying to make Aaron feel better?"

He took a swallow of coffee, gazing out at the shadows that moved with the breeze and the clouds. "I'll tell you if you'll answer one question for me."

Sighing, she looked past him to the night.

"Will you answer my question?" he asked.

She knew it was foolish to place so much power in his hands, and she couldn't understand why she wanted to, but she did. "Yes."

She heard him set down the cup and felt his finger come to rest beneath her chin, turning her face until she was gazing into his eyes. "Do you wear your hair down after you've taken a bath?"

She was grateful for the darkness covering the deep flush fanning her cheeks. "Yes."

He moved his hand away. "My brother's a lucky man."

She watched him, silhouetted by the night, gazing out, perhaps gazing in, and she waited.

"It was during the war. I was fourteen. A drummer boy. We marched into battle alongside those with muskets. Once the battle began, smoke hung over the battlefield like a heavy morning fog. The rhythm we beat on the drum told the soldiers what they were supposed to do. During one battle, as we moved forward, I stepped over men who had ruffled my hair at dawn. I looked down at the still faces of boys not much older than me who had faced an enemy not much older than them. That day the casualties were too great, so I put down my drum and picked up a rifle from a man who wouldn't be needing it anymore. I went in search of a man dressed in gray."

"And you found him."

He nodded sagely. "Wasn't hard to do. Shot the first man I was close enough to shoot. He looked so surprised just before he died. I hadn't expected him to know I'd killed him. I dropped the rifle and ran, but a Reb cavalry officer with a saber stopped me."

"He gave you the scar on your back?"

"Yep. When I recovered, I was a soldier. No more beating the drum, and I didn't run the next time I killed a man."

"Will you share that story with Aaron?"

"Someday."

"Aaron's special to you, isn't he?"

"I love them all, but yeah, Aaron is special. He's so much like Charles that being with him is like catching up on all those years when Charles and I were separated."

"How old was Cassie the last time you saw her?"

He shifted his body. "Six. Charles and I were lucky. Good families took us in. I don't know about the family that took Cassie. I can only hope she's had a happy life."

"Have you had a happy life?"

"I've done a lot of things for which I'm proud, had moments that I wouldn't trade for anything, but when you have no one to share the good moments with, they somehow seem empty. That's why it was important to me to find Charles and Cassie."

For long moments, she listened to the soft whispering of the wind and thought about his words. He needed more than Cassie and Charles to share his moments. He needed his own children, his own family. She imagined a black-haired, black-eyed boy keeping pace with Jesse's long strides, learning the difference between right and wrong at his side. And she imagined a little girl with hair as black and eyes as dark sitting on the floor, pouring imaginary tea into a tiny teacup for her father. She wondered about the woman he would choose to share his life, his children. She knew that unlike herself, the woman would be untarnished.

"I should probably take Charles some coffee," she said at last.

"Yeah, you probably should."

She stood. "Keep a careful watch."

"I will."

She walked around the upper veranda to the back of the house. Her eyes had adjusted to the night, and she saw Charles tucked away in the corner. The rifle looked out of place resting across his lap.

"How are you holding out?" Maddie asked.

Charles took her hand and pulled her down. "Fine. How about you?"

She intertwined her fingers with his. "Feeling like a mother, I guess. I'm worried about the children. Charles, if it comes down to it, I know how to shoot a rifle. Not accurately, but I can make a lot of noise."

He drew her into the crook of his shoulder and placed his arm around her. "It's not going to come down to it. Jesse and I have already talked it over. If those outlaws show up, we're shoving the strongbox out onto the porch. They can have it."

She pulled back. "You'll give them the money?"

"All the money in the world isn't worth the lives of my children." He touched his fingers to her cheek. "Or my wife."

She felt a tightening in her chest with the realization

that unlike the men she'd known before, neither Charles nor Jesse would put her in harm's way. "I just took Jesse some coffee. Do you want me to bring you some?"

"No, Jesse might need it to stay awake—he's used to this kind of thing—but I'm strung as tight as a barbed wire fence. Even if you shoved our bed out here and curled in it with me, I wouldn't be able to sleep. But you should go on to bed."

"I'd rather stay here. I'm not certain I know how to sleep alone anymore." She snuggled against him. "I don't imagine I'll be able to sleep, anyway."

As the sun eased slowly over the horizon, Jesse walked around the veranda and hunkered down before Charles. Maddie was nestled against his side, asleep.

"I'm going to ride shotgun for Carter until he hits Austin."

"That's a long haul. You sure you're up to it?"

Jesse nodded. "Two guns on top ought to discourage any robbers. Why don't we get breakfast going and get these people out of here?"

Barely breathing, Maddie strained her ears for any sounds, yet all she could hear was her husband's rhythmic breathing. She had argued vehemently against Jesse going with the stage. The man had no business being out of bed, much less traipsing across the country on top of a jostling stagecoach.

She heard the solitary bong of the clock downstairs. Jesse'd tethered his horse to the back of the stagecoach, but she prayed he wouldn't ride back tonight. She stiffened when she heard a distant door open. Ranger gave his welcoming yip and settled into silence. She relaxed, knowing that Jesse had come home, fighting the urge to check on him.

"Why don't you go see if he's hungry?"

Startled, she lifted her head. "You're awake?"

"Been waiting for the same thing you have."

"I probably should see if he's all right."

"I think you should. I'll be down in a minute."

She scrambled out of bed, thrust her arms into her wrapper, and tied it tightly around her waist. Her bare feet padded across the floor.

Like an old man who hears Death's whisper, Jesse eased himself into the chair. Resting his elbows on the table, he wondered how he was going to get himself to bed. He decided he'd probably just sleep right where he was.

Damn Maddie for being right. He'd only ridden halfway to Austin before he'd told Carter he was going to have to head back. Carter had told him to ride inside the coach until they got to Austin, but Jesse had begun to think he was going to die up there, and if he was going to die, it was going to be at home.

"Oh, look at you!"

He lifted the leaden ball he called a head and looked at the woman rushing into the room. She placed a cool hand on his cheek.

"You're all warm and clammy. Did you start bleeding?"

"No, just tired."

"Are you hungry?"

He nodded, and she moved away, leaving him wishing he'd denied being hungry. Reaching out, he increased the flame in the lamp so he could see her more clearly. He'd never returned home and had a woman fuss over him.

She slammed a pot onto the stove, its metallic clank resounding throughout the room. "I don't like wasting my time and energy."

He grimaced as she banged another pot.

"You ride out of here without even caring that all my hard work might have gone to waste." She spun around and planted her hands on her hips. "Next time, you can just bleed to death."

As she marched past him, he grabbed her swinging arm and groaned as her movements jerked him. She stopped and knelt beside him.

"You did start bleeding."

He shook his head. "Don't think so. Just don't be mad at me tonight."

She moved the lamp to the edge of the table, then ginger-ly eased his shirt out of his pants and lifted it. She pressed her fingers to the still white bandages and felt him tense.

"Just tender," he forced out.

With tears brimming in her eyes, she lifted her gaze to his. "You don't have to be everyone's big brother. Why can't you be content just to be Charles's brother?"

He brushed his knuckles along her cheek, capturing a fallen tear. "This time, I didn't mean to make you cry."

She laid her forehead against his thigh, the sobs causing her narrow shoulders to quake. Dropping his hand, he gent-ly rubbed her back. "I'm sorry, Maddie. I can't help the way I am."

"You could try," she said, her voice muffled against his leg.

"I can't look the other way when a wrong is being done."

She lifted her gaze. "But it wasn't being done to you."

"Makes no difference. A wrong is wrong."

"And there are no exceptions for you, are there?"

Her eyes were a well of sadness, and he somehow knew her question was of monumental importance, and that the moments when he enjoyed her company would be no more if he answered wrong. "I've never looked the other way when a wrong was done another."

Her eyes drifted closed, and he had a sinking feeling in his gut that he'd given the wrong answer. Footsteps sounded throughout the house, and then Charles walked into the kitchen. Standing, Maddie walked away from Jesse and arranged pots and pans more quietly as she began to warm some chipped beef for him. Charles placed his hand on Jesse's shoulder. "How are you feeling?"

"Like I was standing in the middle of a stampede. I just left Midnight out there. I planned to get to him once I'd rested."

"I'll take care of him." Charles headed for the door.

"Give him some extra oats, will you? He earned them."

"Will do." Charles closed the door quietly behind him.

Jesse watched Maddie moving solemnly, wordlessly around the kitchen. He had a strong urge to put his arms around her and apologize for something, for anything. He placed his hand over his thigh. He'd never had a woman cry over him. Cry because of him, but not cry over him. Something in his chest had constricted when he'd felt her tears seep through the wool of his pants.

He almost wished he had been able to answer her question differently.

❧ 13 ❧

The sultry night air clung to Jesse as he walked away from the creek. His strength was returning and his side had lost most of its tenderness. He'd been able to haul the tub into the kitchen earlier and prepare a bath for Maddie. Slowing his steps, he only hoped he'd stayed away long enough.

With a leisurely gait, he approached the backyard. The house was wrapped in night shadows. He glanced toward the barn and saw a pale light spilling out through a narrow opening in the door.

Stealthily, he crept across the yard and peered into the barn. He saw shadows dance eerily against a far wall. Then Maddie came into view, stretching up on her bare toes, her fingers reaching toward the rafters, her body swaying from side to side.

She twirled and her blue calico dress lifted to reveal her bare calves. She dipped down and her braided hair fell over her shoulder. Then she dropped to her knees, and Ranger bounded across the floor, landing in her lap, nose down, tail up. She picked him up and rubbed her cheek against his neck. "Oh, Ranger, do you think he'll know that I've never danced before?"

The door creaked as Jesse opened it and walked into the barn. Maddie twisted around, hugging Ranger to her until he yelped. She released him, and he scampered back into a stall.

Jesse hunkered before her. She was bathed in the yellow

light of a solitary lantern hanging from a peg in a beam. Damp tendrils of her hair kissed her cheeks. The fragrance of forget-me-nots wafted around her.

"Where's Charles?" he asked.

"He fell asleep while I was bathing."

Jesse sat and draped his arm over his raised knee. "Why didn't you tell him you've never danced?"

She glanced at her hands folded in her lap. "I don't know. Sometimes I get tired of feeling so different." She lifted her gaze to his. "These people have all had such normal lives, the kind of life I've always wanted."

"In what way?"

She lifted her shoulder slightly. "They've had so many people surrounding them. They've had friends to share their joys and sorrows with. They've never been alone."

"And you've been alone too often."

"I've never had a friend. When the people were here before, I noticed some of the women whispering to each other, sharing secrets. I've never had a friend to share secrets with." She felt his gaze filled with understanding fall upon her as though it was a caress. Although he was the last person in the world with whom she should share any confidences, she was surprised to discover that he was the only person she wanted to share anything with.

"What secrets would you share?" he asked quietly.

"I don't know." She waved a hand helplessly in the air. "Little things like I don't know how to dance. Nothing important."

He stood and held his hand out to her. "Come on."

"Where are we going?"

"Nowhere. I'm going to teach you to dance."

Her heart raced. She thought dancing with Jesse would feel as intimate as a kiss, and it was an intimacy she dared not feel. "Oh, that's not necessary."

"Thought you wanted to make Charles happy."

"I do."

"Well, there's nothing he enjoys more than he enjoys dancing, and I imagine tomorrow night, he's going to want to dance with his wife."

Reluctantly, she stood. He placed his hand on her waist and felt her stiffen. "You need to relax. People touch when they dance." He placed her limp hand on his shoulder and took her other one in his. Her eyes were riveted to the ground. "Don't watch my feet."

"How will I know what to do?"

"You'll feel the movements. Just follow them, but you'll have to lift your eyes first. I can't start while you're watching the ground."

She lifted her gaze to the center of his chest. He stepped back. "Come on."

Awkwardly, she stepped forward, then pulled herself free, folding her arms beneath her breasts. "I can't do this."

"Why not?"

"Because you're so judgmental."

"All right, then, let's try this another way. Close your eyes and pretend I'm Charles."

"Why?"

"Because you're comfortable with him. Close your eyes and pretend I'm him, or I'll go wake him and tell him to get down here and teach his wife how to dance."

She placed her hands on her hips. "You would, wouldn't you?"

He smiled. "Yep."

"Oh, all right." She moved back into place.

"Now, close your eyes."

She widened them.

He sighed. "Trust me. Just this once."

She squeezed her eyes shut. "Just remember, I can open them anytime I want to."

He placed her hand back on his shoulder, wrapped one hand around her free hand, and settled his other hand on her waist. "Now, pretend I'm Charles."

"Your hands are too rough."

"Pretend they're not. Imagine that I look kind and compassionate instead of like something that's ridden out of hell."

Her eyes flew open, capturing the solemnity in his face. "That is what you think, isn't it?" he asked. "I've had more than one desperado describe me in those terms."

"I imagine they'd think that with you following their trail, but you're not following my trail, are you?"

"No, I'm not. Now, close your eyes and pretend I'm your husband."

She closed her eyes. Imagining he was her husband was somewhat different from imagining he was Charles. She didn't have to pretend his hands weren't rough or that she had to reach a little higher to place her hand on his shoulder. The only thing she had to pretend was that if he knew the truth, he'd still want to be her husband. She heard a horse nicker in a distant stall, heard a barn owl swoop down from the rafters. Then she heard a soft humming. "What's that?" she asked, quietly.

" 'Nobody's Darling.' It's a favorite of mine."

"It's lovely."

"Concentrate on the melody and when I move, follow."

He went back to humming. When her mind was filled with nothing but the resonant timbre of the music he created, she felt him take a gentle step back. To her surprise, she followed as though she'd been placing her foot where his had been for most of her life.

Ever so slowly, she opened her eyes and lifted her gaze to his, wanting to swim within the black depths of his eyes.

A smile eased onto his face. "That's it. A man likes to look into the eyes of the woman he's dancing with. This is a waltz."

"I like it."

"I thought you would."

She was mesmerized by the deep resonance of his voice, could almost hear the gentle strains of a violin. It seemed as though they were merely swaying on the breeze like the petals of a dandelion blown free with the breath of a child.

"Breathe, Whiskey. You don't want to swoon when Charles is dancing with you tomorrow night."

"How can you think of all the things you have to do at once: move your feet, listen to the music, breathe?"

"I'm only thinking about one thing," he said quietly as his eyes delved deeply into hers.

"Mind if I have a turn?" Charles asked.

"Christ Almighty!" Jesse roared as he jumped away from her.

Maddie staggered back before catching her balance. And she was breathing now, breathing hard.

Jesse plowed his hands through his hair. "Scared the living hell out of me!"

Charles laughed. "Yeah, I thought I might."

"You're damn lucky I didn't have a gun strapped to my thigh. Jesus! You ought to give a man some warning."

"But this was so much more fun. You two often waltz in the barn after midnight?"

"She doesn't know how to dance. I was just teaching her."

Charles quirked a brow. "Oh?"

"Don't 'oh?' me. You keep saying you know so much about her. Then you should have known she doesn't know how to dance, and you should have taken the time to teach her so she wouldn't feel out of place tomorrow night. Before I got here, she was taking lessons from the damn dog!"

"Well, maybe I should finish the lessons."

"Yeah, maybe you better." Without a backward glance at Maddie, Jesse stormed out of the barn.

Charles glanced at Maddie. "I guess that was rude of me to interrupt."

"Honestly, he was just teaching me to dance."

"I know."

He took her in his arms and guided her through the steps. His hands weren't rough and his eyes weren't black. The melodic strains of a violin didn't drift into her mind. She didn't feel as though she was floating on the wind.

But he was her husband. She lifted her gaze to his, returned his smile, and followed his movements as she planned to for the remainder of her life.

The sun sank slowly beyond the horizon, creating a subdued haze of late summer colors across an azure sky, taking with it some of the stifling heat that had hung over the day.

The wagon creaked as it rolled along the dirt road. A wheel dipped into a shallow rut. The children in the back of the wagon squealed, Charles laughed, and Maddie toppled against Jesse's side as she sat beside him on the bench seat. He steadied her with one hand and helped her regain some of her dignity. Once righted, she smoothed out her skirt, then glanced over her shoulder at the family riding along in the back of the wagon. Her family.

She'd wanted to ride in the back with them, but Charles had insisted she ride on the bench seat so she wouldn't muss her dress. She was wearing the same emerald green dress she'd worn the night she'd first met their friends and neighbors. She didn't understand why Jesse was guiding the team of horses, why she was forced to sit by his side. Each time the motion of the wagon caused her to brush against him, she wished more fervently that she was sitting with the children.

"Did Charles teach you the quadrille?" Jesse asked, his eyes focused straight ahead.

"Yes," she said quietly. "He taught me several different ways to dance." But the waltz was her favorite, would always be her favorite.

He nodded. "Imagine he'll keep you busy most of the night."

"Do you enjoy dancing or were you just being kind last night?"

"Whether or not I enjoy it depends on who I'm dancing with."

In the back of the wagon, Aaron stood and leaned against Jesse's back. "You gonna dance with the widow Parker?"

Jesse threw a glance over his shoulder. "Reckon I might."

Maddie felt an unexpected twinge of disappointment at his answer and realized she would no doubt see him dancing with several women throughout the evening.

"You ain't gonna marry her, are you?" Aaron asked.

Using his thumb, Jesse tipped his hat off his brow and studied the sky as though seriously contemplating his answer. A small smile eased across his face, and he glanced back at Aaron. "Reckon I might."

Maddie felt her heart plummet. She knew she had no reason, no right to care what his answer had been. Yet she had cared, and the depth of her disappointment in his answer frightened her. She had a husband. There was no reason Jesse shouldn't have a wife.

Aaron howled. "But she looks like a bullfrog! Sounds like one, too!"

Charles patted Aaron's backside. "Aaron Lawson, don't speak unkindly of people."

"But it's true!" He reached around, placed his palm against Jesse's cheek, and turned his head until their gazes could meet squarely. "You won't marry her, will you?"

Jesse licked his lips and winked. "She makes an awful good sponge cake."

"So does Ma. You could marry Ma if you've got a hankering to marry someone."

Jesse's gaze clashed with Maddie's. Her face took on a hue more lovely than that of the sunset. "She's already married," he said quietly, turning his attention back to the road, wishing to God Charles would pull Aaron down and tell him to be quiet.

"But you like her well enough, don't you?" Aaron asked.

"I like her just fine."

"Then you ought to marry her."

"A woman can only have one husband, and Maddie's got your pa."

"Well, that don't hardly seem fair. What if a woman likes more than one man?"

Jesse clenched his jaws. His head would be hurting by the time they arrived at the Turners' place if this line of questioning continued. "It takes more than liking a person. Generally, people get married because they love each other."

"Don't you love Ma?"

Jesse came halfway off the bench seat, twisted his body, and glared at Charles. "He's your son. Why the hell aren't you explaining all this to him?"

Fighting back his smile, Charles shrugged slightly. "Thought you were explaining it well enough." He tugged on Aaron's shirt. "Come on. Sit back down."

"But he didn't answer my question."

"Sometimes it's best if questions are left unanswered."

Aaron dropped onto the floorboards and squirmed until he made himself comfortable. "Why's that?"

"Because then you can spend the evening wondering what the answer was."

That made no sense to Aaron. If he'd wanted to wonder what the answer was, he wouldn't have asked the question to begin with.

The widow Parker, Maddie was pleased to discover, did look exactly like a bullfrog. Her skin was weathered, her eyes bulged, and her neck was thick with layers of wrinkles that shook with each of her movements, no matter how slight they might be. She also realized it was kindness that prompted Jesse to ask the woman to dance three times. Her face lit each time he escorted her to the center of the barn. As the widow Parker swayed to the tune of the fiddle, Maddie could almost imagine her as a young woman and could see the inner beauty that had caused Mr. Parker to marry her. She felt her feelings for Jesse expand, for he alone took the time to give back to the aged, lonely woman a moment of her youth.

Within the barn, kerosene lanterns glowed, creating a warm intimacy within the cavernous structure. Feeling more at ease, Maddie walked through the barn, skirting the children playing with the new batch of kittens. She was disappointed that Charles didn't dance with her as much as Jesse had indicated he would. And quite often, she wished, much to her chagrin, that she looked like a bullfrog so Jesse would ask her to dance.

Jesse studied the whiskey in his glass. The color was perfect. He could almost see her eyes. He downed the amber liquid. He'd never enjoyed a dance or socializing so little in his entire life.

He'd planned to dance with Maddie at least once, but Aaron's inquisition on the way over had put an end to those intentions. The last thing he wanted was to draw attention to his feelings for Maddie. As much as he hated it, his best tactic was to ignore her.

"Pour me one of those, will you?" Charles asked as he came to stand beside Jesse.

"Certainly." He poured one for Charles, another for himself. He downed his before Charles had lifted his off the table.

"You should dance with Maddie," Charles said.

"You dance with her."

Charles smiled. "I have. Several times in fact. People will begin to talk if her own brother-in-law doesn't dance with her."

"So let them talk. I've never given a damn what people think."

"But Maddie does."

"Meaning?"

Charles took a small swallow. "Meaning you should dance with her."

Jesse slammed his glass onto the table. "I'll think about it."

He headed away from the side of the barn where Maddie was standing. He didn't want Charles to know that at any given moment he could have told him exactly upon which piece of straw his wife was standing. He planned to let two or three dances go by, then casually stroll up to her as though the idea of dancing with her had just come to him. It was a good plan, and it would have worked, if he hadn't caught sight of Thelma Jones grabbing Maddie's arm and pulling her aside. Abruptly, he changed directions.

"You would not believe how shocked I was to hear that Charles had gotten married."

A rat. Thelma Jones reminded Maddie of a rat with her tiny beady eyes. She wondered if it was the size of her eyes that made her nose wrinkle or if she was perhaps continually sniffing for cheese.

"I was visiting my sister in Houston, and when I got back, I heard the news. I almost fainted dead away. He loved Alice something fierce, you know. None of us, especially me, ever expected him to marry again."

Maddie smiled, not certain how to respond to statements delivered in such a squeaky voice.

"Why, if I had known Charles would even consider marrying again, I would have gone after him, myself."

She tried to envision Charles lying in bed with his arms wrapped around the bony woman standing before her. She shook her head at the thought.

"Alice was an angel, so sweet and kind. Never would hurt anyone. Always caring for people. Charles loved her so very much."

"He still does."

Thelma's mouth dropped open. "But he married you."

"Because he got drunk staring into her eyes."

Maddie jumped as Jesse's voice boomed behind her.

"And now, if you'll excuse us, Miss Jones, I'd like to dance with my sister-in-law."

Jesse whisked her away to the dance area before she could object, not that she would have. Maddie couldn't remember putting her hand in his or resting her other hand on his shoulder. She couldn't remember when he'd placed his hand on her waist or exactly when they'd stopped walking and begun to waltz, but she was gliding across the dance floor.

"You don't owe these people any explanations, Maddie."

"But I don't want them to get the wrong impression."

"You shouldn't care what they think."

"Why not?"

"Because their opinions aren't important. You should do things because of the way they make you feel, not because of the way you think it'll make them feel."

She tilted her head. "Is that why you dance with the widow Parker? Because of the way it makes you feel?"

Groaning, he momentarily closed his eyes, not missing a step as he moved in rhythm to the music. "I ask her to dance because she's the only woman here who doesn't think I'll slap a wedding ring on her finger. Nothing worse than a woman who thinks an invitation to dance is an invitation to marriage."

"Is that why you asked me to dance? Because dancing with married women is safe?"

Safe? Dancing with her was anything but safe. If she realized that he held her closer than was proper, closer than he held any other woman . . .

"Charles thought I should ask you to dance."

Nodding slightly, she averted her gaze, but not before he saw the flicker of pain reflected in her eyes. "Has he told you that you look beautiful tonight?"

Returning her gaze to his, she shook her head.

"Well, he should."

"Has he told you that you look handsome?"

He stared at her. She had that familiar impish smile on her face, the one that always made him aware that he did indeed have a heart thumping within his chest. "No, hasn't."

"Well, he should."

Jesse laughed, tightened his hold on her, and swept her across the dance area.

It was wrong to enjoy dancing with Jesse as much as Maddie did. She liked the feel of her hand within his, the way his body moved, and the way her body responded in kind as though they'd been moving together since the beginning of time.

Suddenly, he jerked her toward him, then cast her aside and barrelled through the throng of dancing couples. Maddie screamed as she saw Charles crash into a distant table, his hand upsetting a lantern. It toppled to the ground. The fire within escaped to ignite the straw.

It was advantageous to be surrounded by country folk who knew the exact dangers of a fire in the barn. Jesse was the first to reach the area. He dragged Charles away from the flames licking at the straw. He bent over and pressed his head against Charles's chest, relieved to hear the steady pounding of his brother's heart.

Then he retrieved a blanket and took his place among the other men beating the fire into submission. When the final flames died, he returned to Charles's limp, unconscious form and checked him for burns. The only thing visible was a red splotch on his hand where it had touched the lantern.

"Never knew Charles not to be able to hold his liquor."

Jesse glanced at Ray Turner, Billy's father. It was his barn that had been threatened by the fire.

"I'll be over tomorrow to take care of the damages."

Ray shook his head. "Don't concern yourself with it. Not much damage done."

"I'll be here, anyway." Jesse glanced around the crowd of anxious faces. "Maddie, gather the children." Ignoring the dull pain in his side, he began to lift Charles.

"Wanna try dousing him with water?" Ray asked.

"Nope," he said as he struggled to his feet, cradling his brother in his arms. He worked his way through the crowd of curious onlookers.

Maddie had sought out the girls and taken them by the hand when she realized a fire had begun. She found Aaron in one of the lofts, his eyes wide from witnessing the event. She was putting the children in the wagon when Jesse caught up to them.

"Aaron, I want to put your father's head in your lap."

Aaron positioned himself, and Jesse laid his brother in the wagon with his head on Aaron's lap. He grabbed a blanket and tucked it in around his still body. Taylor placed her tiny hand on Charles's cheek. "Pa hurt?"

Jesse touched her curls. "He'll be all right." And he prayed he would be. Turning to Maddie, he recognized the fire of anger in her eyes. He'd had it directed at himself too many times in the past not to know what it meant. "You want to ride in the back with him?"

Without a word, she hefted her skirts and marched to the front of the wagon. Jesse loped after her and assisted her onto the seat. He had a feeling it was going to be a long ride home.

A full moon graced the night sky, casting a silvery glow across the countryside. The horses plodded along. Jesse could feel the tension surrounding Maddie like a shroud. He wished he could think of a rational explanation besides the truth. With the children in the back, attentive to any conversation, he knew there was little he could say.

"Uncle Jesse?"

He glanced over his shoulder at Hannah bathed in moonlight. "What, angel?"

"Is Pa gonna die?"

He felt his heart slam against his rib cage. Holding onto the reins with one hand, he reached back with the other, lifted the tiny child, and settled her on his lap. He heard a scuffling in the back and looked back to see Taylor standing in the wagon, her doll draped over her arm.

"Maddie, this has frightened the children. Will you hold Taylor?"

He was grateful that without hesitation, she turned around and plucked Taylor out of the back of the wagon.

Maddie hugged the child against her, remembering the first night she'd felt such a keen disappointment in her father, a man she'd never truly known, but had admired and loved just the same. How much harder it must be for these children whose father was always within their reach to learn he was fallible.

"I think your father just drank too much whiskey," Maddie offered in way of an explanation.

Jesse heard the soft understanding in her voice, and he heard the slight accent woven around her words. She was still angry, probably seething. There was no denying that, and yet she was trying not to let the children know. His admiration for her grew.

Then she began to hum a soothing melody, soon giving voice to the gentle words and filling the night with a sweet lullaby.

By the time they arrived home, the girls had fallen asleep. Jesse brought the wagon to a halt before the house and shifted Hannah in his arms. "If you'll carry Taylor, I'll carry Hannah to bed. Then I'll come back for Charles."

Maddie snapped her head around, her face set in hard, unforgiving lines. "Let him sleep out here all night. Serves him right for getting drunk, putting everyone's life in danger, and embarrassing us like that."

With Taylor nestled in one arm, she worked her way out

of the wagon. Holding Hannah, Jesse climbed down and walked to the back of the wagon. "Wait here with your father," he instructed Aaron. "I'll be back in a minute."

He carried Hannah inside and laid her on her bed. Maddie was already undressing Taylor. "Will you undress Hannah?"

She nodded.

"Maddie?"

Quickly, she held up a hand, her fingers splayed as though she wanted nothing to intrude on her anger. "You'd best see after Aaron."

Not until he'd walked out of the room did Maddie relax her stiffened posture and bury her face in her quaking hands. She wanted to do to Charles what he'd done to Aaron when he'd shot Jesse. She wanted to shake him, lay her hand against his backside, and ask him what the hell he'd been thinking. She shuddered as a vision of what might have happened raced through her mind.

Preparing the girls for bed took an inordinate amount of time as her fingers refused to cooperate. Buttons snapped off Hannah's dress and rolled along the floor. She was surprised she didn't wake the girls with her clumsy attempts to get their clothes off.

Eventually, she succeeded in slipping their nightgowns over their heads. She tucked the quilts around each girl, dimmed the lamp, and stepped into the hallway.

She walked into Aaron's room. He was sprawled across the bed, his eyes closed in slumber, his clothes still on, one boot lying on the floor, the other still hugging his foot. She worked the second boot off, gingerly slipped a blanket over him, and left the room.

She walked to her own room, stood in the doorway, and watched Jesse ease Charles's shirt off as though he was a child exhausted from spending the day at the circus. He pitched the shirt away without a backward glance and moved to the foot of the bed.

"You damn fool," he whispered harshly as he tugged off Charles's boot and dropped it to the floor. Then he looked up, and his eyes latched onto hers.

"You should have left him in the wagon," she said tersely before walking away.

Watching her go, Jesse tunneled his fingers through his hair. He heard a door downstairs close. He'd certainly understand if the woman never came back. He finished undressing his brother and tucked the quilt around him. He stood over him for several minutes, watching him, listening to his breathing. He thought he'd rather face a gang of outlaws than Maddie at this moment, but he also knew he couldn't leave her to suffer this alone.

The moonlight sifting through the leaves in the trees guided his path. The dew had already settled in for the night, and she'd carried it away with her footsteps, leaving him a trail he could easily follow. He found her at the creek, the moon creating a silver halo around her. He sat beside her on the moss covered bank.

Maddie didn't divert any of her attention from the stream, but she felt Jesse's presence as though he'd wrapped his arms around her. She swiped the tears from her eyes and pulled her shawl more closely about her.

"When the family that took me in decided to go farther west, I fought against it," Jesse said quietly. "They tied me in the back of the wagon, giving me no choice. I knew they didn't mean to be cruel. They were just doing what they thought was best. My last memory of Charles was watching him run after me with tears streaming down his face. I swore then that I'd find him, keep my promise to my father, and look after him."

"He's no longer a child," she said softly as she glanced over at him.

"No, but he's still my brother."

She shook her head. "I can't forgive him for this. He got drunk right after we were married, and he promised me he wouldn't do it again. He put everyone's life in danger tonight." She looked to him for understanding. "I was so embarrassed that he got drunk and made a fool of himself. I don't know how you carried him out of there with so much dignity."

With his thumb, he removed a glistening tear from her

cheek. "He's not a drunk, Maddie."

"I was there. I saw him weaving through the barn."

Jesse plowed his hands through his hair. "He's not a drunk. Dammit. Dammit," he whispered as though any fight he would have fought was already lost. "I told him to tell you. He had no right—"

"No right to what?"

"To marry you and not tell you."

She watched the emotions cross his face as though he was gathering courage to face an unbeatable foe. He wrapped his hand around hers. "He's dying, Maddie."

She felt her heart plunge, her throat constrict. She shook her head and tightened her hold on his hand as though she could drive away the words he'd spoken. "He can't be dying. He looks well. He's up and about. And this hasn't happened since we got married—"

"It's happened . . . several times. He gets these pains in his head. When they get too bad, he passes out. Haven't you noticed how weak his left side is? When he's holding you, haven't you noticed he has no strength?"

"I just thought it was because he doesn't work as hard as you do, that he wasn't as strong."

He shook his head, the words clogging his throat. "The doctor thinks there's something wrong inside his head." His handsome face contorted with the pain of knowledge. "The pains are getting worse, coming more often. He's probably . . . probably . . ." He burrowed his hands through his hair. "I don't know how much longer he's got."

Her denial of his words was drowned out by her sobs. He took her in his arms, cooing to her, not using words, just soft sounds of comfort.

"He can't die. I don't want him to die," she forced out through her grief.

He cradled her face in his hands. "Ah, Maddie, have you come to love him, then?" he asked hoarsely as his lips trailed over her eyes, her cheeks, tasting the salt of her tears.

Her answer came through her parted lips, silently, warm, welcoming.

He groaned, settling his mouth over hers, kissing her deeply, thoroughly, with all the passion he'd withheld the first time he'd kissed her. His tongue swept through the silken caverns, stealing the treasures of her mouth: the taste, the feel, the hunger.

From her hair, he removed the pins, one by one, allowing the honeyed tresses to pour over her shoulders, to pour into his large hands as he laid her on the moss covered bank and stretched his body along the length of hers.

He lifted his mouth from hers and gazed on her beloved face, bathed in the light of the full moon.

His eyes were as black as the creek, and Maddie thought she'd rather swim in the pools of his eyes than in any waters that rushed by. "There are times," she said softly, "when I wish it had been you who'd bid on me in Fort Worth."

Shaking his head, he buried his face in her abundant hair. "No, Maddie. Never wish that. I never would have bid that much money. And if I had, I never would have had the compassion to take you out of there with me."

He brushed his lips along her cheeks, her chin, the tip of her nose, her closed eyes. Then he released a shuddering breath and nestled his face in the curve of her neck. He kissed the sensitive spot behind her ear, feeling the shivers course through her body. Slowly, he unbuttoned the high collar of her dress, trailing kisses along her neck until he could dip his tongue into the hollow at the base of her throat.

"This is wrong," she whispered. "Charles is my husband."

He lifted his head, his eyes caressing her features. "I know that. I carry that thought to my bed every night and curl up with it and tell myself I can't feel for you what I feel. But damn it, I do."

His mouth swooped down to cover hers, communicating silently what he did not have the right to voice aloud. He slashed his lips across hers, his tongue delving deeply.

Whimpering, she arched against him, burying her hands in his hair, pressing him against her, daring to take what he was offering. For the first time, she had a clear understanding of all that was missing from her marriage. Pressed hard against her thigh was the evidence of his desire, and it fanned the flames burning within her heart. And within her heart, she now understood the full extent of her sacrifice: what she felt for this man was what a woman should feel for the man she'd married. She wanted to share his joys, his sorrows, to hold him during the bad times, to have him hold her during the good ones. And she wanted children, his children.

She began to struggle against the feelings in her heart, against the embrace she wanted, the kisses she longed for, the man she loved. She shoved on his shoulders until he lifted himself enough that she could slip out from beneath him.

"Maddie," he said hoarsely.

She scrambled to her feet and ran. She heard him call her name, imagined him laced with pain that equaled that piercing her own heart. And she ran that much faster.

❧ 14 ❧

Charles fought against waking. Besides his usual discomfort, a dull ache had settled in above his brow. He touched the hardened knot and winced at the tenderness. He tried to remember, unable to recall much of the evening at the dance.

He smelled the aroma of the coffee. Squinting against the early morning light sifting in through the windows, he glanced around the room. Dressed for the day, Maddie sat on the bed. He felt the burn on his hand, then grimaced. "I did it again, didn't I?"

She nodded slightly. He studied her expression, her eyes filled with a wealth of knowledge. He gritted his teeth. "Jesse told you, didn't he?"

"Yes."

"Dammit! He had no right!" He jerked upright, threw the covers off, then quickly threw them back over his hips. "Who the hell undressed me?"

"Jesse."

"Would you please get me some clothes? I can't very well be indignant when I'm buck naked."

She walked to the dresser. She supposed his modesty was the result of his accident. Even though he held her at night, she was only familiar with his shoulder, his arms. His lower body never came into contact with hers, and she realized it was no doubt a source of embarrassment for him to have a body that would never again react in the manner Jesse's had last night. She took out some clothes, carried them to the bed, and sat, holding them firmly in her lap. "Why didn't you tell me?"

"May I please have my clothes?"

"Why?"

"So I can get dressed and go beat the hell out of my brother."

"No, I meant, why didn't you tell me?"

"Maddie—"

"Why didn't you tell me?"

Charles saw the tears brimming in her eyes and felt the anger flee. "Because I think if I don't say the words, it won't happen."

"But it will," she rasped, and he watched the tears flow onto her cheeks.

Nodding, he took her into his arms. "Don't cry, Maddie. You weren't supposed to come to care about me."

Her arms went around him, and she pounded her fist into his back. "Well, I did."

"You were only supposed to care about the children. And maybe Jesse a little."

"I love the children."

"I know you do." Cradling her face with his hands, he brought her away from his shoulder, his eyes holding hers. "You don't have to stay. Our marriage hasn't been consummated. An annulment would be easy enough to obtain. You could go somewhere else, start over. I'd see to it that you had the means to do so."

Sniffing, she shook her head. "You were there when I needed someone. You helped me, Charles, when you didn't even know me. How can I not be here for you when I've come to care about you so much?"

Tenderly, he combed the wisps of hair back from her face. "It was my pleasure to take you out of Bev's. What I have to offer you in the months ahead will probably be anything but pleasurable."

"I want to stay, to do what I can to make it easier."

"Do you have any idea how much easier you've already made it? You love my children as though they were your own. That's the gift I wanted to leave with them, Maddie."

"Are you afraid?" she asked quietly.

He gave her a soft smile. "I'm not afraid of the dying, but I am afraid that Alice won't be there waiting for me. That I won't see her, she won't be with me. Eternity without my Alice would surely be hell."

Softly, Maddie caressed his cheek. He took her hand, turned her palm toward him, and pressed a kiss to its center. "Someday, Maddie, I hope you'll find the kind of love I shared with Alice. There's no greater gift than a love returned in equal measure."

Jesse led Midnight into his stall. He placed the oats in the trough before removing the horse's saddle.

"Jesse?"

He hadn't needed to hear Maddie's voice to know she was standing behind him. He swung the saddle onto the railing separating the stalls, then slowly turned around. Her hands were clasped before her, her eyes filled with sadness.

"Was there much damage done last night in the Turners' barn?" she asked.

"No, and I took care of what little there was."

"Do they still think Charles was drunk?"

"Subject didn't come up. I didn't offer any information. I don't want Aaron hearing something from a friend that he should hear from family."

She nodded, and he noticed that the knuckles on her hands were turning white.

"I love Charles." She lowered her troubled gaze to the ground momentarily before lifting it back to his. "Last night, I was understandably upset. I needed comfort, and I took what you offered, giving little thought to the consequences or what you may have interpreted my reaction or my words to mean. I want you to understand that what happened by the creek will never happen again. Charles is my husband, and if my love for him is not as strong as it should be, my loyalty to him is unwavering. I've told you before that I want to make him happy. That hasn't changed."

Jesse watched her walk away, her mien one of bravery. She was a reluctant soldier called forth into a battle not of her choosing, yet she would stand her ground. It was strange, but he loved her all the more for the words she'd just spoken.

Charles strolled through the tall grasses. He'd left the children and Maddie by the creek. She'd suggested the outing during breakfast, making it perfectly clear that Jesse wasn't welcome to join them. Her attitude had baffled him.

Jesse's attitude hadn't enlightened him, either. When he'd argued in favor of Jesse going with them, Jesse had argued vehemently against it.

Charles pulled off his hat and wiped his brow. The breeze blowing through was too warm to do much good unless a man had been sweating, and he figured Jesse'd done a fair amount of sweating. The pounding of his hammer had echoed steadily across the land most of the morning.

"How's it going?" he asked as he neared the unfinished fence.

Jesse pounded the board into place. "Good."

Charles rested his arms on the top railing of the fence. "You know, in ancient times, emperors generally killed a messenger if he was the bearer of bad tidings. I'm wondering if Maddie's not holding the bad news you delivered last night against you."

"Why would you think that?"

"You two seemed to be getting along, and now it's like you're avoiding each other again."

Jesse untied the red bandanna circling his neck, dropped it in the bucket of water, and slung the wet cloth back into place. "I think it's more likely she realizes she doesn't have much time left with you, and she wants to make the most of it."

Charles contemplated the clouds rolling by. "Maybe. You ever think about taking a wife?"

Jesse pounded a nail into the wood. "I've thought about it."

"And?"

"And what?"

"You think you'll ever take a wife?"

"I might."

"When?"

"How the hell should I know? I'm not like you. I don't take a wife just because the wind changes direction."

"You're thinking it to death, aren't you?"

"Damn right! I've got no desire to marry a woman and wake up the next morning with the passion spent and discover I've made a mistake that I've got to live with for the rest of my life."

Charles shook his head. "You'll never get married."

"I might."

"No, you won't." He slapped a hand on the railing. "That's exactly why I married Maddie."

Jesse furrowed his brow. "Why?"

"Because I know you, and I know you'll think it through until you're an old man, and my children would grow up never knowing what it was to have a woman around."

"Yeah, well, did you ever stop to think that maybe you might be wrong, and I might take a wife? Then I'd have to live with two women under one roof."

"I'm sure Maddie'd move on if you asked her to."

Jesse pounded his seventh nail into the same piece of wood. A tornado tearing through wouldn't be able to rip that piece of wood from that post. "That wouldn't hardly be fair. She loves your children. They love her, too."

"How do you feel about her?"

"Maddie?"

Charles fought back his smile. "No, the widow Parker. Yes, Maddie."

Jesse shrugged. "Got no feelings about her one way or the other. She's your wife—"

A cry of alarm echoed from the distant trees. Both men diverted their attention to Aaron as he ran across the field. "It's Ma!"

Jesse vaulted over the fence and raced toward the trees. Charles figured it was a good thing Jesse didn't have any feelings for Maddie. No telling how fast the man would have run then, and he was unable to keep pace with Jesse's frantic strides as it was.

"What the hell are you doing?" Jesse roared.

"Just get me down," Maddie pleaded.

"Shoulda seen her shinny up that tree, Uncle Jesse. She was just fine till she looked down."

Breathless, Charles ran into the clearing. Jesse spun around and pointed an accusing finger toward the top of the giant oak tree. "Do you see your wife?"

Charles squinted against the sun filtering in through the abundant leaves. "What's she doing up there?"

"She was hanging the rope." Aaron grabbed onto the knotted rope dangling from the tree. "We're gonna use it to swing out into the creek, but then she went and got scared."

With a look of disgust, Jesse shook his head. "She's your wife. You get her down."

"You're stronger than I am. Why don't you shinny up there and hand her down to me?"

Cursing, Jesse dropped to the ground and tugged off his boots. Aaron hunkered beside him. "Want me to tell you which branches are the best ones to use?"

Jesse gave him an icy stare. "I know how to climb a tree."

"I didn't know. Pa said you was born fully growed, that you never was a boy. I didn't know fully growed men climbed trees."

Jesse looked at Charles. "I was not born fully grown."

Charles placed his hand on Aaron's shoulder and pulled him back. "I didn't mean it as an insult. I simply meant you've always handled responsibility well."

Jesse unfolded his body and glared at the woman wrapped lengthwise around a thick branch. He folded his arms across his chest. "You know? I haven't tasted a sponge cake in a good long while. Reckon there's anyone around here that'll make me one?"

"I will!"

"Me!"

He looked at the two expectant faces and all his irritation melted away. He chucked each girl under the chin. "Soon as I get your ma down."

He swung onto the lowest branch of the tree. Then he reached for the one above it and pulled himself up. He couldn't imagine how Maddie had climbed so far up into the tree. He felt the coarse bark scrape his arms, hands, and feet. Maybe in gratitude, she'd work ointment into his cuts. He shook the thought away. She'd made her position perfectly clear that morning. Now it was his turn to be indifferent.

But once he reached the tree branch and straddled it, pressing his back against the bark and watching her prone figure, he knew he could no more be indifferent toward her than he could make the waters of the creek stop flowing.

Bending low at the waist and reaching out, he worked his arm between her flat stomach and the rough bough of the tree. He tugged slightly. She didn't budge.

"You're going to have to let go, Maddie."

"I can't."

"I won't let you fall."

"Just move like you're a caterpillar crawling backwards!" Aaron yelled to the treetops.

Jesse tightened his hold on her. "Trust me."

"It's not a matter of trust, you bleedin' idiot. It's a matter of fear!"

He sighed. "If fear brings out your accent as well, how will I ever know if you're mad at me or afraid of me?"

"I've never been afraid of you."

He wished he could see more than the back of her head, wished he could look into her eyes. "Never?" he asked quietly.

"Never you, but the things you believe in."

"I don't believe in anything that should frighten you."

She heaved a deep sigh. "For you, everything, everyone is either good or bad. You don't understand that sometimes good people do bad things, bad people do good things." Forcing open an eye, she glanced back at him. "Have you ever done something bad, something you were ashamed of, something that if you could do over you'd do differently?"

For long moments, perched out on the tree branch, she studied him. She closed her eyes. "You haven't."

Her words made him feel as though his character possessed shortcomings. He scooted along the tree branch until his hips were pressed against hers.

"Keep your eyes closed and relax your hands," he said quietly. With his arm still beneath her waist, he slowly brought her up until their bodies were pressed together, her back against his bare chest, her backside nestled between his thighs. She shifted her hips, and he groaned. "Don't squirm."

"I was going to fall."

"You weren't going to fall. I won't let you fall. Now we're going to swing your leg over to the left." He slipped his hand beneath her thigh, guiding her leg over the branch, turning her hips until her side was pressed against his chest. "Now wrap your hands around my hand."

She did, and he closed his hand around hers, holding tightly.

"You're going to stand on my foot, then I'm going to lower you down to Charles. You might have a little fall, but he ought to break most of the impact."

Slipping his other arm beneath her arms, he eased her off the limb until her bare foot touched his.

Maddie felt the ball of her foot rub across the top of his foot, creating a sensation more intimate than pressing her back against his chest. An image of this man in bed, her foot seeking out his, came into her mind. She squeezed her eyes shut. She never sought out Charles's bare feet in the middle of the night.

Her foot left his as he removed his hand from beneath her arms and lowered her farther. She dangled in the air.

"Let go, Maddie. I'll catch you!" Charles yelled.

She took a deep breath, tensed her body, and screamed as Jesse's fingers slipped away from hers. She felt Charles's arms go around her just before they both plummeted to the ground.

Charles laughed as he rolled her off him. "You can open your eyes now."

She did and smiled at the concerned faces surrounding her.

"Whatever prompted you to climb a tree if you were afraid to be up so high?" Charles asked.

"I didn't know I'd be afraid." She jumped to her feet and squinted up at the tree. "Make sure the rope is tied tight!"

"Yes, ma'am!"

Jesse eased himself out farther on the tree branch and secured the rope. Her knots might have held, but he had no desire to climb back up this damn tree. By the time he'd worked his way to the ground, the family was gathered near the creek bank.

Aaron scrambled up to the lowest branch that spread out over the water, grabbed onto the rope, and with a small running start, swung himself out over the creek waters. He released his hold on the rope, hollered, and fell into the water with a mighty splash. Jesse smiled as Charles climbed onto the branch.

Taylor left the gathering and came to stand before him. "Make ponge cake?"

He lowered his body. "Maybe later. Right now, why don't you go enjoy the creek?"

A smile of joy lit her face before she ran back toward the bank. Picking up his boots, Jesse unfolded his body and began walking back toward his labors. He heard Maddie's squeal of delight, followed by a distant splash. Quickening his pace, he forced himself to keep his gaze focused on the distant horizon, to keep his feet moving toward a fence that wouldn't be finished until the weight of the years bent his back.

Sweat trickled down his temple. The thought of the cool creek waters tempted him. The creek was long and winding with other places designed by nature for swimming. Maybe he'd work on his fence a little longer, then go in search of a new swimming hole.

He heard the whispering of the wind and smiled. It almost sounded like Maddie calling his name. Then he heard his

name more clearly, leaving no doubt it was her voice behind
him.

He turned to watch her approaching, breathless and soaked
to the skin by the waters of the creek.

"I didn't thank you for getting me out of the tree."

He shrugged. "It was well worth my time. The girls
promised to bake me a cake."

"We'll have it after supper."

" 'Preciate it." He jerked a thumb toward the area behind
him. "Better get back to my fence."

He took a step back. She took a step forward.

"Don't go," she said softly. "I was wrong to think we
could have a family picnic without you."

He wasn't certain if it was the way she was looking at
him or that he was standing before her with bare feet that
made him feel so vulnerable at that moment. He wished
he'd taken the time to put on his boots so he would have
known. He took another step back. "I really need to get
some work done on my fence."

She took two steps forward. "Please stay. Charles and
the children want you here."

"And what do you want?"

"I don't want to spend the day climbing trees just to have
your company for a little while."

"How the hell'd you get up there, anyway?"

She smiled. "I don't know. Will you come back?"

He heaved a deep sigh. "Reckon so. Don't want to spend
my day climbing trees, either."

They began walking back toward the creek. He bent
down, pulled up a yellow flower, and held it out to her.

"What's this for?" she asked as she took it.

"For making Charles happy."

They approached the creek bank, and Jesse found himself
surrounded by little urchins urging him toward the rope. He
dropped his boots, climbed to the low branch of the tree,
and swung out over the creek. He released his hold on the
rope and plummeted into the warm water.

Charles wrapped his arm around Maddie's waist. "Thank
you for inviting him back."

"I want you to be happy, and I could tell you missed having him here."

"You'll always share the children with him, won't you? He'd be lost without them."

"Of course I will."

"Good. Now, let's see if we can't make this the best picnic we've ever had."

For the remainder of the day, their laughter echoed along the creek.

❧ 15 ❧

Unable to sleep, Maddie roamed the house, the lamp within her hand lighting the way. Charles had drifted to sleep, but sleep no longer came to her as easily. She would lie in his arms until she heard his rhythmic breathing, then she'd raise herself up on an elbow and watch him, silhouetted by the night. She noticed things now that had eluded her before: the thinness creeping over him, the deep furrow between his brows that remained after he fell asleep, and the embrace that was not as strong as it had once been.

She saw the pale light slipping out into the hallway beneath the door of the study. On raised toes, she scurried quietly down the hall and pressed her ear against the door. She could hear no sounds. Prepared to wage war if she discovered Silas had returned, she turned the handle, eased the door open, and peered inside.

Jesse was hunched over papers and ledgers strewn across the desk. He made notations, reached for a sheet of paper, studied it, dropped it, and made further notations. His hair was disheveled, and she could see the furrows his frustrated fingers had plowed through the thick strands. It was long past midnight, and it suddenly occurred to her that he never retired when they did, and yet he was awake, tending to chores, long before anyone else.

Closing his eyes, he bowed his head, sighed deeply, and rubbed the back of his neck. He rolled his head from one side to the other and back.

By the time he opened his eyes, she'd walked to the center of the room. "I thought you said Charles did the books."

Tossing the pencil down, he forced a tired smile. "I guess it's time you learned the truth. Texas Rangers lie."

"You do it all." The question was stated as fact, a fact he didn't deny.

"It seems more important for Charles to direct his energy toward spending time with the children." His eyes held hers. "And his wife."

She felt the heat flush her face. Always, that one truth stood between them. She was married to his brother.

"You don't seem too pleased with the figures you were recording."

He heaved a deep sigh, rubbing his hands over his face as though they could erase the figures he'd just recorded. "We need the cattle."

Guilt prompted irrational anger to surge through her. "And I suppose you're blaming me—"

Jesse held up a hand. If he weren't so tired, he'd let her vent her anger just so he could enjoy the slight accent her rage induced. "I'm not blaming anyone. I'm just stating the truth. You see how few stagecoaches stop here. It's dwindling down to nothing. People are using the trains."

Walking to the window, she gazed out upon the night. "Maybe you could take me back to Fort Worth. Maybe they'd give back your money."

"I doubt they'd pay us what you're worth."

She spun around. "And how much would that be, Mr. Lawson?"

"A hell of a lot more than a thousand dollars, Mrs. Lawson."

She blinked away the tears. She had expected him to belittle her worth, not enhance it.

He studied her, his black gaze penetrating. "Do you know who killed your father and brother?"

"What difference does it make?" she asked.

He dropped his head into his hands, rubbing his eyes, reining in his anger. Fear had ignited her eyes and thrown her defenses in place. She guarded her past the way a mother wolf protected her young. He picked up the pencil and tossed it back down. "I'm seriously considering doing some bounty hunting. Figure I might as well make it personal. Go after whoever it is that gives you nightmares, put them away so you aren't afraid anymore."

"Bounty hunting?"

He flinched as disgust marred her face. "I don't see a lot of choice. Texas Rangers don't make a whole hell of a lot. It took me years to save enough money for a start on a herd. I don't have years. I figure if I target two or three with good bounties on them—"

"Target? You sound like you're hunting animals."

"They are animals. They murder—"

"You killed!"

"But I never murdered."

"And there's a difference?"

"Yes, ma'am, there is, and I think you damn well know what it is."

"I won't stay in a home that's supported with blood money."

"And what the hell are you going to do, Maddie? You'll have three children hanging on to your skirts wherever you go. You think you've learned some skills since you left Fort Worth?"

She stormed across the room, planted her palms on the desk, and leaned toward him. "Yes, as a matter of fact, I have. I'll run an inn somewhere else."

"You're not listening to me. Inns are shutting down all over the state. Inns in the larger towns are converting to hotels if there's something in the town to draw people. Otherwise, they're closing, too."

"Then I'll just find a hotel to run."

He rolled his eyes. "And how the hell are you going to do that?"

"I'll think of something."

"Maybe you think you'll find some dying man as desperate as Charles—"

The crack of Maddie's palm hitting Jesse's cheek echoed

throughout the room. "Go to bleedin' hell."

She stormed out of the room. He dropped his head into his hands. Only a desperate man would marry her. A man desperately in love.

The slight tapping on the door stirred Maddie from a restless slumber. Easing out from beneath Charles's arm, she padded barefoot across the hardwood floor, opened the door slightly, and peered out into the shadowed hallway.

"Get dressed. There's something I want to show you," Jesse whispered.

"Go to hell."

"Maddie, please." His voice echoed with a desperation she'd never before heard from him.

She squinted. "It's not even sunup."

"That's why we've got to hurry. Meet me in the kitchen."

Jesse slipped away before she could issue any further protests. She clicked the door back into place and glanced over at her sleeping husband. She wondered how he would feel if he knew his wife was sneaking out with his brother in the early hours of the morning.

Jesse was taking a long swallow of coffee when Maddie came into the kitchen. In the dim light, he could still see the puffiness around her eyes, the disorientation that often marks the beginning of a new day.

"Want some coffee before we head out?" he asked.

"Head out? Where are we going?"

"You'll see. Want some coffee?"

She shook her head.

"Then let's go." He set down his cup, shoved open the door, and waited for her to pass through. Reluctantly, she did so. Closing the door behind them, he jaunted across the back porch and hopped to the ground. "Come on. We've got to hurry." With long, sure strides, he headed into the woods.

Maddie scurried after him. As she reached him, he extended his arm back, wrapped his hand around hers, and guided her through the dark forest.

His strides were purposeful, his manner intent. It was obvious he was familiar with this path he traversed in the darkness.

Jesse stopped, and Maddie found herself no longer surrounded by trees. Whatever lay before her was invisible, still cloaked in night shadows. Hunkering down, he tugged her down beside him. He slipped his arm behind her, clamping his hand on her waist, leaning her against his side, steadying her. And for long moments, they waited in silence, his eyes trained on the far horizon.

Maddie saw the first fingers of the sun playing timidly along the horizon. Then they reached up and painted the sky in lavender, orange, a sweeping pink. As they created a masterpiece in the heavens, so they revealed the masterpiece on the earth: the valley, lush and green; the pond, still in the morning light, mirroring the beauty of the sky.

"It's beautiful," she whispered reverently, not wishing to disturb Mother Nature in her glory.

"In the midst of all these woods, Maddie, it's like God just scooped His mighty hand down," he made a dipping, sweeping motion with his cupped hand, "and said, 'Here, you shall graze cattle.' "

She studied the profile of the man she'd come to love, and, for the first time, felt no guilt about the feelings she harbored for Jesse. Her love for him was as beautiful as the sunrise. And his dream. She wanted him to have his dream.

"When will you be leaving?" she asked quietly, her voice conveying the understanding and acceptance of his decision, her heart expanding beyond its limits because it was important to him that she give him both. She watched his throat work as he swallowed.

"End of the week."

She could do no more than nod and pray the realization of his dream would not mean the death of hers.

"Couple of our neighbors owe me some favors. I'll make arrangements for them to check in on you from time to time. If anything needs doing, you leave it for them to do. I'll take care of everything else before I go so all you and Charles will have to do is the small things. And I'll let you know where I am, so you'll be able to get in touch with me if you need me."

The unspoken thought hung between them: if Charles dies.

"How long will you be gone?"

"Hopefully not too long. I'll go after the ones with the biggest bounties."

The ones. He hadn't referred to them as men, and she realized he didn't want to think of them as men, that the thought of what he was contemplating was as distasteful to him as it was to her. And yet dreams required sacrifices. The more magnificent the dream, the more a person had to be willing to give up in order to own it.

"Those with the larger bounties are the most dangerous, aren't they?" She couldn't stop her voice from quivering. He refused to look at her or answer. "I couldn't stand it if I lost both you and Charles. I've come to love you both."

He turned then, his gaze delving into hers, and she wondered if he could see through her eyes into her heart and know that the love she held for him was so incredibly, beautifully different, so much deeper than the love she held for Charles.

"I'll be careful. And I'll come back. My dreams are here, Maddie. Everything I've ever wanted, everything I've ever searched for . . . I keep finding right here."

She thought he would kiss her then, so intense was his gaze, so much longing was mirrored in his eyes, but he didn't. Instead, he pulled her more securely against his side and looked out again over the land.

They stayed for long moments, thinking about dreams and the price they might each be asked to pay to achieve them.

The stagecoach rolled in at twilight. Jesse hoisted up onto the footrest and helped the driver take the trunks down. Maddie approached the passengers milling around beside the stagecoach. A buxom woman patted her generous bare cleavage with her lace handkerchief.

"My word, but it's hot," she said.

A man standing beside her laughed. "You're always hot, Lilly."

She punched his arm with enough force to send him staggering back. "For which you should always be grateful, Thomas." Smiling brightly, she turned to her arrested audience. "He is, of course, referring to my performance upon the lighted stage." Her eyes widened. With a flourish, she rushed over to the stagecoach and clamped her painted talons around Jesse's thigh. "Sir, sir, I beg of you. That's my trunk. Please take care with it."

Jesse gave her a half smile. "Yes, ma'am."

Her hand traveled slowly up and down his thigh. "My, you're not a city boy, are you?"

"No, ma'am, but I'd think your eyes could have told you that as easily as your hand."

Coyly, she peered at him through her thick lashes. "But it wouldn't have been as much fun now, would it?"

Maddie forcefully cleared her throat. Lilly screeched and jumped back, her hand to her throat. Maddie produced her sweetest smile. "Please let me acquaint you with our home and show you where you can freshen up after that long, hot journey."

Lilly threw a glance back over her shoulder at the man, who was now laughing. "Should have told me you were married. I don't mess with married men." She flounced off, catching up with the other passengers as Maddie escorted them into the house.

Maddie entered everyone's name into the guest register, then showed them to their respective rooms.

Aaron tossed the stick so it landed a short distance away from him. Ranger scampered after it, growled at the offending object, studied it, yelped, then took it in his mouth and trotted back to Aaron's side.

"Good dog." He patted the pup on the head and tossed the stick so it landed a little farther away than it had before. Ranger went through the same routine before bringing the stick back to Aaron.

"Smart dog you have there," a deep voice said.

Aaron twisted around on his haunches and looked up at the finely dressed man. He wasn't nearly as tall as Uncle Jesse. "Yes, sir."

The man knelt and rubbed his hand briskly over Ranger's side. "What's his name?"

"Ranger."

The man smiled. "How did you decide on a name like that?"

"Named him after my Uncle Jesse. He was a Texas Ranger."

"Where's your uncle now?"

"Helping the whip, I imagine."

The man took the stick from Aaron and tossed it. "So he'd be the tall man with the black hair."

"Yes, sir, that's him."

"And what's your name?"

"Aaron."

The man held out a hand. "I'm Paul."

Aaron cleared his small throat. "Ain't supposed to call guests by their first name."

The man's smile increased. "Somner. Paul Somner."

Aaron stuck his hand into the one that was offered him. "Nice to meet you, Mr. Somner."

Maddie stepped out onto the porch. "Aaron, I need you and Hannah to gather some kindling."

"Yes, ma'am." He glanced over at Paul Somner. "Gotta do what Ma says. Pa's real particular about that." He leapt to his feet and began running. "Come on, Ranger!"

Maddie stepped off the porch and approached the man standing in the yard. He wore a brocade vest and a tailored jacket. She didn't think the wind would dare blow through his blond hair. His face was that of a young man, but something in his blue-gray eyes spoke of experience. "Can I help you with something, Mr. Somner?"

"No, Mrs. Lawson, I was just looking around. After being cooped up in that stagecoach for most of the day, I felt a need to stretch my legs. That's a fine boy you've got there."

"We're proud of him."

He shoved his hands into his pockets. "If you'll excuse me for appearing forward, you hardly look old enough to have a boy that age."

Maddie felt the heat warm her face. "My husband was married before."

A deep scarlet flushed his smooth cheeks. "I seem to have tripped over myself with that compliment. I am sorry for your husband's loss. Have you been married long?"

"Only a few months."

He bestowed upon her a gracious smile. "My congratulations to you then."

"Thank you."

His smile broadened, creating a small dimple in his left cheek. "I'm soon to be married myself. My betrothed is waiting for me back East. I had some business to attend to here and wanted to get it out of the way before the marriage."

Smiling, she tilted her head. "My congratulations to you then."

"Thank you. I was thinking of bringing her here on our marriage trip, but each town I visit in this state is so different from the one before it, I hardly know what she would enjoy the most. Where do you think she might like to spend some time?"

Maddie folded her hands together. "I don't know. I like the area around here, the hills, the greenery."

"Did you grow up around here?"

"No."

He waited as though expecting clarification. When none came, he studied his boots. "I recently visited Galveston." He lifted his eyes to hers. "Do you think she'd like that?"

She shook her head. "I really wouldn't know. I've never been there."

He smiled. "I like listening to the surf wash upon the shore. I thought that would make for pleasant memories."

"It sounds lovely."

"Perhaps, but then again she's spent some time at the Atlantic Ocean. I don't suppose the Gulf of Mexico is that much different. What about Fort Worth or Dallas? Is there anything of interest there?"

"There are some fine theaters."

"Which one would you recommend?"

Maddie laughed lightly. "I've never been to any of them."

"Truly? You seem a lady of culture. I thought surely you'd grown up in high society."

She shook her head. "No, my life has always been quite simple and plain."

"No adventures, no excitement?"

"I have all the excitement I need right here with three children."

"But before you were married, did you never long for something more than this?"

She smiled softly. "No, Mr. Somner, for as long as I can remember, the life I have here is what I've always wanted. Now, if you'll excuse me, I need to see about getting a meal prepared for you and the other guests."

Maddie walked into the kitchen, lifted the lid on the pot, and sniffed the stew.

"They're a hungry bunch," Jesse said as he and Charles walked into the kitchen. "They're already sitting down to the table."

"Everything's ready. We just need to get it out there," Maddie said.

"Be careful when you're serving Miss Lilly that you don't spill any of that stew on her," Jesse teased.

Tilting her nose in the air, she began to spoon the stew into the serving bowl. "The thought never crossed my mind."

Jesse chuckled. "You're no good at telling lies, Maddie."

"She's a brazen hussy. Don't you think so, Charles?"

Charles picked up the pitcher of water. "What I think is that we'd best start serving them." He headed toward the dining room.

Maddie finished filling the large bowl with stew, picked it up, and carried it out of the kitchen.

Lilly was once again patting her chest, drawing every man's attention to her generous endowments. Maddie was disgusted to see the woman's enraptured audience included her husband and her brother-in-law. Jesse and Charles exchanged adolescent smiles, and she was tempted to leave the caring of their guests in their hands.

Lilly leaned across the table. "Mr. Somner?"

Sitting across from her, Paul Somner smiled. "Paul. Please call me Paul. Traveling by stage creates an intimacy between passengers that traveling by train doesn't."

She flashed him a smile. "And you look to me to be a man who would prefer the intimacy."

He blushed clear up to the roots of his blond hair.

"I believe you mentioned you live in Washington. Are you a politician by chance?"

"No, ma'am."

"Then, pray tell, what does a handsome man such as yourself do in Washington to earn a living?"

"I'm a detective with the Pinkerton Agency."

The sound of a bowl crashing to the floor and breaking into a thousand pieces echoed throughout the room. Charles sent water sloshing over the table as he dropped the glass he was holding before he rushed over to join Jesse at Maddie's side.

She was on her knees, fighting back tears, her trembling fingers picking up the broken remains. "Oh, I'm so sorry."

Jesse put his hand on her shoulder. "Doesn't matter."

"Oh, but it does. It was so beautiful. I was careless. It was so beautiful. Imported from England." Her gaze remained transfixed on the floor, the splattered stew, and the broken bits of china.

"I know the truth, Maddie," Jesse said quietly.

She jerked up her head. Jesse was totally unprepared for the stark terror reflected in her eyes. Gently, he squeezed her shoulder. "I know you've never been fond of my stew, and you were trying to spare these people having to eat it, but I'm afraid I've made enough to last through ten accidents."

She covered her mouth with a trembling hand as the terror retreated and profound relief washed over her. Tears flowed onto her cheeks as she tried to laugh, but the sounds she emitted more closely resembled sobs. Jesse leaned back. Charles put his arms around her and helped her to her feet. "Come on, Maddie. We've got other bowls. I was never fond of that one, anyway."

"Liar," she whispered as he led her toward the kitchen.

Jesse picked up several pieces of the shattered bowl before he twisted his body slightly and looked toward the table. The guests had turned their attention to lighthearted banter. All the guests, except Paul Somner.

Somner sat, his elbow resting on the table, his chin resting in his hand, his expression thoughtful. His gaze locked onto Jesse's, and then, as though some profound question had been answered, he turned his attention back to those seated before him.

Closing the door behind her, Maddie stepped onto the back porch. Cleaning the dining room and kitchen after the evening meal had seemed to take forever. She'd been unable to make her hands function. Her mind had been absorbed with thoughts of the man from the Pinkerton Agency, trying to remember exactly what questions he'd asked her earlier, what answers she'd given. The man probably wasn't even betrothed, but had simply used the ruse to determine with which parts of the state she was familiar.

She knew several stage line companies took robberies against their coaches as a personal affront. She walked to the railing, wrapped her hands around it, and took a deep breath. A person always paid when they wronged others. One way or another, they always paid.

Paul Somner stepped out of the shadows. "Mrs. Lawson."

Maddie spun around, fighting to calm her erratic heart, to disguise the fear she felt. "Mr. Somner."

"I didn't mean to startle you."

She returned her gaze to the yard. "You didn't."

"I was apologizing for earlier when my revelation about being a Pinkerton detective seemed to upset you."

"I assure you, it didn't. I was so engrossed in watching Miss Lilly that I forgot about the bowl. It slipped. That's all."

"Ah, yes, Miss Lilly. She's enough to distract anyone." He cleared his throat. "The accommodations and food here are exceptional. Certainly worth the two dollars we'll pay before we leave in the morning."

"My husband takes a great deal of pride in his inn."

"As well he should." He moved until he was standing beside her, close enough that she noticed he smelled of lemon. Fresh and clean. She could feel him studying her, could feel his eyes take in every detail of her face.

"You have unusual eyes, Mrs. Lawson. Their shade is one a man is not likely to forget once he's gazed into them."

Quickly, Maddie stepped off the porch. "If you'll excuse me, Mr. Somner, I have a few more chores to tend to before I retire."

Somner watched as the woman was swallowed by night shadows. He withdrew a thin cheroot and a small pair of silver scissors from his breast pocket. Snipping off the tip, he placed the cheroot in his mouth, struck a match, and lit it, allowing the flame on the match to burn long after he needed it. He took several small puffs before releasing the smoke in one grand gesture. He removed the cheroot from his mouth, held it out in his hand, and studied it a moment. "I don't much like being spied upon, Mr. Lawson."

Jesse stepped out of the shadows. "And I don't much like seeing Maddie upset."

"It was not my intent to upset her."

Jesse moved until he was towering over Somner. The man was small of stature, and yet there was nothing small in his manner. "I spent a lot of years working as a Texas Ranger. I know the look of a man who's searching for someone. I know the look of a man when he's found the person he's looking for. You found who you were looking for today."

Somner tilted his head and smiled. "Yes, Mr. Lawson, I did."

"What do you intend to do about that?"

Somner looked out into the night. He took a long draw on his cheroot and then released three perfect circles of smoke into the air. "For the moment . . . nothing. I have a reputation for delivering surprises. More than one person is involved in this case. I have little doubt that eventually they'll all come together. When they do, I shall spring my little surprise."

Jesse leaned down until his face was close enough to Somner's that he could have told the man which plantation had raised the tobacco he was smoking. "Well, while you're waiting to spring your little surprise, contemplate this. You do one thing to cause that little woman to experience any pain or sorrow, and just before you die, you'll regret the day you were born."

Somner casually quirked a brow. "I would expect such an impassioned threat from the woman's husband, not her brother-in-law."

"I place family above all else whether that family be through blood or marriage. Anyone harms any member of my family, they'll answer to me. And they'll answer dearly."

Somner tilted his head in acknowledgment of Jesse's feelings. "I'll keep that in mind, Mr. Lawson."

"See that you do."

Jesse stepped off the porch and disappeared beyond the trees. Somner listened to the wind, leisurely smoked his cheroot, and thought about the future. Surprises were such a joy to deliver, but this one, he had little doubt, would be the most rewarding of his career.

Standing before the creek, watching the muddy waters flow, Maddie heard Jesse's soft footfalls. She wanted to turn around and throw herself into his arms, to feel the protection he had offered to so many during his life. But he'd only ever offered his protection to those who deserved it, and she knew she was one of the undeserving.

"Maddie, tell me," he implored quietly, the deep timbre of his voice a caress through her soul. "Tell me what you're afraid of. Tell me why you think Somner is a threat to you."

"I don't think any such thing."

He touched her arm, and she skittered away.

"I won't let anyone hurt you. I won't let any harm come to you, but I've got to know what we're dealing with here."

She laughed. "You're not invincible, Jesse. Aaron proved that easily enough."

He dropped his head back, running frustrated fingers through his hair. "You said a marriage should be built on trust—"

"I'm not married to you."

"You seem to remember that only when it's convenient for you."

She spun around. "I've never strayed from the vows I made with Charles."

"No, you haven't, but I'm not talking about you and Charles. I'm talking about you and me."

"There is no you and me." She looked at his beloved face, wishing the truth wasn't so painful. "And there never will be, Jesse."

"In two days, Maddie, I'll be going to the Ranger headquarters in Austin. Their information won't be outdated like McGuire's. I'll find out what I need to know."

"I know you will."

"Then for God's sake, tell me now. Trust me tonight, before I go."

She brushed her fingertips along his cheek. "It's not a matter of trust, you bleedin' idiot," she said softly.

Turning away, she searched the waters. When he returned and looked upon her, she would once again be as she was before and would have to leave behind all that she loved.

❧ 16 ❧

"You're going, then?" Charles asked.

Jesse slid the Winchester rifle into the scabbard resting alongside his saddle. The stage had departed shortly after dawn, and he'd decided against waiting another day to leave. He had little doubt that Somner would double back and, with a careful eye, be waiting to deliver his surprise. He wanted to know by nightfall whatever it was Somner knew now. "Yep."

"Any idea how long you'll be gone?"

"Long as it takes." He slung the saddlebags into place.

"I'm sorry, Jesse. I had no right not to buy the cattle you wanted."

With a thumb, Jesse tipped his hat back off his brow. "About damn time you realized that and apologized."

"I realized it the minute I handed the money over to Bev. I just thought things would work out."

Jesse extended his hand. When Charles grasped it, he pulled him close, hugged him tightly, and prayed it wouldn't be the last time he saw him. He released his hold, mounted his horse, and brought the hat brim low over his brow. "If it makes any difference, I think you made the better investment."

He urged Midnight out of the barn into the sunlight. Glancing toward the back porch, he felt disappointment settle within his chest. He hadn't expected Maddie to be standing there, but damn, he'd hoped she'd see him off.

Charles walked out of the barn. "You take care now."

Jesse gazed down at him. "I will." He heard the door open and turned his attention back to the house.

The girls ran toward him. Hannah, with the advantage of years, reached him first. She held up a small cloth-covered bundle. "We made you a sponge cake to take with you."

Taking the offering, he felt the warmth spread from its center. " 'Preciate it." Out of the corner of his eye, he caught a movement and looked again toward the porch. Maddie stood there, hugging the beam. Bending down, he touched each girl's cheek. Then he sent Midnight into a trot and reined him in beside Maddie as she stood on the porch.

Their eyes met and held, his imploring her to tell him the truth, hers pleading with him not to ask. He lifted the bundle. " 'Preciate the cake."

"Eat it while it's warm."

"I will." He had a thousand things he wanted to say to her, a lifetime's worth. "Maddie—"

"You take care," she urged, tears brimming in her eyes.

If she was his only responsibility, he'd dismount right then and there and say to hell with the cattle, Somner, and her past. The weight he carried on his shoulders had never seemed heavier. He tipped his hat and kicked Midnight into a slow lope.

She watched Aaron and Ranger run after him. Jesse stopped and ruffled Aaron's hair. Then he rode away. She was certain her dreams were being carried within his saddle-bags.

Charles ambled over to the porch. "I don't imagine he'll be gone too long."

"No, I don't imagine he will." She smiled at her husband. "You look tired. Why don't you take Aaron fishing?"

"Fish for dinner sounds good to me. Why don't we all go?"

Stepping off the porch, she took Taylor's hand. "Come on, let's go see if we can find a catfish."

She was a coward.

Gazing out the bedroom window into the blackness of

night, Maddie acknowledged that solitary truth. In her heart, she already knew the path she would walk, and she would walk it with whatever dignity she could.

Regretting so much, she squeezed her eyes shut. She should have been honest with Charles. She should never have allowed him and his children to care for her. She should have rejected his proposal and returned to Bev's where small brown-eyed children wouldn't look upon her with love. Now she would destroy their faith with the truth.

Charles was her husband. She'd tell him tonight what Jesse would undoubtedly discover in the morning. She'd offer to stay with him as long as he needed her. Then she'd quietly surrender to the authorities. If he could no longer stand the sight of her, she'd surrender tomorrow.

She moved away from the window and folded down the quilt on the bed. She'd miss the children desperately. She'd miss Charles. Wiping the tears from her cheeks, she knew she would miss Jesse most of all. She'd wanted to tell him before he left, but she couldn't . . . not after all the times he'd promised that he wouldn't let anyone or anything harm her. The truth about her past would give him no choice but to break his promises, and she hadn't wanted to see that knowledge reflected in his eyes.

Perhaps if she didn't love him so much, she could have told him. Perhaps that was why she could tell Charles now. As much as she had come to care for him, Charles did not hold her heart. It belonged exclusively to his brother.

She heard Ranger bark and fall into silence. She glanced out the window, but could see nothing among the shadows. She walked across the room, opened the door slightly, and peered into the hallway. Charles should have returned from checking downstairs. She wondered if he'd had one of his spells, if that's what had caused Ranger to bark. Perhaps the dog was now licking his unconscious face. She rushed across the room, grabbed the lamp, and headed into the hallway. Descending the stairs, she glanced around as different portions of the lower floor came into view. She walked into the dining room and saw a pale light spilling out from the kitchen.

She hurried into the kitchen and came up short at the sight that greeted her. "Silas," she whispered hoarsely.

"You lied to me, Maddie girl," the giant man said, his scarred visage a testament to the life he lived.

Maddie looked at Charles as he sat in a chair, his hands tied behind his back, a cloth stuffed into his mouth. Unspoken apologies filled her eyes; understanding filled his. A movement caught her attention, and she saw the lumbering hulk of humanity known as Walsh. He sat on the floor running his huge hand over Ranger.

Resembling a buffalo, Silas shook his large head as though he was filled with great sorrow. "The money weren't buried where you said, Maddie girl."

"You were probably digging in the wrong place."

"I had Walsh digging the area for a week."

"Maybe you misunderstood my directions."

He let a stream of tobacco juice fly. It landed near her bare feet. "Maybe. We woulda been back sooner, but we had a damn posse on our tail for near a month and had to go down to Mexico for a while. You wouldn't of set 'em on us, now, would you, girl?"

"How would I have managed that without giving myself away?"

He glanced around the kitchen. "You're living fine, Maddie. You must have traded something for it. Maybe you dug up the money yourself. Maybe it's here somewhere." He drew his gun from his holster. "Which of his legs should I shoot first?"

Charles slid his eyes closed, and Maddie felt the fear rip through her. What was it Jesse had said about men who had no souls? When they were finished with Charles, they'd harm the children, whether she told them what they wanted to know or not. "If you hurt him, I won't tell you anything. I'll go with you and show you exactly where Father buried that money."

Silas spewed his tobacco juice so it landed on Charles's face. "That's my girl." He lumbered toward the door. "Come on, Walsh."

Walsh stood, cradling Ranger in his large hand.

"Leave the dog, Walsh," Maddie said.

"But I like him, Maddie." He rubbed the dog against his cheek. "I want to keep him."

"Leave him," she ordered.

"He can take him if he wants," Silas said.

She planted her hands on her hips. "I am the only one left who knows where my father buried that strongbox. You'd better give some thought to keeping me happy."

"Leave the dog," Silas growled.

Petulantly, Walsh dumped Ranger into his box and lumbered out of the room. Silas grabbed Maddie's arm. She looked toward Charles. "Forgive me," she whispered before she was jerked outside.

Charles struggled against the rope that chafed his wrists. He pulled, strained, and thought about toppling the chair over, but it would gain him nothing but Ranger's tongue in his face. He dropped his chin against his chest. Thoughts rumbled through his mind like a storm encroaching on the sunshine. How could he have been so wrong? What would he tell the children?

He strengthened his resolve, gritted his teeth, and worked the bindings. It was still dark when he slipped his hands free. He yanked the soiled cloth from his mouth, untied his feet, and rushed to the water pump. Filling his cupped hands, he drank and splashed the cool water on his face at the same time.

He didn't want to burden his son, but at the moment, he didn't see much choice. He had no desire to trust this matter to the local sheriff or have nosy neighbors asking questions. He'd wake Aaron and explain only enough so the boy would be alert, but not frightened. He'd leave him to watch the girls while he rode hell-bent-for-leather to Austin. He and Jesse could be back here before nightfall. It'd put Jesse a day behind the men who'd taken Maddie, but knowing his brother, Charles knew one day wouldn't make a difference.

He walked quickly through the dining area into the foyer. Unexpectedly, he felt the storm rage through his head and

the pain rush at him stronger, with more fury, than it ever
had before. He squeezed his eyes shut, pressed the heels of
his hands against his temples, and staggered back. "Dear
God, not now, please not now!" The anguished prayer went
unanswered. He collapsed across the stairs and sank into the
black abyss.

Jesse sat in the chair, his hand cupping his chin. He'd
drifted off to sleep a couple of times during the afternoon,
but stark images of men wanted for murder kept intruding
on his peace. He'd ridden most of the night to get back to
the inn, knew he should be riding now, but he'd be damned
if he was going to leave before Charles came to.

Charles groaned. Jesse eased up in the chair and placed
his hand on his shoulder. Charles opened his eyes, then
slammed them shut. "Sweet Lord."

"You in a lot of pain?"

"There comes a time when you stop measuring it by its
intensity. I'm at that moment."

"What can I do for you?"

"Laudanum. Top drawer of the dresser."

Jesse retrieved the painkiller. He spooned the liquid into
Charles's mouth. Groaning, Charles dropped his head on
the pillow. "When did you get here?"

"Around noon. Found you at the bottom of the stairs with
a blanket draped over you."

"The children?"

"They're fine. They ate sponge cake for breakfast, then
kept vigil at your side. Aaron was afraid to go for help,
afraid to leave the girls."

"How'd you know to come back?"

"I didn't. I needed to talk to Maddie."

Alarmed by the resignation he heard in Jesse's voice,
Charles opened his eyes. Jesse touched the raw wound on
his wrist. "Want to tell me what happened here?"

Struggling, Charles managed to sit up. "Two men came
and took Maddie."

Jesse bolted from the chair, charged across the room,
braced both hands on the window, and gazed out at nothing.

"She go with them willingly?"

"I wouldn't exactly say she was willing. They said she knew where some money was buried and threatened to shoot me if she didn't tell them where it was." When Jesse didn't respond, Charles forced himself to ask the question he wasn't certain he wanted answered, afraid he already knew the answer. "What'd you find out in Austin?"

Releasing a great gust of air, Jesse bowed his head. "What I suspected all along. Her father and brother weren't passengers on that stage, Charles." He cast a sidelong glance at his brother. "They were the ones robbing it." He pulled a piece of paper from his pocket and unfolded it. "Her father was known as the Highwayman because of his pronounced accent. Whenever he stopped a stagecoach, he yelled, 'Stand and deliver,' which is common among highwaymen in England. In the beginning, he rode with his son. Then later, what was believed to be another son joined the ranks. Since they never killed anyone, they were considered relatively harmless but irritating when they relieved passengers of their valuables. A few years back, their popularity faded when they hitched up with two men who were rough and quick to pull the trigger."

Charles groaned. "The two men . . . Maddie called them by name."

"Silas and Walsh?"

Charles nodded. "Don't you dare say you told me so."

Jesse threw his head back and tunneled his fingers through his hair. "I wouldn't dream of it."

Charles rubbed his brow. "What are you going to do?"

"I'm going after them. They've killed four men."

"Wonder why Maddie never mentioned that she had another brother."

"Because she didn't have another brother." Jesse tossed the paper onto the bed.

Charles read the description of the youth. It was too vague for an artist to draw a likeness, but it contained enough description that if a man knew the outlaw, he'd recognize her. He jerked his head up. "What are you going to do?"

"I told you. Go after them."

"What are you going to do about Maddie?"

Averting his gaze, Jesse walked toward the door. Charles struggled out of bed and stood unsteadily. "Jesus Christ! Jesse, for once in your life, don't think this thing to death."

Jesse stopped, his hand on the doorknob. "I haven't thought anything through since you brought her home, and I've regretted it every time I didn't." He opened the door and walked out.

Pressing the heel of his hand against his forehead, Charles rushed after him. "Well, while you're thinking this to death, consider this. She doesn't know where the money is. She only told them she did so no harm would come to me or the children."

Partway down the stairs, Jesse halted and glanced over his shoulder. "How do you figure that?"

"If she knew where the money was, she wouldn't have had to step into Bev's parlor."

"Maybe she didn't have the means to get to it."

Charles held his brother's unflinching gaze. "I'd think if a woman had a choice between stepping into Bev's parlor or crawling on her hands and knees to a strongbox filled with money, she'd crawl."

With the lightness of a shadow, Jesse approached the weathered shack hidden deep within the dense thicket. He'd been trailing them for three days. Twilight surrounded him. He knew it would be to his advantage to wait until the break of day, to catch them unaware at first light. That's the way he'd been taught to do it.

He heard the sickening thud of a fist hitting flesh before he reached the side of the shack. Anger brewing within him, he peered through the narrow slats of the splintered shutter. Maddie was sprawled on the dirt floor. A giant towered over her.

"You're lying, Maddie girl."

Shaking her head, she struggled to sit up. "I don't know where the money is, Silas."

Silas slammed her to the ground, and Jesse felt the molten

rage shoot through him. He released his stranglehold on his revolver and reined in his anger. Now was not the time to lose control of his emotions.

"Walsh, get me a rope."

Jesse watched the other man lumber out of the shack. The larger man knelt over Maddie, grabbed her hair, and yanked her up. "I know ways to make you talk. Give you my word before this night is over, you'll tell me where the money is buried, and you'll be damn glad to dig it up for me."

Jesse stepped away from the window and heard something snap beneath his boot. He glanced down at two small twigs held together with a piece of string so they formed a crudely shaped cross. Turning his attention back to the task at hand, he crouched low and stalked his prey.

Maddie felt as though she was a rag doll when Silas slung her onto the bed in the corner of the single room. She scrambled up and pressed her back against the wall.

"Walsh surely is taking his time," Silas said as he unbuckled his gun belt and dropped it onto the table. "Probably forgot what the hell I sent him after." His mouth formed a distorted smile as he raked his eyes over her.

She clutched the wrapper around her throat. "If you do anything, Silas—"

"What? You won't tell me where the money is?" He grabbed her ankle and jerked her down to the bed. He fell on top of her, captured her wrists with one beefy hand, and held them in place over her head. His free hand roamed insolently over her curves.

His breath was hot and rancid as he ran his mouth across her throat. Deep within, Maddie screamed, but she knew to voice her horror would only ignite his lust and violence. He worked her nightgown up, and a small whimper broke free of her restraint. He chuckled and dug his fingers into her buttocks. She heard a rope thud to the ground, grateful Walsh had come back in time.

"You can stay and watch, Walsh," Silas growled without lifting his head from where it was buried next to her throat, "or you can leave, but you stop me from taking her this time, and I'll kill you."

Silence permeated the room. Then chains rattled to the floor. Silas jerked his head to the side and met the gaze of a silver gun barrel. He looked up and discovered Satan had risen from the bowels of hell.

"Get off her, or I'll kill you," Jesse said, his voice ominously low.

Silas eased back. With one rapid, smooth motion, Jesse holstered his gun, swung his fist around, and sent Silas crashing to the packed earth. "Get up, you son of a bitch," Jesse growled.

Struggling to his feet, Silas flailed his stocky arms. Jesse delivered a solid blow to the man's gut, then another to the center of his face. Silas dropped to the ground with a resounding thud. Jesse grabbed the shackles and rolled Silas to his back. He clamped his hands and feet into the restraints before dragging him across the earthen floor. He deposited him in a corner and walked back to the bed.

Curled in a ball, Maddie stared at him. Swollen flesh and black bruises marred one side of her face. Tears welled in her eyes as he gently touched her abused flesh. "They won't hurt you anymore, Maddie." He extended his gun toward her. She raised her eyes from the silver barrel to his hardened face. "Hold the gun on that one. If he moves an inch, shoot him. I've got the other shackled up outside. I want him in here where I can see him."

Taking the gun, Maddie held it with trembling hands. She watched him walk through the door. She'd prayed he'd come, prayed he wouldn't. She'd seen in the cold depths of his eyes that he knew the truth. He was no longer the man she'd kissed by the creek, nor was he the man she'd waltzed with in the barn. He was a Texas Ranger determined to carry out his duty.

Confusion marking his face, Walsh stumbled in ahead of Jesse. He walked to the corner and dropped beside Silas. Jesse picked up a rope.

"Shoot him, Maddie girl," Silas urged. "Shoot him or you'll hang along with us. You were there, girl, when we killed the first one. Makes you as guilty as us."

His back to her, Jesse wrapped the rope around the men

as though Silas wasn't talking. She felt as though someone had sliced her heart. He trusted her, and for some reason she couldn't explain, it pained her all the more that he did.

When the two men were adequately immobilized, Jesse hunkered down and addressed them. "I'm short on patience, and I'm anxious to get home. I figure you're both going to hang anyway, but if you do one thing to aggravate me, I'll shoot you dead right here and now."

He got up, walked over to Maddie, took the gun from her, and slipped it into his holster. She dropped her gaze to the shackles resting on the ground. Closing her eyes, she held out her hands, palms up.

"Why don't you see to fixing some coffee? I'll need it to keep awake tonight. I'm going to hobble my horse, then I'll be back."

She watched him disappear. Wishing he'd treat her like the dirt she was, she knelt before the small fire in the hearth. She felt as though she was a little girl who knows she's done wrong and is expecting a whipping, but the whipping never comes, and therein lies the punishment.

"Did he make you promises, girl?" Silas threw out across the room. "He's got no power over the law. He can't save you. Only old Silas can do that. My gun's still on the table. Get it and just wound him. I'll finish him off. Know what they do to women in prison? They'll do to you all the things I've wanted to do, but no one will stop 'em."

"I stole his dreams from him once before, Silas. I won't do it again." A sound in the doorway gained her attention, and she glanced up. Holding his rifle, Jesse strode into the ramshackle structure.

"You can sleep in the bed tonight," he said as he laid his rifle on the table.

She poured some coffee into a cup and set it on the table. Then she limped across the earthen floor and lay on the bed, rolling to her side so she faced the wall. She felt the bed dip under his weight.

"Here. Hold this to your cheek."

Reaching back, she took the damp cloth he offered and pressed it against her cheek. She wished it would ease the ache in her heart as easily as it did the pain on her face. She didn't move when Jesse placed her foot on his thigh. She heard him rip a blanket. Then she felt him wrap the woolen strip around her foot.

"They didn't even let you put on your shoes?"

She didn't answer, didn't think he expected an answer. Tenderly, he wrapped her other foot in silence. When she felt him leave the bed, she reached down and drew up a blanket. The room suddenly seemed as cold as a winter storm. She heard him scrape a chair across the floor and set it against the wall beside the bed. It moaned in protest as he dropped his body into place.

"Does Charles know everything?" she asked quietly.

"Yes."

"And the children?"

"No."

Finding some comfort in his answer, she wondered how he would explain her absence to the children when he returned home. She felt him pull the blanket over her shoulder. As simple as the action was, it caused a far greater pain within her heart than any of the harsh words he'd ever flung at her.

"Try and get some sleep. We'll be starting a hard two-day ride tomorrow."

"Where are we going?" she asked.

"I'll be taking you to the Ranger headquarters in Austin."

She drew her knees up and let the tears wash silently down her cheeks.

Jesse concentrated his attention on the two men huddled in the corner. The army had taught him discipline. The Rangers had taught him restraint. It took every bit of will-power he possessed not to crawl into that bed and wrap himself around Maddie.

He had to maintain a tight rein on his heart. His heart had no say in this matter, but it sure as hell wanted to say its piece. If he allowed his heart to speak, he'd have come into this shack with his guns blazing and killed two men for daring to take her. If he allowed his heart to talk, he'd take her to Mexico and build a ranch there. He'd send for the children, but what sort of life could he give them? Certainly not one they could be proud of. No, his heart had to stay silent on this matter.

He glanced around the shack. He didn't think it had changed much over the years. All the furniture was homemade, and it didn't appear anyone had taken much time to make it. He imagined Maddie as a little girl, playing on the dirt floor. She would have had no tiny teacups. He wondered if she'd had a rag doll. He dropped his head back and listened to the wind howling through the cracks in the walls.

Jesse jerked awake. The interior of the cabin was gloomy. Beyond it, through the slats in the shutters and the cracks in the door, he could see the emerging dawn. In the corner, the two men snored like hibernating bears. He glanced toward the bed at his side. It was empty.

He bolted out of the chair, and it crashed to the floor. He rushed outside and came to an abrupt halt. All the horses were hobbled nearby.

Taking in every detail surrounding him, his eyes and ears alert, he began to stalk the area. He moved around to the side of the shack and felt like a damned fool when Maddie glanced over at his crouched, hunting stance. Then she returned to her task.

He knelt beside her. "Your mother's grave?"

Nodding, she straightened the crude cross his big foot had nearly destroyed the day before. "I used to think if I ever had any money, I'd mark her place with a proper cross."

"Imagine she prefers the one you made when you were younger."

"I hate to ask, but if they hang me, will you bring me back here and bury me beside my mother?"

He took the twigs from her trembling hands, leaned over, and poked them into the earth. "No one's going to hang you."

"I think I'd rather hang than go to prison. Prison for a woman can't be pleasant."

"No, I don't reckon it is."

She balled her fists, fighting the tears, wishing it was anyone but Jesse turning her in, grateful it was Jesse now at her side. Sometimes, she thought she'd go insane with the mixed emotions she felt for him. "The money that Silas was looking for—"

"I know you don't know where it is."

She took a shaky breath. "It's buried beneath the dirt in the hearth."

Grabbing her arm, he spun her around. "What?"

"It was taken from a Wells Fargo stage. Posse was hot on our trail, so we split up. Father and I came here, and he buried the money. Then we met the others outside Fort Worth. They decided to do one more job before coming back here for the money. Only they didn't know the Texas Rangers were expecting a robbery and had set up an ambush. Father and Andrew were killed. Silas and Walsh didn't know where the money was buried."

He studied her face. "Why didn't you come back and get the money?"

"Because it didn't belong to me. I never used the money from any of the robberies."

"Why didn't you tell Silas where it was?"

She shrugged. "It wasn't his, either. I knew he'd kill me whether he had the money or not. I wanted to die with some dignity, knowing I'd thwarted his mean heart."

His fingers tightened around her arms, then he gently cupped her face. Her heart cried at the anguish she saw reflected in his eyes.

"Why didn't you trust me?" he rasped.

"I trust you as I've never trusted anyone in my life, and that makes all this that much harder to bear. I was ashamed, Jesse. I didn't want to see the truth of what I am reflected in your eyes. You, Charles, the children. You're all so good, so upstanding. Charles thought when I walked into Bev's, I was moving down in the world, but I was actually moving up."

"How the hell do you figure that?"

"At least at Bev's, I wouldn't have taken a man's money without giving him something back."

"And that was important to you?"

Her warm tears ran in a rivulet along her cheeks. "I never knew what Father and Andrew did until my mother died. When it was time for their next job, they took me with them. The first few times I only held the horses while they robbed a stagecoach, but as I got older, I threatened to shoot people if they didn't cooperate. I hated it, and I hated myself for not walking away. I believed Father when he said the next time would be the last."

She released a strangled laugh. "I know it's hard to understand, but he was a good father, and Andrew was a good brother. I loved them, even after I learned what they did. But they weren't good men. They took things to which they had no right. It was so hard . . . loving them, but hating the things they did."

"You ever kill anyone?"

She shook her head. "I was afraid I'd kill someone, so I never loaded my gun."

"You little fool. Do you know how easily you could have gotten killed?"

"I didn't care. My life was worthless until Charles asked me to be a mother to his children. It was a chance for me to give without taking." Fresh tears filled her eyes and spilled onto her cheeks. "Does Charles hate me?"

He brought her face so near to his that she felt his breath whisper across her lips.

"How could anyone hate you?"

"Don't you?"

His eyes delved deeply into hers. "No, Whiskey, I could never hate you." He grazed his knuckles across her cheek. "But I have to take you to Austin."

Bravely, she nodded. "I know. If you didn't, you wouldn't be the man you are." Or the man she loved.

At that precise moment, he wished he was anyone but who he was. He stood. "I'll dig up the money, and we'll take it back with us."

Reluctantly, she followed him into the shack, whispering farewell to her dreams on the way.

❧ 17 ❧

It was past noon, three days later, before Jesse herded his captives into the Ranger headquarters. A man behind a desk stood and shook his hand. "Well, Jesse, I didn't think I'd see you back so soon."

"Got lucky, Bob. I'm turning over these two outlaws along with this money they stole from a Wells Fargo stage." He dropped his saddlebag on the desk.

Bob signaled to two Rangers standing nearby. The men grabbed Silas and Walsh. Silas struggled. "You're coming too, Maddie. You're one of us." The Ranger pulled him toward the cells. "Don't know what he promised you, girl, but you'll hang with us!" His voice echoed along the corridor until it faded into silence.

Bob sat behind his desk and pulled out some papers. "This is them, isn't it?"

Jesse glanced at the wanted posters. "Yep."

Bob nodded. "And what about this last member of the gang? This young fella." He studied Maddie. "Been some speculation that maybe he's a girl."

"She's the leader's daughter."

Maddie dropped her gaze to the floor. She expected Jesse's next words to sound like a death knell, but no words came, only the silence hovering around her. Sadly, she realized he was waiting for her to openly admit the truth.

Squaring her shoulders, she lifted her eyes to the man behind the desk. She would face what was to come without the cowardice Silas had shown. She took a breath, ran the words quickly through her mind, and opened her mouth to speak.

"But she was laid to rest in Fort Worth," Jesse said.

Maddie snapped her head around. Stone faced, Jesse was looking directly into the eyes of the man sitting behind the desk. Bob cleared his throat. "I see. Know that for a fact, do you?"

"I'll stake my life on it."

Bob leaned back in his chair. "Don't recall you introducing me to the lady here."

"Maddie is my brother's wife. Those two kidnapped her. I guess they were looking for a ransom."

Bob ran his finger over his lips. "What was that fella yelling about her hanging?"

"You know as well as I do, Bob, you can't give any credence to anything an angry prisoner says."

Bob chuckled. "I guess maybe I've been behind this desk too long. Course I wouldn't be here at all, if you hadn't saved my life back in seventy-eight."

Jesse shifted his stance. "Rangers don't keep a tally on the debts they owe each other."

"I know most don't, but I do." He scrutinized Maddie a moment longer, then cleared his throat. "Without a body, I can't give you a reward on the last member of the gang."

"Wasn't looking for one."

Bob scribbled on some forms and handed them to Jesse. "Just sign on the bottom line, and I'll see that the money for those two gets sent to you."

Jesse signed the papers. Then he put his hand beneath Maddie's elbow. "I'll be seeing you around, Bob."

Bob leaned forward. "I'll get the word out about this young lady. No sense in bounty hunters wasting their time looking for her."

" 'Preciate it," Jesse said as he opened the door.

"Jesse?"

He glanced over his shoulder.

"You just make damn sure she doesn't come back to haunt us."

Jesse gave a brusque nod and escorted Maddie outside. She wrapped her arms around a rough pillar. She had never expected to walk in the sunlight again or breathe untainted air. Her legs wobbled. It was several moments of breathing deeply before she dared glance over at Jesse.

Stepping off the boardwalk, he gave her a cursory glance before turning his attention to the passing activity. "I can't take you home looking like that. There's a bathhouse just off Congress Avenue. We'll go freshen up, have a quick meal, then we'll ride home." He grabbed the reins of their horses and began walking.

As though in a trance, Maddie followed as he weaved through the throng of people. She wanted to touch the buildings just to make sure she hadn't fallen asleep and dreamed all this, but his long strides left no time for wanderings.

They entered the bathhouse, and a small woman bustled over. Jesse talked with her a moment. Then the woman approached Maddie, smiled at her, and took her arm. "Come with me, señora."

Maddie felt a moment of panic and looked at Jesse.

He gave a curt nod. "Rosa will see to your needs. Just go with her."

Obediently, she followed the woman to a small room at the end of the corridor.

"You sit here, señora, while I have my boys fill the tub."

The young men traipsed in time and again filling the wooden tub with steaming water. Sitting on the wooden bench, Maddie studied her hands. Her fingernails were cracked and broken, her knuckles grazed, and her skin rough. For a while they had been the hands of a mother, before that the hands of an outlaw. Now, she didn't know what they were.

The young men dumped the water from the last pails into the tub, tipped their hats, and walked out, closing the door quietly behind them. Maddie unwrapped the strips of blanket from her feet and rubbed her toes. Every muscle and bone in her body ached. A brisk knock on the door sounded before Rosa stuck her head inside the room.

"Señora, are you decent?"

Decent wasn't a word she would have ever associated with herself. "I'm still dressed."

Rosa bustled into the room. "Your husband told me to give you these things." She handed Maddie a large parcel wrapped in brown paper.

Slowly, Maddie unwrapped the parcel. She ran her fingers over the riding skirt, blouse, boots, and underclothes.

"Oh, señora, you are so fortunate to have such a caring husband who loves you so much." Rosa rolled her eyes toward the ceiling. "And one so handsome, too." She held up a small vial. "He told me to pour these into your water." As the bath salts hit the water, the scent of forget-me-nots wafted through the room.

Hugging the clothes, smelling the sweet fragrance of the water, Maddie collapsed to the floor. The first sob wracked her body. Somewhere in the distance, she heard Rosa's voice. Her light footsteps as the woman ran from the room were soon replaced by heavier footfalls as Jesse rushed in. He dropped to the floor and took her in his arms.

She pressed her face against his bare chest and cried for all the things she'd been, all that she was, all that she'd ever wanted to be.

"Shh, Maddie, it's over now."

She shook her head vigorously against his chest. "He knows you weren't telling the truth."

"Probably."

She tilted her tear-streaked face, her eyes searching his. "Don't you know what you've done? They'll send you to prison—"

"No one's sending me to prison. As far as the state of Texas is concerned, the fifth member of that gang no longer exists."

"But the man from the Pinkerton Agency—"

"I don't think Somner will be bothering you." He sighed deeply. "He told me more than one person was involved. I'm assuming he meant Silas and Walsh. I think once he got on the stagecoach, he doubled back to wait for them. Since he didn't stop them from taking you, I can only assume he wasn't as smart as he thought. I figure they ran across him and killed him."

"Maybe he's just hurt somewhere."

"Maybe. I'll have a good look around when we get back. If I don't find anything, I'll send a telegram to Washington."

She studied his calm face and remembered words he'd spoken long ago about the mistakes a man made when he didn't think through his actions. "You can't take the law into your own hands. You'll come to regret—"

"No." He brushed the loose strands of hair away from her face. "No, Maddie, I'll never regret what I did today." He ran his finger over the worry lines etched within her brow. "This isn't something I did lightly. I thought long and hard about it; I thought it nearly to death." He gave her a small smile.

She shook her head. "You can't make this a person-al—"

"I didn't. Why the hell do you think I've been such a cold bastard since I walked into that shack? Because I didn't want my heart talking instead of my head."

"Jesse, what you've done isn't right."

"Dammit, Maddie, why are you fighting me on this? I spent years hunting outlaws and desperadoes. I know a bad person when I see one." He cupped her face, his eyes holding hers. "There's not a spark of bad in you." When she opened her mouth to protest, he rushed on. "All right. You rode with some bad men. You held the horses and you pointed an unloaded gun at some people, but there's more honesty and goodness in you than there is in half the people walking that street out there." He rubbed his thumbs over her cheeks. "Trust me on this."

"But Charles and the children—"

"Would only suffer if you went to trial and in the end, you'd be found innocent. By the time I stepped down from that witness stand, not a person on that jury would dare vote guilty."

"What would you do—threaten them with nightmares?"

"No, I'd tell them how well you care for my brother and his children. I'd tell them how you'd rather sell your body than your soul. I'd tell them about a strongbox buried in a hearth that could have given you a life most people only dream about."

Tears filled her eyes. "I don't deserve this," she whispered hoarsely.

Wrapping his arms around her, he drew her against his chest. He felt her warm tears trickle down his chest. "I don't know anyone who is more deserving of a new start, Maddie."

They rode long after the sun set. Maddie thought Jesse intended for them to ride through the night, but without warning, he stopped and dismounted. He lifted her down from the mare and proceeded to set up a camp without a word. He unsaddled the horses and hobbled them, then built a fire.

Maddie sat on the blankets she'd spread before the fire and watched as Jesse stalked silently around the perimeter. Satisfied that all was secure, he returned to the fire and added some more dry wood. His gaze was focused on the writhing flames. She wondered if his thoughts burned as steadily as the fire, if he was beginning to regret the lie he'd delivered with such ease to a fellow Ranger. She would harbor no ill feelings, would understand completely if he took her back to Austin at first light.

He stirred the fire, and when he spoke, his voice blended in with the roar of the fire's blaze. "I want tonight, Maddie." He twisted his body away from the fire until his attention was focused entirely on her. "Tell me you don't love me, and I'll sleep on the other side of the fire. Otherwise, I intend to take tonight."

Tears brimmed within her eyes. "I care for Charles," she whispered hoarsely. "I don't want to hurt him."

In silence, he moved lithely across the narrow space separating them and sat beside her. He cradled her cheek as his thumb caressed her soft skin. "I won't take anything that belongs solely to Charles, but I'll push his ownership to the edge."

She lowered her gaze. "Please don't ask this of me."

"I'm not asking you to dishonor your vows. I'm only asking that you give me something to carry away with me when we leave here tomorrow." He leaned close until she felt his breath fan her cheek. "Tell me you don't love me."

A sob escaped her clogged throat. He tilted her face, his thumbs gently wiping the tears trailing her cheeks. "I love you, Whiskey."

Another sob sounded, and the tears increased. If he hadn't said the words, she thought she could have overlooked the tender expression in his eyes.

"You're my brother's wife. I carry that thought with me every minute of every day, every second of every night. My dearest wish is that Charles will live long enough to hold his first grandchild, but that means I'll be an old man before I ever have another opportunity to hold you in my arms throughout the night."

Laying her face against his chest, she listened to the steady rhythm of his heart. She inhaled the lingering scent of his bath, mingled with the sweat of travel. "You can't wait for what may never be."

"How can I not?" he asked, feeling the warmth of her tears soak through the cloth of his shirt. "You touch me in ways I didn't even know I could be touched." He wrapped his large hand around her smaller one. "I'm not talking about this kind of touching, though God knows I think about it often enough." Gently, he placed a finger beneath her chin and tilted her gaze up to meet his. "I'm talking about the way I feel when I watch you with the children." He pressed her palm flat against his chest. "I'm talking about what I feel deep in here when you smile, the terror that rips through me when I see fear in your eyes, the joy that explodes within me when I hear you laugh. Do you feel any of that for me?"

She felt all of it and more, but she couldn't give him hope where there was none. As he tentatively touched his lips to hers, she forced her mouth to remain immobile, to ignore the warmth of his mouth, the lure of his touch.

"Dammit, Maddie," he rasped. "Either tell me you don't love me or show me that you do."

No anger marred his voice, only an anguished pain. A fleeting moment was all he asked for, was all she could give him. She could not deny his heart, nor could she deny her own.

When he again lowered his mouth to hers, she welcomed his kiss with the certain knowledge that true love brings. Groaning at her response, he swept his tongue inside her mouth, stealing the treasures she offered. Her fingers clutched his shirt, and he pressed her closer, relishing the feel of her within his arms.

Tonight. They would have tonight, and he intended to make sure it was enough to get him through all the nights that lay ahead when he wouldn't have her in his arms. He lifted his mouth from hers and gazed into her eyes. He saw doubt flicker briefly within the passionate depths.

"I swear, Maddie, when I take you home to Charles tomorrow, we'll both be able to look him in the eye and feel no guilt. Trust me."

She gave him an impish smile. "It's not you I'm worried about trusting, you bleedin' idiot."

Smiling, he pulled her close. "God, I love you. There's a little river just beyond those trees. Swim with me." Not waiting for her answer, he wrapped his hand around hers, pulled her up, and walked toward the river.

The full moon reflected off the dark waters as they meandered downstream. Somewhere a fish splashed, a frog croaked, and crickets chirped.

"I'll get undressed over there and meet you in the water," Jesse said.

Maddie watched as he became one with the shadows. Slowly she unbuttoned her shirt. She removed her boots and socks and set them beside a boulder. Then she took off her shirt and her riding skirt. Standing in her linen chemise and drawers, she listened for the sound of Jesse getting into the water.

He emerged from the shadows in all his naked splendor, sleek and powerful with the moonlight dancing around him.

She thought she'd never seen anything as beautiful. She touched her trembling fingers to his chest. "You're not in the water," she whispered.

"I always wondered what your hair would look like if I gave it its freedom. That night by the creek, I was disappointed that I didn't get a good look at it." He took her braid and slowly unraveled the strands. A smile of appreciation graced his face as he poured her hair over his hands. He began to untie the ribbons on her chemise.

She closed her hands over his. "We shouldn't."

"Maddie, you may be an old woman before I ever make love to you. At least let me have the memory of your body when you were young."

She rubbed her hands over the backs of his hands, along his wrists, and up his forearms before dropping her hands to her sides. His hands worked the ribbons loose, then freed the buttons. He ran his finger along the lace at the top of the chemise until his hand curved over her shoulder. He slid the linen down her arm.

She felt the cool night air whisper along her flesh, but it was his warm touch as he palmed her breast that sent the shiver of delight coursing through her body.

He lowered his mouth, tasting her flesh. Moaning softly, Maddie threaded her fingers through the thick strands of his hair. His tongue swirled over her nipple, and she felt her knees weaken. He braced his large, strong hands against the small of her back to support her. His face gently nudged aside the linen that covered her other breast so his mouth could give it the same tender ministrations. He trailed his mouth to the valley between her breasts, then slowly followed the slope of her throat, marking his trail with tiny love bites. He melded his mouth over hers and slowly sipped of the nectar within. He had no need to rush; she was his for the night, but he knew it wouldn't be enough. A lifetime with her wouldn't be enough. He removed the rest of her clothing before lifting her into his arms. "I'm not in the mood to swim."

Wrapping her arms around his neck, she buried her face in his shoulder as he walked into camp. Carefully, he laid her on the blanket and stretched out beside her.

Resting up on an elbow, he ran his hand from her shoulder to her wrist and entwined his fingers with hers. He brought her wrist to his lips and placed a tender kiss on the flesh Silas had bruised. "When I saw him on top of you, I wanted to kill him," he said in a rough voice. "I never had to work so hard in my life not to kill a man."

She laid her fingers against his taut jaw. "It's over now, remember?" she asked softly.

His gaze traveled up to her discolored cheek, and he touched the back of his hand to her face. "I wish my hands weren't so rough. You've had enough rough hands touch you."

She pressed her palm against his. "I like the feel of your hands."

His eyes darkened. "Do you?"

Smiling warmly, she nodded. "That night you taught me to waltz, I only complained about the roughness in your hands so you wouldn't know how much I liked it when you touched me."

He glided his hand along the length of her body. "You're so beautiful," he whispered. "When you're an old woman, and I make love to you, this is the way I'll see you."

Maddie watched the golden flames from the fire throw their light against his sculptured form. Following his example, she ran her hand over the hard lines and planes that comprised this man. "I'll be wrinkled and look like the widow Parker. You'll wish you hadn't wasted your youth, that you hadn't waited."

"My eyes will see you as you truly are." He took her hand and pressed her palm against his beating heart. "But here, I'll always see you as you are tonight."

His arms went around her, pulling her body close. She fit perfectly, soft where he was hard, curved where he was straight, narrow where he was broad, smooth where he was rough. Before dawn eased over the horizon, he intended to memorize everything about her. He combed his fingers through her long, honey strands, so silky. He inhaled deeply of forget-me-nots.

They lay for the longest time, making no sound, few movements, just memorizing the feel of each other.

He placed his finger beneath her chin, bringing her face up until her eyes locked onto his. "There are so many things I want to say to you, things I want to hear you say to me, so many ways I want to touch you. Damn me for loving my brother so much." He tenderly brushed his lips across hers. Then his tongue teased the outer edges of her mouth.

Maddie parted her lips slightly. The tip of her tongue touched his and issued an invitation he couldn't ignore. Their lips, their tongues, their mouths became as one, slowly searching like a child who has been given a poem to memorize and learns it line by line, adding one line to the next, until the poem in his mind is complete. So each leisurely explored the mouth of the other. Their bodies sought to create their own refrain, pressing closely, memorizing the lines, the curves, the textures. Their hands patiently explored what wasn't forbidden, by unspoken agreement, maintaining a propriety that only their hearts could understand.

In time, he lifted his mouth from hers, gazing into the whiskey of her eyes, drinking his fill. "I've always wondered what it would feel like to hold you while you sleep."

Lethargically, she shook her head. "I don't want to waste any of tonight sleeping."

But eventually, as Jesse knew it would, the exhaustion of the past few days caught up with her, and she closed her eyes. He felt her body relax within his arms. He brought the blankets over them and curled around her. Listening to the night, he memorized the feel of her in his arms.

Opening her eyes to the early morning darkness, Maddie drew the blankets more closely around her. Her clothes were folded neatly upon the blankets. Hunkered before the fire, Jesse slowly brought a cup of coffee away from his lips.

Clutching the covers against her chest, she sat up, and he offered her the cup. With trembling fingers, she brought the cup to her lips and took a small sip, her eyes never leaving his. She handed the cup to him, and he tossed it aside.

"Oh, hell," he rasped, taking her in his arms. "The sun's not up yet."

Then he kissed her, a soul-searching, heart-searing kiss, filled with beauty and agony, for one more moment shared, one more farewell to endure. With a whimper, she fell against him and his arms tightened around her, his mouth as desperate as hers to take its fill, to steal the wondrous sensations and hoard them away for the long, lonely nights to come when memories alone would share his bed.

He pressed her face into the nook of his shoulder, took great gulping breaths, and waited for his breathing and his heartbeat to return to normal. He combed his fingers through her hair one last time, inhaled her scent, and touched the softness of her cheek. "In the days and nights to come, Maddie, remember that nothing you give to Charles takes anything away from me."

She nodded, unable to speak for the tears clogging her throat. She felt his withdrawal begin deep within his chest, long before his arms ever released their hold on her.

"You'd best get dressed now so I can get you home."

She watched him douse the fire, cover it with dirt, and pack their few belongings. Not until he left to ready the horses did she begin to dress.

The early morning mist had melted away by the time the inn came into sight. Maddie heard Aaron's voice heralding their arrival.

Jesse dismounted and came around to lift her down. For one brief moment, they were hidden from view, their eyes daring to say what their voices could not. "What I feel for you will never fade, Maddie. Remember that." Briefly, his hands tightened their hold on her small waist. "Now, go on."

He released her and studied the saddle as though he'd never before seen one. She slipped away from him, and he wrapped his hand around the saddle horn to stop himself from pulling her back. Letting her walk into the arms of another man was the hardest thing he'd ever done in his life.

Her steps quick, her heart straining to return for one more moment to a place of solace within Jesse's embrace, she forced a smile that rapidly changed to a genuine expression of her feelings as she saw the girls running toward her.

"Ma! Ma!"

She dropped to her knees taking both girls in her arms and hugging them tightly. With tears in her eyes, she looked up, surprised to see the hard glare in Aaron's eyes.

"Did those men do that?" he asked, pointing at her cheek.

She nodded.

"Uncle Jesse, did you give 'em what for?" he asked, his stance warning his uncle that he'd better have come to his mother's defense.

Jesse took the reins of both horses. "I gave out a couple of black eyes and a busted nose."

Aaron nodded in approval. When Maddie stood, he flung his arms around her. She held him tightly, looking over the top of his head at Charles. Charles looked worn, his eyes tired. Releasing Aaron, she gazed at the children and touched the splotches of whitewash that decorated their faces and clothes. "What's this?"

"Pa said you always wanted a white fence around your house so we're building you one," Aaron explained.

With tears brimming in her eyes, she turned to her husband. He gave her a soft smile before he embraced her.

"I'm so sorry," she whispered.

"Shh. You're home now. That's all that matters."

She felt the small tugs on her riding skirt and looked down at the beaming faces.

"Wanna see the fence?" Hannah asked.

She nodded and followed the children.

Charles ambled over to where Jesse stood silently holding the horses. "Not much of a hero's welcome for you."

Jesse shrugged. "Wasn't expecting one."

"The men that took her—"

"Are in jail right now. Imagine they'll eventually hang for the murders they committed. They won't be giving Maddie any more trouble."

"What about her own past?"

"Took care of it."

Charles released a sigh of relief. "I owe you more than I can ever pay."

"You don't owe me anything." He nodded toward the children. "So you're building her a fence?"

"Yep. It was something she told me she always wanted."

"How'd you know I'd bring her back?"

Charles smiled. "I just knew. Guess you'll be leaving again soon."

Jesse shook his head. "The bounties on those two men were generous." He smiled. "I've got more than enough to get my cattle here."

❧ 18 ❧

The pounding on the bedroom doors began at one end of the hall and traveled down to the other.

"Come on!" Jesse shouted. "Everyone get out of bed! It's a day for dreams."

Bleary eyed, Aaron staggered into the hall. Jesse turned him around and pushed him back into his room. "You've got to put clothes on, boy."

The door to the girls' room opened. Maddie stepped out, both girls in tow, dressed in their coveralls. He'd known she'd be awake. She smiled at him and released her hold on the girls. He hoisted both of them into his arms.

"Want to see what a dream looks like when it comes true?" he asked.

The girls nodded vigorously. He hugged them tighter and watched as Maddie disappeared into her own room. The love he'd felt for her before did not compare with the love growing inside him with each passing day. It was ludicrous, downright insane for a man to fall more deeply in love with a woman because of the love she showered on his brother, but Jesse was doing just that.

She was filling Charles's remaining days with laughter, smiles, and a radiant warmth. Jesse was drawing so many baths and spending so many nights standing by the creek that he lost count.

Drawing her shawl around her shoulders, Maddie walked out of the bedroom. "Come on, Charles. It's Jesse's day."

Jesse wanted to tell her that it was their day. Then her

gaze met his, and he realized he didn't need to tell her anything. She knew.

Charles came out of the room, slipping his suspenders over his shoulders. "Here, I'll take Taylor. Come on, Aaron."

"Coming!" He hopped on one foot into the hallway as he tugged a boot onto his other foot. Then he dropped his foot and started running down the stairs. "Come on!" he hollered.

They scrambled down the stairs and walked through the house into the gray darkness. Jesse took the lead with Hannah clinging to his neck. Aaron struggled to match him step for step as Ranger followed close on his heels. With her hand wrapped around his arm, Maddie walked beside Charles as he carried Taylor.

The early morning mist coated the ground, muffling their passage. Jesse stopped and dropped to his haunches. He shifted Hannah onto one thigh while Aaron pressed against his side. Maddie knelt beside him. Charles hunkered down beside her and put his arm around her waist.

And they waited.

In the darkness, with the cool morning air circling about them, they were little more than shadows crouched at the edge of the woods.

From the corner of her eye, Maddie watched Jesse. For the remainder of his life, he would never have a day like this one. She wanted to be in his arms, sharing this moment with him, knew that had he asked, she would have come here with him alone. But he hadn't asked. So great was his love for his brother that he would deny his own heart the things that it wanted, sharing his dreams with another man's children instead of his own.

Charles removed his hand from Maddie's waist. "Taylor, this is your Uncle Jesse's day. Why don't you sit with him?" He lifted the child off his knee, and she scrambled over Maddie to reach Jesse. He pulled her onto his lap.

The sun eased over the horizon, blanketing the earth in sunshine. In the distance, they heard a deep bawl, followed by the shouts of men, the clomping of hooves. Then slowly, the green valley took on a new appearance, the appearance of a dream fulfilled, as the herd of cattle with long horns wandered in.

"I see 'em!" Aaron shouted.

Jesse threw his arm around the boy, pulled him close, and hugged him. The girls jumped off Jesse's thighs. Hannah grabbed Taylor's hands and swung her in a circle until they giggled so hard they tumbled to the ground.

Charles stood and helped Maddie to her feet. She glanced over at Jesse. A beautiful smile graced his face.

"I think Pa would have been proud," Charles said.

Jesse unfolded his body and looked out on the land, the cattle, the family surrounding him. "He would have been very proud."

Maddie held her hands out to the girls. "Come on, girls. We need to see about fixing breakfast." She glanced at Jesse. "Only I don't guess you'll need coffee to stay in a good mood today."

"No, ma'am. Nothing could put me in a bad mood today."

Charles slipped his arm around Maddie. The family walked away, carrying the memory of the dream's arrival with them.

"You're gonna teach me to be a cowboy instead of an innkeeper, right, Uncle Jesse?"

Jesse ruffled the boy's hair as they trudged toward the house. "Right."

"How long are the men that brought the cattle going to stay?" Charles asked.

"Long as I need them. I need to give some thought to building some sort of shelter. Can't ask them to sleep outside every night."

In the distance, a horn blast signaled the unexpected arrival of a stage.

Jesse looked across at Charles. "I'm not in the mood to work today. What say we change out their horses, shove some food into their hands, and send them on their way?"

"Sounds like a good idea to me."

They quickened their pace and arrived at the front of the inn just as the stagecoach rolled to a stop.

Jesse opened the door and froze as Paul Somner stepped to the ground.

"Good God, man, you look as though you've seen a ghost," Somner said, "but then considering the telegram you sent to my superiors, I guess you do think you're looking at a ghost."

"What the hell are you doing here?" Jesse snarled.

"Now is that any way to welcome a guest?"

A short distance away, Maddie moved in closer against Charles's side. He tightened his comforting hold on her as he whispered in her ear, "Don't worry. Jesse will take care of it."

"Paul!" A feminine voice floated out of the coach. "Paul, will you please help me out of here. It's stifling hot."

"Certainly, love." Paul extended a hand into the coach and helped a young woman step down. She was tiny, small boned, her brown hair swept up beneath a fashionable hat, her face partially hidden by a black blindfold.

"I shall kill you if I discover I am in the middle of a busy town and people are gawking at me."

"Listen. Does it sound as though we're in a busy town?"

She tilted her head. "No." She sniffed. "It doesn't smell like a town either. It smells like . . . the country."

"Very good."

"Now, will you tell me why you blindfolded me?"

Leaning close, he spoke quietly. "Because, my love, your wedding gift is here, but you must find it." With a flourish, he removed the blindfold.

She glanced quickly at the people standing before her. Then her eyes fell on the house, and she gasped. "Oh, Paul. You've quit your job with the Agency. You've bought me a house, and we're going to settle here."

Slowly, he shook his head. "I'm afraid you're stuck living in Washington, at least for a while. This is the inn where we're going to spend a few days resting."

She jutted out her chin, flung her hands to her hips, and stomped her small foot. "Then give me a hint—a good hint—or I shall ask for separate bedrooms," she threatened with a teasing glint in her eyes.

Lovingly, he traced his fingers along her cheek. "It's someone you've been looking for since you were six years old."

She spun around and looked at Jesse intently. "Oh, my God!" Her hands flew to her mouth as her eyes flooded with tears. "No one had eyes as black as Jesse's."

Jesse looked at the small woman falling apart before him. Her brown eyes and brown hair were so reminiscent of his mother's. His eyes darted over to Paul Somner.

Smiling smugly, the man was leaning against the side of the coach. "Surprise!"

Jesse's gaze flew back to the woman with the tears streaming down her face.

"Jesse?"

He could do no more than nod. Then her arms were around his neck, his arms were around her waist. He lifted her off the ground and hugged her tightly against him. "Cassie?" he asked hoarsely. She bobbed her head vigorously, and he pressed his sister closer.

Charles released Maddie and walked toward his brother. Jesse turned to Charles and gently set Cassie back on the ground.

As she studied Charles, she again covered her mouth. "Oh, Paul! You found them both!" She flew into Charles's arms and nearly knocked him over. He hugged her tightly.

When she released him, she studied the children. "And whose children are these? No, no, don't tell me. They have to be yours, Charles." She knelt in front of Aaron and brushed the hair from his brow. "He looks just like Charles did the last time I saw him. Doesn't he, Jesse?"

"Yes, he does. This is Aaron." He dropped beside the boy. "This is your Aunt Cassie."

"She looks a lot like Pa, don't you think?"

"She and your Pa took after your grandmother."

"And you look like Grandpa."

Jesse nodded.

"Does that mean I have to hug her?"

"Reckon it does."

Aaron nodded acceptance of his sentence and slung his arms around the woman's neck. He knew the hugging sort of woman when he saw her, and he knew it was best just to get the hugging over with.

"And who are these angels?" Cassie asked.

"Hannah and Taylor," Jesse said.

They needed no prompting to hug their aunt. Holding them close, Cassie relished the feel of the little girls. When she released them, Paul helped her to her feet.

Charles brought Maddie forward into the crowd. "This is my wife, Maddie."

Maddie smiled hesitantly at Paul, then at Cassie. Cassie felt no uncertainty. She hugged Maddie as though she'd known her all her life.

"We were just getting ready to have breakfast," Maddie said. "Would you like to join us?"

Cassie slipped her arm through Maddie's. "That would be wonderful. And I want to see the house and hear all about how you met Charles. We have so much to catch up on, years and years."

"When smallpox struck the community, Mr. and Mrs. Lawrence decided to leave. I'm not certain where we were to go, but Mr. Lawrence passed away on the journey. Mrs. Lawrence returned to her family in Virginia.

"Then last year, when she died, I discovered she'd left everything to me. At first, I didn't know what to do with all that money. I thought about trying to find you myself, but it seemed an impossible task, so I went to the Pinkerton Agency in Washington. And they assigned Paul to my case." She smiled warmly at her husband.

"He is an extremely skilled investigator. After our first meeting, I realized I didn't remember enough about my childhood to really aid him in his search. He suggested we go out to dinner where we could discuss things in a more casual atmosphere. He thought that approach might unleash memories."

"And did it?" Jesse asked, his voice taut.

"Well, yes, as a matter of fact, it did. I remembered so many small tidbits that we went to dinner more often. Then Paul asked me if I had any gentlemen callers. He felt there might be something about them that reminded me of my brothers, so he interviewed them." She furrowed her brows and glanced at her husband. "Funny, though, none of them ever called upon me again after that." She squeezed his hand. "Not that it matters now. And of course, he found you."

"And this was quite a sizable inheritance?" Jesse asked, tapping his fingers on the arm of the chair, his gaze riveted on Paul.

"Yes, it was," Cassie answered.

Jesse leaned forward. "And Somner just decided to marry you without obtaining permission from your brothers first?"

"Well, we couldn't very well have traveled across the country together if we weren't married."

"He could have asked permission when he was here before."

"And ruin my surprise?" Paul interjected.

"I want to know why you married her."

"I'd think my reasons were obvious."

"Why don't you enlighten me?"

Paul leaned forward until his gaze was even with Jesse's. "I love her."

"Whatever is going on between you two?"

"Jesse's just playing the older brother," Charles informed her. "After all these years, Cassie, you're going to have to get used to it."

"I need some fresh air," Paul said before standing and walking out of the room.

On the back porch, he puffed on his cheroot. Cassie wasn't too fond of his smoking, and he supposed he needed to consider giving up the cigars. On the other hand, what woman wanted to be married to a man who was perfect? "Still spying on me, Jesse?"

Jesse stepped onto the porch. "I don't recall giving you permission to address me as anything other than Mr. Lawson."

Paul clicked his teeth. "You are an ornery old cuss, aren't you? Can't imagine why Cassie was so anxious to find you."

"Well, I can't imagine why she'd marry you."

Paul glanced at him sideways. "Can't you? Somewhere beneath your gruff exterior I believe there beats the heart of a man who knows what it is to look across the room at a woman and know he'd never let anyone or anything harm her. Cassie's safe with me, just as Maddie's safe with you."

Jesse heaved a sigh. "How long am I going to have to suffer your annoying presence?"

"I've been wondering that myself. Charles seems to have aged considerably since I was last here. I had planned to stay only a few days. Then I was going to take Cassie to Galveston, but I was thinking it might mean more to her in later years if we stayed on here a bit longer." He quirked a questioning brow.

Jesse nodded. "She might prefer to stay here a bit longer."

"In that case, why don't you tell me what I can do around here to help lift some of the burden from your shoulders?"

As Jesse hefted the board, he admitted to himself what he wouldn't admit to anyone else. He felt a certain degree of admiration for Somner. In the past week, the man had undertaken with tenacity every chore Jesse had suggested. It was a bit disconcerting to realize that they had more things in common than not.

Paul pounded the nail into the board. He felt a certain measure of pride in his accomplishments this week. He'd managed to keep pace with Jesse, a feat he thought few men were able to do. He straightened his back, removed his hat, and allowed the breeze to ruffle his hair. He glanced over his shoulder. "What's that sound?"

Jesse dropped his hammer into the bucket, jerked the shirts off the post, and tossed one to Paul. "The reason this fence will never get finished." He stepped over an incomplete portion of the fence. "Come on."

Rushing to catch up with Jesse's long strides, Paul followed him into the woods. He heard the laughter and a distant splash. Then they walked into a small clearing.

"Paul!" Cassie shouted. She released the rope and waved just before she plunged into the water.

"Good Lord, what's she wearing?" Paul asked.

"The latest in fashionable creek side wear," Jesse answered.

Aaron rushed over. "Uncle Paul, let me show you the mud slide."

Paul followed the boy to the muddy slope. "You say this is a—" His final words were but a yell as Aaron slammed his shoulder against his uncle's thigh. Paul slid down the muddy embankment and hit the water. He looked up and saw Jesse proudly patting Aaron's shoulder.

Jesse looked at the man sprawled in the water. "Surprise!" Then he threw his head back and laughed, a deep rumble that sent the birds fluttering from the trees. Paul returned his laughter.

Jesse turned his attention to his brother. Charles was stretched out on the ground, his head resting on Maddie's lap as she continually ran her fingers through his hair. He walked across the clearing and hunkered before them. "He asleep?"

"No, I'm not asleep," Charles said, opening one eye. "Not with all the hollering and commotion going on."

Jesse glanced off in the distance, at the thick cloud formations coating the sky. "Looks like cooler weather heading in."

"That's why I decided to spend today at the creek," Maddie said. "Cassie never swam in a creek before."

Jesse smiled broadly. "Judging from the expression on Paul's face when he hit the water, he hasn't, either."

"I think you like him," Charles said.

Jesse looked at the couple splashing the girls at the water's edge, allowing them to splash back, feigning direct hits. "I guess Cassie could have done worse," he said grudgingly.

Charles sat up and rubbed his left arm, trying to get the feeling to return to it as he leaned against the tree. "I think you're just upset because he bested you. You thought he was searching for Maddie when he was really searching for you."

"He could at least have had the decency to explain the situation to me when I confronted him."

"When did you confront him?" Charles asked.

Jesse started pulling up weeds. "When he was here before."

"Exactly what did you say to him?"

"I don't remember exactly. I may have threatened to kill him."

"What?" Maddie and Charles exclaimed in unison.

He shrugged. "Only if he made Maddie unhappy. Now, I'll just kill him if he makes Cassie unhappy."

"I don't think he's in any danger then," Maddie said.

He smiled. "No, I don't reckon he is."

Shivering, Taylor walked over, dropped onto Jesse's lap, and pressed her wet back against his chest. Maddie handed him a towel. He draped it over Taylor and rubbed briskly.

Cassie soon joined them and wrapped a blanket around her drenched body. "That was invigorating." She glanced around her. "This is wonderful. It's so strange, and I don't know how to explain it, but I don't feel as though we were ever really separated."

"I know what you mean," Charles said. "I felt the same way when Jesse showed up on my doorstep."

"I guess that's what it means to be a family," Cassie said softly, "to know that years and miles can never really separate you. Do you know where Mother and Father are buried?"

"Not really," Jesse said. "There were a lot of graves over the prairie."

Disappointment wove itself through Cassie's features. "I had hoped to erect a monument over their resting place, but I shall have to be content with naming the endowment fund after them."

"What endowment fund?" Jesse asked.

Cassie laughed self-consciously. "My inheritance. We put it in a trust and find worthy causes to dole it out to."

"You're not living off it?" Jesse asked.

"My word, no. It was a mere pittance next to Paul's inheritance when his parents died. We didn't need it, so rather than have it get lost among his wealth, he suggested I put it in a trust and use it for charitable works."

Jesse's eyes narrowed. "He's got a lot of money?"

"Oh, my goodness, yes."

"And he just neglected to mention this little fact about himself the other day when I accused him of marrying you for your inheritance."

"He's really quite modest and I'm sure—"

"He wanted it to be a surprise," Jesse growled.

Cassie smiled. "Well, he does enjoy his surprises."

❧ 19 ❧

The cool autumn breeze ruffled Aaron's hair as he sat on the upper veranda with his father. If Billy saw him, Billy'd call him a sissy for sitting on his father's lap, but Aaron didn't care. He knew secrets, secrets his father told him when they watched the sun fall beyond the horizon. Secrets that made him hug his father a little tighter at night. Secrets that made him glad he could sit on his father's lap in the evening when no one was looking.

"Wish it was spring," he said wistfully.

"Why's that?" Charles asked.

"So we could make a kite and fly it."

"Why do we have to wait for spring?"

"Never seen no one fly a kite in the fall," Aaron answered.

"Then we'd be the first, wouldn't we?"

Aaron shifted around until he could face his father. "You reckon it'd be all right?"

"I don't see why not. I'd like to fly a kite, too."

Aaron bounded off his father's lap. "Should we keep this a secret, too?"

"No, let's share it with the others. See if they want to join us."

"I bet they will!" Aaron called out as he raced across the veranda and rushed through the door.

Charles took one last look at the sunset before following his son inside.

Aaron tromped down the stairs, two at a time, and skidded into the parlor. Jesse and Paul looked up from the checkerboard. Maddie stopped embroidering the eye on Taylor's doll. Cassie, Hannah, and Taylor set down their teacups.

"Me and Pa are going to make a kite tonight! Fly it tomorrow," Aaron announced, the excitement clearly visible in his face.

"Where are you going to fly it?" Jesse asked.

"In the meadow. You'll have to move your cows to one end."

Jesse arched a brow. "Oh, I will, will I?"

"Yes, sir, if you don't mind."

Jesse glanced at his brother as Charles sat beside Maddie on the sofa and took her hand. "You're going to fly a kite tomorrow?" Jesse asked.

"If we have a breeze like the one we had today. Aaron doesn't want to wait until spring. Neither do I."

"Well, then, just let me claim my victory here, and we'll make one."

"Why make only one?" Paul asked. "We've got three children here. Seems like we ought to make three."

"We?" Jesse snorted. "What's a city boy know about making kites?"

Paul smiled. "I'll have you know I can make a kite that would make Benjamin Franklin jealous."

"Oh, really?" Jesse goaded.

"Really."

"What is it with you two?" Cassie asked. "Why do you have to compete on everything?"

"Madam, we haven't even begun to compete." Jesse leaned back in his chair, his eyes on Paul. "Pick your partner."

Paul glanced around the room. "Who wants to help me make the best kite that ever graced the skies?"

Hannah waved her hand. "I'll help you, Uncle Paul."

"How about you, Taylor? You want to help me?" Jesse asked.

Taylor bobbed her head.

"All right," Jesse said, glancing over at his opponent.

"Why don't you concede, and we'll work on kites?"

Paul shook his head. "I'm not conceding. This game is mine."

Jesse slapped his hand on the table. "I'm feeling magnanimous tonight. I'll concede."

"Oh, no, you're just trying to deny me a victory."

"Paul! If he concedes, you've won," Cassie said.

"No, I haven't. I won't win unless I beat him, and he knows it."

Jesse smiled. "Will you settle for a draw?"

Lifting his hands off the table, Paul returned the smile. "Might as well. It's the closest I'll come to an honest victory—until tomorrow anyway."

They scraped their chairs across the floor in unison, and the girls ran to their sides. Jesse hoisted Taylor into his arms. "Let's go see what we can find to make a kite."

As everyone else walked out of the room, Charles squeezed Maddie's hand. "You want to help?"

"No, I have something else in mind for my contribution to this evening. You and Aaron get started, and I'll surprise you with it."

"All right." Standing, he wavered, leaned over, and rested his hand on the back of the sofa.

Maddie placed her palm flat on his back. "Are you all right?"

"Yeah, just dizzy for a minute."

She slipped her arm through his. "My surprise will take place in the kitchen. Why don't you walk me as far as the dining room?"

Shifting his weight, he leaned against her. "A real gentleman would walk you all the way to the kitchen."

"Not when he has something as important as a kite to make."

By the time they made their way to the dining room, the large oak table was covered with kite makings: thin sticks, twigs, newsprint, string. Aaron was busily mixing flour and water to make a paste for holding his kite together. He lifted the spoon. Not content with the consistency of the white matter, he added more water and stirred again.

Maddie pulled out a chair. "You sit here, and I'll get started on my surprise." As Charles sat, she glanced across the table to Jesse, his eyes discerning as always, studying Charles. He lifted his gaze to her. "I have some scraps of calico you can use for the tails on your kites," she said.

She walked into the kitchen and pressed her hands against the table, bowing her head, fighting back her tears, knowing she couldn't release them until after everyone had gone to bed. She forced herself to listen to the laughter coming from the other room, the innocent laughter of children mingled with the knowing laughter of adults. She heard the lighthearted banter, the feigned arguments, the excited voices of the children. Then she heard the deep voice she needed to hear.

"Where did you say the calico was?"

Turning, she walked straight into Jesse's strong embrace. He did nothing more than hold her, but it was enough. Taking a deep breath, she stepped back and smiled. "The scraps are in my sewing basket in the parlor."

He touched his knuckle to her cheek, mouthed the words "Love you," and quietly left the room, leaving his love and strength behind. She wrapped her heart around his gifts, took a pot off the wall, shoved wood into the stove, and began working.

Some time later, she walked back into the dining room and set a plate beside Charles.

"Pa, you gotta tie the string tighter or the sticks won't stay together," Aaron said.

Taking hold of his left hand and moving it to his lap, Charles glanced at Maddie. "My fingers don't seem to want to work."

She forced a brave smile for him and for the children who were staring at him. "I have a hard time dealing with string myself, but I'll help Aaron if you'll taste the fudge and let me know if it's worth sharing. Open your mouth." She popped a piece of fudge into his mouth.

He closed his eyes and smiled. "Yep, it's worth sharing."

"Then pass it down here," Jesse said.

Maddie moved the plate to the middle of the table, then began helping Aaron with his kite. Charles reached across the table for another piece. "Can't remember the last time I had fudge," he said.

"Know why I made fudge?" she asked.

"No."

She smiled. "Because the first time I looked into your eyes, I thought of the fudge my mother used to make at Christmas."

Charles leaned back. "That's interesting. My eyes reminded you of fudge. Your eyes remind Jesse of whiskey. What do Jesse's eyes remind you of?"

She glanced down the table, gazing into black eyes.

"Coffee!" Hannah cried, her hand covering her broad smile. "Cuz Uncle Jesse drinks so much coffee, it fills up his belly and goes to his eyes."

"And what do your eyes remind me of?" Jesse asked, his own eyes narrowing.

Hannah leaned over the table until the tip of her nose was almost touching Jesse's nose, and her eyes were big and round.

"Chocolate cake," Jesse said as he grabbed her and tickled her tummy. "It's cuz you eat so much chocolate cake it fills up your belly and goes to your eyes!"

Squealing, Hannah collapsed on the table.

"Get your hands off my partner," Paul said as he worked his hands around Jesse's and tickled Hannah. She screeched as both her uncles continued their assault.

"What are you laughing at, Aaron?" Cassie asked. Together, she and Maddie pulled Aaron out of the chair. He writhed on the floor as they tickled him.

Taylor climbed down from her chair and crawled into Charles's lap. "Fud," she whispered. Charles pulled the plate nearer. Together, they watched the commotion taking place around them as they plucked piece after piece of fudge off the plate.

Jesse stopped tickling Hannah and glanced at the far end of the table. "Hey, what happened to the fudge?"

Paul stopped tickling Hannah, Maddie and Cassie stopped

tickling Aaron, and everyone became very quiet. Jesse stalked over to Taylor. She squeezed her eyes shut tight.

"What color are your eyes, Taylor?" Jesse asked.

She shook her head vigorously.

"They wouldn't remind me of fudge, would they?"

She screamed when he picked her up and set her on the table. "No, I guess they wouldn't, but your pa's would!"

Charles didn't know how it happened, but he suddenly found himself under attack. He tried to escape Jesse's wiggling fingers and instead found himself sliding to the floor, his laughter echoing around him. "Good Lord! Jesse, stop!"

"You ate all the fudge!"

"Taylor did! I didn't!"

"No!" Taylor cried as she crawled across the table to the far end.

Aaron jumped to his feet and started tickling his father. When Hannah soon joined him, Jesse eased back. Paul set Taylor on the floor. "Go tickle your pa," he said, and she ran to the writhing man, her tiny fingers working to increase his laughter.

Charles laughed and rolled from side to side until he was out of breath. Watching him closely, Jesse lifted Aaron and Hannah away. "That's enough now." Taylor rested her head on Charles's chest.

"But what about the fudge?" Aaron asked.

"Maddie'll just have to make some more," Jesse said. "If we don't get these kites finished, they aren't going to be ready to fly tomorrow."

Maddie knelt beside Charles. "Are you all right?"

"Yep, I needed that."

She helped him up, and everyone gathered around the table. Turning their attention to the kites, they no longer worked in teams, but worked as a family.

Maddie eased out of bed and padded over to the window. Glancing out, she saw Charles sitting in a rocking chair on the veranda. She retrieved her wrapper, thrust her arms into it, and joined him. "What are you doing out here?" she whispered, drawing her wrapper more tightly about her to ward away the predawn chill.

"Just wanted to watch the sunrise." He held his hand out to her.

She placed her hand in his, remembering a time when his had seemed so warm and strong. Now, it felt as though the first frost of autumn had settled over it. He gave a slight tug. "Come sit with me."

"Just a minute." She walked back into their room and returned, carrying the quilt from their bed. Easing onto his lap, she draped the blanket around them and snuggled in against him. Charles smiled. "We should have done this before now."

"It was never this cold in the morning before now."

"It'll be warm by noon, but do you feel the breeze? It's a good breeze for flying a kite."

Beneath the quilt, Maddie took his hands in hers and rubbed briskly, trying to restore some warmth to his fingers. "I thought I'd pack a picnic, and we'd just make a whole day of it."

Charles wrapped his fingers around hers, stilling her hands. "Maddie, I want you to know that if a man is allowed to take his memories with him, heaven will be that much sweeter for the gifts you've given me."

Tears brimming in her eyes, she looked upon his beloved face, wanting to deny the implication of his words, but knowing no good would come of it. Instead, she voiced the words she knew would bring him the most peace. "I'll take good care of your children and love them as though they were my own."

"I know you will. And you keep making Jesse's coffee strong and black as pitch. Seems to improve his mood."

Then, because she'd never done so before, she pressed her lips to his, kissing him sweetly. Cupping her cheek, tilting her face away from his, he gazed into her eyes, a smile gracing his face. "Maybe we should have done that before now, too."

Smiling softly, she lay her head in the crook of his shoulder. "Maybe so," she said quietly.

Wrapping his arm around her, he glanced toward the far horizon, past the tree-covered hills, clothed in their autumn colors. "Ah, Maddie, look. It's going to be a beautiful day."

She turned her head slightly, but the new dawn was little more than a haze of colors viewed through a rainbow of her tears.

"Let it go!" Charles called out as Aaron ran, his hand holding onto the kite, his arm extended toward the sky.

Aaron released the kite, and it caught the wind, soaring into the blue sky. Hannah released her kite and the wind carried it toward the clouds. Taylor clung to Jesse's neck as he ran with her. Then she opened her fingers, and the kite momentarily dipped down before fluttering upward. The children squealed, the adults clapped, and smiles filled every face in the meadow. The children ran back and claimed the sticks that anchored the string of the kites.

"Think it's touching heaven, Pa?" Aaron asked.

Charles hunkered down. "Yeah, I think it is."

"Think Ma can see it?"

"Yep."

"I'm going to fly a kite every fall, Pa. Will you look for it?"

With tears clogging his throat, Charles pulled Aaron close. "Yes, son, I'll look for it."

"Will you touch it?"

"Yes, I will, and your mother will touch it, too."

"I'll share the secrets with Hannah and Taylor when they get old enough."

"I love you," Charles whispered. Then he stood, and his step faltered.

Jesse glanced over at him. "You all right?"

He nodded. "Just tired." He walked over to Hannah and hugged her close. Then he knelt and hugged Taylor. After she turned her attention back to flying her kite, Charles continued to kneel, one hand pressed to the ground, bracing his arm to hold himself up.

Jesse hunkered down beside him. "Why don't we go sit under the tree for a while?"

Charles nodded. Jesse helped him to stand. Maddie moved in beside him. "Charles?"

He took her hand, wishing he had the strength to squeeze her hand in reassurance. "You stay with Taylor. She'll be upset if she loses her kite."

She had neither the courage nor the desire to smile, but placed a light kiss on his cheek before turning her attention back to Taylor.

Charles leaned into Jesse as they walked slowly toward the stand of trees. Jesse supported him as he eased to the ground beneath the cool shade of the oak tree. Charles leaned against the rough bark of the tree as Jesse sat beside him. "Maddie worked out, didn't she, Jesse?"

Jesse looked across the clearing at Maddie, catching her laughter as she helped Taylor guide her kite. "Yeah, she did."

With effort, Charles shifted his body, dug something from his pocket, and placed it in Jesse's hand. "Remember this?"

Jesse stared at the delicate circle of gold. "Mother's ring. How did you come to have it?"

"Remember that box of odds and ends I used to hoard under my pillow and would never share with you? Somehow it ended up in there. It never seemed right that I had it. I bought Alice and Maddie their own rings."

Jesse closed his fingers over the precious gift. His mother had often told him the ring bound her to the one she loved.

"Will you do me a favor?" Charles asked.

Jesse gazed upon his brother, his complexion sallow. "Anything."

"I want you to promise me that when the man who loves Maddie marries her, he'll place that ring on her finger."

Jesse turned his face away, tightening his fist until he felt the ring cut into his palm. Had he been so transparent these last months?

"Promise me."

Jesse gave a curt nod, his voice hoarse. "I promise."

Sighing in relief, Charles lay back against the tree. "That'll keep it in the family, won't it, Jesse?"

Jesse unfolded his hand. "Yeah."

Charles's eyes filled with regret. "I'm sorry, Jesse. I should have given her her freedom long ago . . . when I realized she was falling in love with you."

Jesse met his brother's gaze. "She never strayed from her vows, Charles. Nothing but words ever passed between us." He grimaced. "Well, maybe a kiss or two."

"I know, and it somehow makes what I did seem that much more selfish, but you see, I'm a coward. I was always afraid I'd die at night . . . and I didn't want to be alone. Hell of a thing to ask of a woman."

"She's your wife—"

"No, Jesse, she was never my wife. She's been a good mother to my children and a treasured friend to me, but never my wife." He rested his palm over his chest. "Within my heart, I've only ever had, only ever wanted one wife . . . and that was Alice. You have to understand how much I love Alice or you'll never understand what I'm going to tell you now."

"Kite, fly high!" Taylor cried, her hands balled into tight fists around the twig where the string was secured. Maddie pulled Taylor close against her and listened to the luting of the wind, a beautiful sound, almost like a love song gracing the heavens. A calmness wrapped around her, and she knew an inner peace unlike any she'd ever known.

In the distance, she heard the anguished sobs and looked toward the trees where Jesse had taken Charles. She felt her heart plummet at the sight of Jesse hovering over Charles.

"I'll watch Taylor," Paul said, placing his hand upon her shoulder.

Maddie turned to Paul. She saw in his face the painful truth her heart did not want to accept. Cassie was nestled up against his side. She watched Cassie's small shoulders shake as Paul's arm protectively shielded her grief from the children. She squeezed Cassie's hand. "Do you want to come with me?"

Turning her face from Paul's chest, Cassie shook her head and forced a trembling smile. "I prefer for my last memory to be of Charles flying a kite." She wiped the tears from her eyes. "Paul and I will keep the children occupied. You go to Jesse."

Grateful for their quiet strength and calm, Maddie nodded. Walking quickly toward the trees encased in the late afternoon shadows, the grief welling inside her, she gathered her own courage and strength. She knelt in the tall grass, knowing if she could have found the words to voice aloud, she would have said them, knowing some things in life were meant to be delivered in silence. She placed her hands on Jesse's trembling shoulders.

Gently, he lay Charles on the cool earth before wrapping his arms around Maddie and pressing his face against her breast. "We were talking. Then he pointed toward the trees and said he saw Alice, that she was as beautiful as she was the day he married her. I looked, but I didn't see anything." He lifted his head, his eyes searching hers for something he couldn't understand. "He was smiling, and there was so much gladness in his eyes, I can't even describe it. He reached out, curling his fingers as though he was taking somebody's hand." He choked back a sob. "Then he was gone."

Maddie drew him against her and felt his body wracked with the force of his grief.

"Damn, it hurts," he whispered hoarsely. "I wasn't ready for him to go."

"But he was." With tears flooding her eyes, she cradled his cheek with her palm. "He missed Alice so much, and now he's with her."

Nodding, Jesse moved away and roughly swiped the tears from his face. He brushed his wrist beneath his nose, sniffing and stifling any further tears. "Yeah, he was telling me just how much he loved her, how much he cared about you." He released a ragged sigh. "I need to get him to the house."

"I'll go with you."

He could do little more than nod. He lifted Charles into his arms, cradling him one last time.

The door squeaked as Maddie opened it and stepped out onto the porch. Aaron sat on the steps, his elbows digging into his thighs, his chin perched in his hands. Ranger lay at his feet as though he, too, mourned.

That afternoon Charles had been laid to rest beside his beloved Alice. Taylor was too young to understand. To Hannah, Charles had just gone on a trip to be with their mother. Aaron alone understood the finality. Maddie sat beside him.

"It's all right to cry, Aaron."

Aaron shook his head. "Uncle Jesse didn't cry."

"Yes, he did," she said softly. "And when he did, I put my arms around him like this." She put her arms around Aaron, pulling him against her breast. "And held him close."

The first sob was silent, no more than a shudder passing through the child's body. It was followed by a sob that sounded as though it had been torn from his heart. "I miss Pa," Aaron croaked, flinging his arms around Maddie.

Maddie allowed her own tears to wash down her face as she pressed her cheek to the top of Aaron's head. "We all do. He was very special and that's what we have to think about and remember: all of his smiles, the sound of his laughter. How much we loved him. How much he loved us."

Aaron moved away, swiping the tears from his face. "You gonna marry Uncle Jesse now? Pa said you would. Said I was to be understanding about it."

Maddie glanced away, guilt manifesting itself within her because Charles had seen through her, had known about the feelings she harbored for his brother.

"You love him, don't you?" Aaron asked.

She pulled him close, resting her chin on the top of his head. "It's too soon, Aaron. Our hearts still hurt."

❧ 20 ❧

Cassie walked out to the small cemetery. As he had so often in the passing days, Jesse stood before Charles's grave. She wrapped her hands around two slats of the fence.

"Paul and I have decided to go to Galveston for a couple of weeks," she said. "We thought we'd take the children with us. Give them a change of scenery, get to know them better."

Jesse glanced over at her and nodded. "That sounds like a good idea. Maybe you could take Maddie with you."

Cassie opened her mouth as though to speak, then closed it. She looked to the golden leaves of the trees. Life never seemed simple. She brought her gaze back to Jesse. "Actually, Jesse, I was thinking perhaps you and Maddie could get married before we left. It would give you a chance to have some time without the children underfoot."

"Jesus!" Jesse moved quickly through the gate and stormed around the fence until he was staring down at her. "It's only been two weeks. Show some respect, for Christ's sake."

"Is that what you and Maddie are doing? Showing respect? Is that why you avoid each other, why you don't talk to each other? Is that why you stand here in front of Charles's grave and she walks to the creek? Out of respect? Or is it out of guilt?"

Jesse plowed his fingers through his hair, his voice ragged. "Charles knew what we felt. I took from him what was his."

Cassie placed her hand on his arm. "No, Jesse. He never intended for Maddie to be his." She pulled an envelope from her pocket. "Charles gave this to Paul the day before he died. He told him to give it to me when the time was right. I want to share a portion of it with you." She removed a piece of paper from the envelope and began to read quietly.

My dear Cassie,

In my life, I have known what it is to be truly loved. I have known the deep love of a wife for her husband, children for their father, and a brother for his brother.

You may think me crazed, and perhaps I was, but as Death hovered over me, I found a need to leave gifts to those I love, those who have loved me, gifts that time would not diminish.

Although separated by long years, I know Jesse as though he had been raised by my side. I know he will look after my children as I would, that he will give to them unselfishly all he has to give. And I feared that when my children grew up and moved away, Jesse would look around and find himself grown old and alone.

For you see, dear sister, unlike you and me, Jesse would never put his own heart first. And so, I took a wife, hoping that the love she and Jesse would share with my children might blanket them as well.

Should my dearest hope be realized, should Jesse and Maddie decide to marry, it is my wish that you encourage them not to wait, not to mourn for a year or even a day.

Though leaving you all brought me great sorrow, I am now with my dear Alice and my heart is once again whole. It is my hope that Jesse and Maddie will find the same joy in each other.

Cassie folded the paper and placed it back into the envelope. "We'll be leaving late Saturday afternoon. I thought a simple ceremony here at the house would be appropriate." She hugged Jesse as he stood silently before her. "Maddie's at the creek."

Then she walked away. Jesse glanced down at the granite

markers. "You had no right, Charles, no right to marry her, hoping she'd marry me." He shoved a hand into a pocket. "But I'm damn glad you did."

With twilight easing in around him, Jesse walked toward the creek. He pulled a leaf from a tree and proceeded to shred it. He knew what he felt in his heart, thought he knew what Maddie felt in hers, but she'd never spoken the words. They hadn't been his to receive even if she'd wanted to say them aloud.

He came to the creek bank and saw her just as he knew she would be: sitting down, gazing out upon the slowly moving water . . . alone. He knew that feeling, had felt it for much of his life. And he knew what it felt like to look across a room, catch and hold her gaze, and tell her a thousand things without ever saying a word.

She didn't move as he sat beside her. He wished he'd gathered more leaves to shred. He sighed, unsure of the best way to approach the subject. Here he was, once again doing something without thinking it through. He sure as hell hoped Charles was happy. "Cassie wants to take the children to Galveston for a couple of weeks."

She glanced at him and smiled. "Oh, they'd enjoy that."

He rubbed his chin. "Yeah, I reckon they would." He shifted his body and reached into his pocket. "Know what this is?"

Maddie took the ring and held it up to the dimming sunlight. "A ring."

"Our mother's ring. Charles made me promise that the man who loves you would put that ring on your finger when he married you."

She furrowed her brows and studied his face. "What?"

He cleared his throat as gently as he could. "Thought I'd do it Saturday."

"Thought you'd do what on Saturday?"

"Put the ring on your finger."

"This Saturday?"

"I know we haven't mourned a year, but if I've learned one thing, it's that you never know what's going to happen tomorrow. Maddie, I'm as old as my father was when he died. And Charles . . . he was younger. I just figured while we're both young and healthy, we ought to do it. It's what Charles would have wanted."

"You're going to marry me because it's what Charles wanted?" she asked, a slight accent punctuating her words.

"No, I'm going to put that ring on your finger because it's what he wanted." He cradled her face between his strong hands. "I'm going to marry you because I love you." Doubt surfaced within his eyes. "That is, if you want to marry me. Do you?"

She placed her hands over his and gave him a smile that told him long before she spoke what her answer would be. "Oh, yes."

Jesse rolled his shoulders, feeling the weight of the jacket surrounding him. Sticking his finger between the knot on his cravat and his throat, he wiggled it around until he could breathe again. With disgust, he looked at the reflection of the man sitting in the chair behind him. He had a strong urge to knock that smile right off his face.

"I look like a dandy dressed like this. Hell, I look like you!"

"Then your bride should be very pleased," Paul said.

"I don't know why we have to be so formal about this wedding. It's not like she hasn't been married before."

Paul stood. "I'd think that alone would be enough reason to see that today is special for Maddie."

Jesse once again adjusted his clothing.

"Not nervous, are you?" Paul asked.

"Hell no, I'm not nervous."

"Shall we go downstairs then?"

"This doesn't look right," Jesse said as he began rearranging the cravat.

"It did before you started messing with it." Paul brushed Jesse's hands aside and set about straightening the tie.

"Make sure it's right."

Paul heaved a weary sigh. "It was right the other three times I did it. It'd stay right if you'd keep your clumsy hands off it." He stepped back. "There. Don't even look in the mirror. Just take my word for it. It's perfect. Let's get downstairs before you mess it up again."

Ignoring Paul's admonishment, Jesse took a last glance at his reflection in the mirror. He sure as hell hoped she appreciated all the trouble he was going to on her behalf. "All right, let's go."

He stepped out into the hallway. Cassie released a sound of joy, rushed over to him, and hugged him closely. "Don't you look handsome?"

He glanced around the hallway. "Where's Maddie?"

"She'll go downstairs in a little while."

"Why can't we go down the stairs together?"

"Because this is her day, and a bride should have an entrance."

"Why does she need an entrance? It's just us, the children, and a nice, quiet ceremony."

Smiling, Cassie tilted her face up. "She had a nice, quiet ceremony when she married Charles. I wanted today to be special."

"Afraid to go downstairs by yourself?" Paul asked.

Jesse jerked his head around and glowered at the irritating man. "No, I'm not afraid."

"Then let's go."

Jesse trudged toward the stairs. "Hurry Maddie along, would you?" He looked over his shoulder. "And see that she wears her hair down."

"What?" Cassie asked, her eyes and mouth equally round. "I just spent two hours pinning it up."

"Then unpin it. I've never seen her hair down in the daylight. If you want her to make an entrance, I'm sure she'll make one hell of an entrance with her hair down." He rolled his shoulders one last time and began walking down the stairs.

" 'Bout time the groom showed up!" McGuire yelled as he leaned against the banister at the foot of the stairs.

Jesse stopped halfway down the stairs and stared at the owner of the general store. He'd recently removed every outdated wanted poster from McGuire's wall. "What the hell are you doing here?"

"Told you before, man, you can't go off getting married n private."

Jesse felt the trepidation shoot through him like a well-imed arrow to his gut. He tread down the stairs more autiously until he could peer into the parlor. All he could ee were the backs of heads, the backs of a lot of heads. Ie stepped down into the foyer, spun around, and sent an ccusing glance back up at his brother-in-law. Paul smiled.

"Don't you dare say it," Jesse warned.

"Why not? It's so much fun to say." Paul's smile ncreased. "Surprise!" Chuckling, he trotted back up the tairs. "I'll fetch the bride!"

McGuire put his hand on Jesse's shoulder. "We just wanted you to know we all approve."

"It was just supposed to be a nice, quiet ceremony."

"Well, we'll keep it quiet if that's what you want, but we lid bring a fiddle player." He winked. "I plan on asking the widow Parker to dance. You wouldn't want to deny me the oleasure, would you? Now that I know you're not after her yourself."

"After her myself?"

"Hell yes, man. You were dancing with her so much I figured you were sweet on her."

"I was never sweet on her."

McGuire slapped his shoulder. "Then come on, man. Let's get this wedding under way."

Shaking hands and greeting guests as he went, Jesse walked through the parlor until he was standing before the hearth. He shook the minister's hand, then glanced at his best man.

"You nervous, Uncle Jesse?" Aaron whispered.

"Yep. You?"

Aaron nodded.

Jesse placed his hand on the boy's shoulder. "You'll do fine." He smiled at Hannah and Taylor, dressed in finery, standing on the other side of the minister.

Hannah cupped her hands around her mouth. "You'll be glad, Uncle Jesse."

His smile growing warmer, he nodded. Then he turned

around and looked out the open parlor doors toward the stairs.

Maddie looked once again at her reflection in the mirror and shook her head. "Cassie, I can't wear Alice's wedding gown."

"Why not?" Cassie asked as she adjusted the train flowing down the back of the ivory gown.

"Because she and Charles shared something special—"

"And you and Jesse don't?"

Maddie studied her trembling hands. "He deserves better than me."

"That's for him to decide."

She lifted her gaze to Cassie's. "Is it?"

Cassie nodded. "And I'd say he's already decided."

"I want to be good for him, to make him happy."

"Then marry him and give him a day and a night like none he's ever had." She hugged Maddie closely. "Now come on. You have one nervous man waiting for you."

Jesse watched Cassie scurry down the stairs and sit on a chair in the front row of gathered people. Catching his eye, she smiled innocently. She was damn lucky the room was filled with people, or he would have throttled her right then and there. They were going to have a long talk when this was over. She was picking up all her husband's bad habits.

He glanced back toward the stairs, and suddenly he didn't care if the whole state of Texas was sitting in the parlor. Maddie, with her honeyed hair cascading around her, was more beautiful than he'd ever imagined. And she was about to become his.

Her eyes sought and held his, and he felt as though everything had narrowed back down to the only people that mattered. She walked through the room, her arm linked with Paul's. People stood as she passed, and suddenly Jesse was damn glad they were all here, damn glad that she'd had this moment, would always know that their marriage had been blessed by the good wishes of friends.

With tears brimming in her eyes, she came to stand before him. The minister cleared his throat. "And who gives this woman to this man?"

"Charles does," Paul said. He squeezed Maddie's hand, then stepped back, and relinquished her into Jesse's keeping.

Jesse didn't care that she was supposed to slip her arm through his and stand by his side. It wasn't enough, not enough for what he was feeling, not enough for all that he saw reflected in her eyes. He took her hand, gently pulled her against him, and slipped his other arm behind her back, holding her close, the way he intended to hold her for the rest of his life.

Maddie tilted her face toward him, looking deeply into his eyes, falling into the obsidian depths, knowing he'd always catch her. She heard the minister's words of love and marriage. She listened to the deep timbre of Jesse's voice as he gave her his vows. Then she recited her own vows, wishing she could tell him that they were so different, so beautifully different from the ones she'd exchanged with Charles. But gazing into his eyes as he slipped his mother's ring onto her finger, she knew that he knew.

Then he lowered his mouth to hers, bestowing upon her a sweet kiss filled with the promise of passion.

When he lifted his lips from hers, the children surrounded them, each wanting their own hugs. Then Cassie, with tears in her eyes, and Paul hugged them.

The guests left their chairs and came forward to express their happiness for the couple.

Maddie didn't hear people drag the chairs out of the way, but she did hear the lilting strains of the violin. Smiling, Jesse took her into his arms and waltzed her across the floor. They danced alone, surrounded by family and friends, until the music faded away. Then another tune began, and other couples joined them on the floor.

"Has your husband told you you're beautiful?" Jesse asked as he moved in time to the music.

"No," Maddie said as she followed his steps.

"You're beautiful."

"Has your wife told you how handsome you are?"

He touched his finger to her temple. "Yes, I think sh did."

The waltz continued, but Maddie was aware of little bu her husband's eyes upon her, his hand holding hers. "/ husband should have no secrets from his wife. What do you think about when you're dancing?"

"Depends on who I'm dancing with."

The music drifted off into silence. He whispered near he ear, "Try and slip away after the next dance, and I'll you what I was thinking about that night in the barn."

Paul stepped up. "I believe it's customary for the bride to dance with the best man, but I'm afraid Aaron's having no part of dancing, so I've graciously offered to fill in for him. You don't mind, do you, Jesse?"

"Nope, it'll give me a chance to dance with my sister." He squeezed Maddie's hand. "Don't forget." He eased his way through the crowd until he located Cassie, took her hand, and led her to the center of the room.

"You're angry with me," she said.

"Nope. I was, but I'm not anymore."

"Good. This is how weddings should be: family and friends celebrating a new beginning. It's the way Charles wanted it."

"God, I miss him, Cassie."

"But there's so much of him here, Jesse. You can't turn around without being reminded of him."

They waltzed across the floor until the lyrical melody came to an end. Jesse brought her fingers to his lips and kissed her fingertips. "Never danced with my sister before. Thank you."

He bumped into her as someone bumped into him. He looked into Aaron's beaming face as he cradled a black and white spotted puppy against his chest.

"Look, Uncle Jesse. Billy's got some more puppies. He wants to give us this one as a wedding present! Will you let him?"

Jesse studied the youthful face, a face so similar to one he'd cherished as a child, missed as an adolescent. He heaved a sigh of resignation that made Aaron's smile increase. "I reckon. What are you going to name him? Rancher?"

"Heck fire, no! I'm gonna call her Princess!"

"Her? Aaron, wait!" Jesse called out as the boy dashed away and disappeared beyond the open doors. He looked at Cassie and discovered her knowing smile was as irritating as the one her husband wore as he stood beside her. "I need some fresh air."

He stalked through the house and stepped onto the back porch, breathing deeply of the outside air, relishing the distant scent of forget-me-not.

Maddie turned around and leaned against the beam. "I was afraid you weren't coming."

"I got waylaid. Appears we've got another dog. Her name's Princess."

She smiled. "That should make Ranger happy."

"That's what I'm afraid of."

She tugged on the lapel of his jacket. "I think you're trying to change the subject, but talking about dogs isn't going to work. What were you thinking about when we were dancing in the barn?"

He braced his strong hands on either side of her delicate face, threading his fingers through her glorious hair, his eyes delving deeply into hers. "How much I wished you were mine."

He kissed her then as he'd never kissed her before: with the unequivocal knowledge that he could give to her all he had to give, ask of her all that she wanted to share. They were no longer thieves, stealing glances, craving touches, harboring forbidden feelings.

She wrapped her arms around his neck, and he lowered his hands to the small of her back, pressing her body against the length of his, kissing her deeply, savoring that to which he now had absolute rights.

In the distance, he heard a horn blast. "That'll be the stagecoach," he whispered, his lips hovering above hers.

"I need to get the children ready," she said quietly.

He nodded imperceptibly before pressing his lips to hers. She slid her fingers into his hair, sighed, and lifted her mouth from his. "We'll have overnight guests if we're not careful."

"Enough said." He brushed his lips over hers. "You get the children ready. I have some things I need to see to."

He released her and stepped off the porch. Watching his long legs take him out of sight, Maddie felt the joy swell within her. "Thank you, Charles," she whispered. "Thank you for all the gifts you've given me this day."

21

Maddie waved until she could no longer see small arms fluttering outside the windows, until the stagecoach disappeared through the cloud of dust and the dust settled to the ground, leaving nothing but the dimming twilight behind.

She squeezed back her tears as Jesse drew her against his sturdy chest.

"They'll be fine," he said, and she felt the deep rumble of his chest.

"I know. It's just that I miss them already."

"Then I guess I'll have to do something to keep your mind off their absence."

Anticipation coursed through her as he buried first his hands, then his face in her honeyed tresses. He released a ragged sigh. "Did Charles tell you about the accident he had with the horse in the stall?"

She nodded, grateful that Charles had told Jesse of his impotence. She'd worried that her new husband would think she was more experienced than she was.

"I was there when it happened. Stallion broke two of his ribs." He placed his hands on her shoulders. "That's all he did." Slowly, he turned her to face him and stroked her chin with his thumbs. "Texas Rangers aren't the only ones who lie."

"Why?" she whispered as the importance of his statement became clear.

"Because he wanted your first time with a man to be with

a man you love. His gift to you for all the gifts you gave to him."

Kissing her tenderly, he tasted the salt of her tears. "Will your first time be with a man you love, Maddie?"

Giving him a tremulous smile, she nodded.

Wiping the tears from her cheeks, he held her tender gaze with his own. "Tell me," he pleaded softly.

"I love you, Jesse."

"Do you know how long I've wanted, how much I've wanted to hear you say that?" Bending, he slipped an arm beneath her knees and lifted her into his arms. "I intend to make sure Charles's gift to you is the most precious gift you ever receive."

Wrapping her arms around his neck, she pressed her face against his shoulder as he carried her to the house. He opened the door, walked through, and slammed it shut with his foot.

"Shouldn't we wait until the sun sets?" she asked as he climbed the stairs.

"Sun's setting now, and we've waited long enough as it is."

He carried her into the Princess room, set her down on her feet, and quietly closed the door. The curtains were drawn, cloaking the room in shadows. A lamp burned low on the bedside table. A lazy fire danced within the hearth. A hazy mist rose above the water in the wooden tub resting before the fire.

"When did you prepare the bath?" Maddie asked quietly.

"Paul took care of it for me."

"I think you do like him."

"He has his moments." He stepped behind her. Capturing her hair, he draped it over one shoulder. He undid several buttons until the high collar of the gown revealed her slender neck. He kissed her nape, then the sensitive spot behind her ear. "I've thought about giving you a bath since the first night I hauled the water up for you."

She felt his fingers travel the length of her spine, undoing the remaining buttons as they went. She closed her eyes, relishing the feel of his hands as they glided over her body, removing her clothes until they were nothing more than a silken pool beside her feet. His clothes quickly joined hers. He carried her to the tub and lowered her into the water, leaving her hair to cascade over the edge of the tub as though it were a waterfall.

She sank into the warm water and the scent of forget-me-nots wafted around her.

Sitting back on his heels, he traced his finger along the curve of her breast where the water gently lapped. The silkiness of the water offset the roughness of his finger to create a harmonious shiver along her flesh. She felt her nipples pucker as his hand dipped beneath the water to cup the underside of her breast.

She threaded her damp fingers through the thick mat covering his chest. "I wanted to do this the day you lifted me down from the stagecoach."

"I wanted to do this every time I drew you a bath." He lifted his palm and sprinkled the water over her shoulders, watching the water trail down, leaving beads of moisture behind.

"When did Charles tell you about his gift to me?" Maddie asked softly.

Jesse met her amber gaze. "The afternoon we flew the kites."

"So, all these months—"

"I thought my brother was already in heaven."

She cupped his face, drawing him near. "You were willing for him to have so much."

"Everything I wanted."

She nuzzled her face against his neck. "The night we spent by the campfire . . . before that, I'd never seen a man . . ."

He brought her away so her face was no longer hidden. Her cheeks were bright with embarrassment, and he loved her for it. He arched a brow. "Never?"

Slowly, she moved her head from side to side, her eyes focused on his. "I suppose I should have felt shy." She allowed her gaze to follow the contours of his body. An appreciative smile eased onto her face as her gaze returned to his eyes. "But I thought you were magnificent, and it felt so right to look at you and touch you." She ran her hand along his chest. "It's always felt comforting to have you near."

He skimmed his hand along the curves he had memorized by the campfire. "I'm going to touch all of you tonight, Maddie." He glided his hand along her hip. "But not in the tub."

Giving her a tender smile, he stood. He reached for the towel warming in front of the fire. She smiled as the shadows played over his bronzed flesh.

He tossed the towel on the bed, then slipped his arms beneath her and lifted her from the water. He laid her on the bed and slowly used the towel to dry her arms. He twisted around and began to dry her legs. She traced her finger along the scar on his back. Then he threw the towel aside.

"I'm still wet."

"I know," he said as he stretched out beside her. "But whenever I'd walk to the creek, this is what I'd think about."

Maddie was cool where the water glistened upon her body. He dipped his face between her breasts, and she felt the warmth of his mouth as he lapped up the droplets. Burying her fingers in his hair, she moaned softly, growing warmer as he trailed his mouth over her flesh, sipping of her.

He lifted his eyes to hers. "Ah, Whiskey, you're so sweet." He kissed her slowly, savoring the feel of her mouth mating with his, plundering that to which he now had an absolute right.

Maddie ran her foot up his calf, then down, reaching until her toes touched the top of his foot. She glided her hands down his back, over his body, reciting the poem she'd memorized so well that night by the campfire. Tonight, the poem would end differently. Tonight, she would explore that which she hadn't dared to explore before.

She slipped her hands between their bodies and wrapped

her fingers around him. He growled deep within his chest and deepened the kiss. Responding as she had so often in her dreams, she took what he offered and demanded more. She stroked him, marveling at the velvety smoothness. He tore his mouth from hers and trailed his lips along her throat.

"Ah, Whiskey." He blazed a trail downward, exploring the peaks, then descending to the valleys, tasting, teasing, caressing with an infinite tenderness. He left nothing unexplored, and she reveled in his exploration, discovering a beauty of sensations unleashed by his touch.

Beside the campfire, he had been tethered, touching her in ways that created a warmth, but now he touched her in ways that created a need, a need to know how the poem would end. "Oh, Jesse!"

He lifted his face from the valley between her thighs and moved up, lowering his mouth to hers. She kissed him deeply with a yearning that rivaled his own. He hoisted himself above her. Instinctively, she lifted her hips to receive him, and he plunged into her sweet depths.

She released a small cry, and he froze.

"Oh, God. I hurt you."

She shook her head. "Only a little."

He squeezed his eyes shut, his voice ragged. "I'm so sorry, Maddie. I wasn't thinking." He eased down to his elbows and grazed his knuckles along her cheek. "I've never had a virgin."

She smiled, the teasing smile he loved, and asked, "Is this your first time, too?"

"It's my first time with a woman I love."

Tears gathered in her eyes.

"I love you, Whiskey."

Plowing her fingers through his hair, she pressed him down and brought his lips to hers. Their tongues danced a slow waltz to a melody created by their hearts. Slowly, their bodies began to follow the same rhythm. He eased out of her.

"Don't leave me," she whispered as she pressed her hands to his hips.

He smiled. "I'll come back." He eased his way back. "Did that hurt?"

"No."

His motions continued, slow and easy, like the ocean lapping upon the shore. When she failed to flinch, his movements intensified. When she smiled, he released all the passion he'd been holding back.

Maddie felt the full power of this man as his thrusts carried her to new heights. She fell into the obsidian depths of his eyes, feeling the sensations increase in intensity, almost beyond bearing. She closed her eyes.

"Don't close your eyes," he ordered through labored breaths.

She opened her eyes, holding his, as he carried her farther from shore. She gasped as a wave of sensations hit her, followed rapidly by another. Then the final wave rolled over her, but instead of taking her under, it lifted her to new heights. She cried out, clinging to him as his body shuddered repeatedly with his final thrusts, his low moans creating the perfect final verse.

For long moments, replete, they did little more than gaze at each other. Then he smiled at her. Her face was relaxed and totally at peace. Her mouth curved up in a small semblance of a smile. "What are you thinking?" he asked.

She sighed softly. "I was thinking about Charles."

"That's what a man wants to hear after he's just made love to a woman. That she's thinking about another man."

He dropped a quick kiss onto her lips and made a motion to move off her. She cupped his face, halting his movements. "Don't move away. I was just thinking what an incredibly beautiful gift Charles gave me." Lovingly, she trailed her fingers over his face. "I can't even begin to imagine what it would feel like to have another man's body nestled within mine without love surrounding us. If I'd known it was supposed to be this beautiful . . . I never would have walked into Bev's."

He buried his face in her hair. "Ah, Whiskey."

"I didn't know it was supposed to be like this, Jesse."

"Neither did I," he replied raggedly.

"Didn't you?" she asked incredulously.

Taking her hand, he pressed her palm against his pounding heart. "What I feel here, I've never felt before, not for anyone. You're the finest gift I've ever received."

With tears in her eyes, she whispered hoarsely, "I want to make you happy."

"You already have," he said just before he lowered his mouth to hers.

Charles had slept with his arm draped over Maddie's stomach. Jesse slept with his body draped over hers. She awoke with the certain knowledge that she was indeed sleeping with a virile man. She stretched her toes until she could rub them across the top of his foot. She smiled. It felt much nicer when she was snuggled beneath him in bed and not dangling from a tree branch.

He shifted his body, and she used the opportunity to roll toward the edge of the bed. His arm snared her and dragged her back beneath him. She studied his face. His eyes were closed and his face was completely relaxed. "Jesse?"

He moved not one muscle. She blew a soft breeze beneath his chin. His nose twitched. She kissed the center of his chest and heard a gentle purring in his throat. She waited, and he began to snore softly. "Jesse?"

When he didn't respond, she began to ease out from beneath him as though she was a caterpillar moving sideways. She thought of Aaron and wondered how he was enjoying his adventure. Everything seemed so quiet without the children around. As she sat up, Jesse's arm snaked out and pulled her back.

"Where are you going?" he asked, his voice thick from sleep.

She shifted so she could face him and threaded her fingers through the hairs on his chest. "Thought I'd get you some coffee."

One corner of his mouth tipped up. "Don't you think I'll be in a good mood today?"

"Oh, I plan to keep you in a good mood, but I thought it wouldn't hurt to start your day off right."

He shook his head as his eyes darkened. "I'm changing my habits. I'm not starting the day with coffee anymore. I'm starting it with Whiskey."

His mouth swooped down to capture hers, and she was the one who purred. Wrapping her arms around him, she felt his muscles undulate as he nestled between her thighs. He entered her slowly and moved lazily against her. She squeezed her thighs, and he groaned, deepening his thrusts.

He kissed the tip of her nose, she kissed his chin. He kissed the sensitive spot below her ear, she kissed his throat, following his Adam's apple as it slid up and down. He kissed her shoulder, she kissed his. Then he raised up, and the lazy movements melted into a frenzy of thrusts. Maddie eagerly greeted his thrusts until she shuddered beneath him, until he shuddered above her.

He dropped to his elbows, his breathing labored. She ran her hands along his damp back, knowing now why she found sweat so appealing on this man. He smiled down on her. "Good morning."

She returned his smile. "Good morning."

He rolled to his side, bringing her with him. "I may never drink coffee again."

She laughed and snuggled against him. The fire had died away long ago, but they'd never bothered to dim the lamp. It still shone on them. Maddie popped up and looked toward the window. Jesse's hold on her tightened.

"Let me up for a minute," she said.

"Where are you going?"

"I want to see something."

His arm came away from her. She slid out of bed, padded on bare feet to the window, and pulled the curtain aside. He raised up on an elbow and enjoyed the splendid view of her backside. Then he enjoyed watching her rush back to the bed and slip beneath the covers.

"The sun's not up yet," she said as she snuggled against him for warmth. "I want to go look at your dream as the sun comes up."

"My dream's here, Maddie, with you. All these years, I just thought it was my cattle."

"A man can have more than one dream. Please?"

He dropped a brief kiss to her lips. "All right." He got out of bed, stepped into his pants, and walked to the door. There he waited.

She clambered out of bed and draped a blanket around her shoulders. "What are you waiting for?"

He glanced over his shoulder. "I'm just wondering if I'll find one of Somner's surprises when I open this door. The whole town could be waiting out in the hallway to see if we enjoyed the night."

Smiling, she walked across the room, opened her arms, and wrapped the blanket around him, pressing her breasts against his bare chest. "Want me to go with you?"

He slipped his arm around her. "Yep."

She went with him to his room and watched him dress. Then he went with her to her room and watched her dress.

"Which room do you want to be our room?" he asked as she slipped into the riding skirt he'd bought her in Austin.

"Your room."

"I'll move your things this afternoon."

In the cool morning just before dawn, they walked through the woods until they came to the meadow. Jesse hunkered down, nestled Maddie between his thighs, and wrapped a blanket around her. They watched the sun peer over the horizon as the breeze brought the scent of cattle to them.

"I wanted to be here with you like this the morning they came," she said quietly.

He tightened his hold on her. "You were with me, Maddie, in my heart."

Jesse had saddled Midnight and tethered him at a near-by bush. He stood, retrieved his horse, and lifted Maddie into the saddle. Then he mounted behind her, drawing her against his chest. They rode slowly along the outskirts of the herd.

Then they rode to the creek. Jesse spread a blanket over the fallen leaves. Snuggling against each other, they enjoyed a picnic.

They did little more for the remainder of the day than

experience the joy of sharing moments together that they'd denied themselves in the past.

Maddie felt the brush slide through her hair. She never would have thought her husband was the type of man who would brush a woman's hair. He'd given her another bath. Then she'd given him one. He'd enjoyed it until he came out of the bath water smelling like flowers, but his disgruntled mood didn't last long.

She sat before the mirror with her wrapper on. Her husband stood behind her as naked as the day he was born. He moved to the side, and she caught a glimpse of his naked splendor in the mirror. He moved back, and she was left with nothing more than a view of his chest.

Slowly, she worked loose the knot on her sash. Then she parted the wrapper and created a tiny opening so a portion of her flesh came into view. She lifted her gaze and caught her husband's as his eyes darkened. Although he continued to brush her hair, he did not apply as much pressure nor allow the brush to travel as far.

Slowly, she slipped the wrapper off one shoulder. Her reflection in the mirror captured all his attention. She heard the brush fall to the floor. Holding his gaze, she eased the wrapper off her other shoulder.

He dropped to one knee, turned her slightly, and buried his face between her breasts. "Dear God, but you're sweet."

"I was trying to be wanton."

He took the strands of her hair between his fingers. "Your hair always reminded me of honey, and I wondered if you were as sweet. Then I'd look into your eyes, and I could almost feel the whiskey burning deep within me. I'd wonder which was truly you."

She threaded her fingers through his hair. "Which am I?"

"Both."

He swirled his tongue around her nipple. She arched toward him as he continued his loving sojourn to her other breast. She dropped her head forward until her cheek was pressed against the top of his head. "I'm burning now, Jesse."

"Wrap your legs around my waist."

She did as he bid. He slid one hand beneath her buttocks and wrapped one arm around her back. He stood, and she clung to him.

"Shake off your wrapper."

She released her hold on him, one arm at a time, allowing the wrapper to fall to the floor. He crossed the room and sat on his bed. He cupped the back of her head and tilted her face so his mouth could latch onto hers. Kissing her deeply, he rolled her over onto the bed, blanketing her body with his own.

The fire in the hearth roared, throwing its warmth toward them, but they had little need of it as they created their own fire within one another. Jesse slid his arms beneath her, pressing her against him, as he again rolled over. She released a surprised gasp as she ended up straddling his hips. A question arose in her eyes, and in his darkening gaze she found the answer. She lifted her hips, then brought them down to sheathe him. He combed his fingers through her hair, spreading it out until it formed a curtain around them.

Smiling, she lowered her lips to his. His mouth welcomed her, enticing hers to explore leisurely. He cupped her breasts and gently molded them to fit his palm. She slowly circled her hips until she felt the first spark. She lifted her lips from his and buried her face in his neck. Placing his hands on her hips, he urged her on. She raised up and followed the rhythm he had set. He again cupped her breasts, gently kneading. She felt the sparks ignite and released a small cry. He lifted his head from the pillow and suckled her breast. And she exploded into a thousand fires.

He dropped to the pillow and she kissed him hungrily, trying to share with him all she'd just experienced. He cradled her hips, and she felt the shudders wrack his body. She collapsed on top of him, listening to the hard pounding of his heart, feeling the rise and fall of his chest beneath her cheek.

"Every time we make love, I feel as though I've received a gift," she said quietly. "Will it always be like this, Jesse?"

"Always, Whiskey."

She kissed his shoulder, his neck, his jaw. "Will you give me another gift?"

Threading his fingers through her hair, he tilted her face until he could hold her gaze with his own. "I'll give you all the gifts you want."

❧ Epilogue ❧

The first rays of the morning sun filtered in through the window as Maddie slowly opened her eyes.

Jesse moved quietly through the room and gently sat on the bed. Tenderly, he combed the wisps of hair away from her face. "How are you feeling?"

She smiled warmly. "A little tired." She shifted her body. "A little sore."

"Want to sit up?"

She nodded. He slipped an arm beneath her back, lifted her, and shoved pillows behind her. She settled against the pillows, feeling a contentment greater than any she'd ever known.

"How is she?" she asked.

Jesse glanced at his daughter, nestled peacefully within her small cradle beside their bed. "Beautiful."

Maddie placed her palm against his bristly cheek. "Have you slept at all?"

He covered her hand, turned his head, and placed a kiss on the center of her palm. "I never gave any thought to having my own family, a family that was mine. From the time I was twelve, all I wanted was to find Charles and Cassie. Then when I found Charles, I was content to share his children." He squeezed her hand, cleared his clogged throat, and touched his knuckles to her cheek. "But the gift you gave me in the early hours before dawn this morning . . . Ah, Maddie, I couldn't sleep for the wonder of her, the wonder of you."

He captured a tear as it trailed slowly down her cheek. "I love you, Whiskey."

A gentle cry took his attention away from her. He glanced at his daughter as she began to exercise her lungs with more ferocity. "What's this? Is that an English accent I hear?"

Filled with joy, Maddie laughed. "I think she's probably hungry and getting impatient with you for not getting her over here."

While she unbuttoned her nightgown, he lifted his daughter out of the cradle and carried her to the bed. Maddie took the babe, cradling her in her arms, guiding her to her breast.

Jesse watched as his daughter worked her mouth vigorously to draw nourishment from her mother. "The children would like to see her this morning, if you're up to it. Think they want to see you, too . . . make sure you're all right."

She smiled. "Why don't you get them ready? We should be finished here by the time you get back."

Leaning over, Jesse kissed her briefly before getting up and heading out of the room.

Maddie brushed her fingers through her daughter's fine, ebony hair. She counted fingers and toes as she had shortly after her daughter was born. She studied the way her thick lashes rested on the ruddy cheeks. "Thank you, Charles," she whispered. "Thank you for taking me out of Bev's. Thank you for giving me a family to love."

Moments later, when her daughter stopped nursing, Maddie lifted her onto her shoulder. With one hand, she buttoned her nightgown, amazed at how quickly she was adapting to her child, how natural everything seemed. She heard a soft tapping on the door. "Come in."

The door opened slightly, and three heads peered in at once.

"Come on in," Maddie urged.

Hannah and Taylor tiptoed into the room.

"What are you doing?" Maddie asked.

"Uncle Jesse said we had to be quiet," Hannah whispered.

"I don't think you have to be that quiet. Hurry over here so I can get some hugs."

The girls raced across the room, claiming their places beside the bed. Maddie reached over and gave each one a hug. Aaron ambled up, and she stuck out her hand.

"Ah, Ma." He leaned over and hugged her, careful not to intrude on the space now occupied by the newest member of the family. He straightened up and studied the baby. "She looks like Uncle Jesse."

Jesse sat down on the other side of the bed. Maddie smiled. "Yes, she does." She tilted the baby's face toward the children. "See, her eyes are even dark."

"What's her name?" Hannah asked.

"Charlene."

"That's sorta like Pa's name," Aaron said.

"Is that all right with you?" Jesse asked.

Aaron glanced over at his uncle. "Yep. I reckon he'd like that."

"Pretty baby," Taylor said, her hands folded primly on top of the quilt as she leaned into the bed.

"Yes, she is a pretty baby," Maddie said. "Just like you were when you were born. And she'll grow up to be as pretty as you are now."

Her face beaming, Taylor looked over at Hannah.

"And as pretty as me," Hannah said.

"And as pretty as you," Maddie assured her.

"I was wondering," Aaron began, "if you're my ma and he's my uncle, is she my sister or my cousin?"

"Which do you want her to be?" Maddie asked.

"My sister."

"Then that's what she is."

Aaron puffed out his chest at the thought of having another sister.

"Why don't you all head to the kitchen, and I'll be down in a minute to see about rustling up some breakfast?" Jesse asked.

The girls rushed out of the room. Aaron walked more slowly, stopped at the door, and glanced back into the room. "Uncle Jesse, I been thinking. Charlene might get confused if I'm her brother and Hannah and Taylor are her sisters and we're calling you uncle. I'm thinking maybe we ought to start calling you Pa. Just so she won't grow up confused. Pa told me it'd be all right when I was ready. Reckon now's a good time to be ready, seein' as how I got a new sister and all."

Maddie felt the tears welling in her eyes. She looked to Jesse and watched his Adam's apple bob. Gently, he cleared his clogged throat. "I'd like that," he said gruffly.

Aaron smiled. "I'll tell Hannah and Taylor." He closed the door quietly behind him.

Laying Charlene beside her on the bed, Maddie reached up and wrapped her arms around Jesse's shoulders. Carefully, he drew her near, burying his face in her hair.

"Another gift?" she whispered.

Lifting his head, he gazed into her eyes. "I have a feeling we'll spend the remainder of our lives discovering all the gifts Charles left us." He cradled her beloved face in his large hands. "But you will always be the gift for which I'll be the most grateful."

He lowered his mouth to hers, kissing her tenderly, holding back his desire, giving her nothing but his love.

She accepted his token into her heart, knowing that in their twilight years when their bodies were old and weary, they would need only to hold hands to experience the joy of their love.

And she knew that their hearts would forever remember not only the gifts, but the special man who had wrapped them in love and delivered them with care.